The Fossil Man

The Fossil Man

by
Jules Gros

translated, annotated and introduced by
Brian Stableford

A Black Coat Press Book

ISBN 978-1-61227-409-6. First Printing. June 2015. Published by Black Coat Press, an imprint of Hollywood Comics.com, LLC, P.O. Box 17270, Encino, CA 91416. All rights reserved. Except for review purposes, no part of this book may be reproduced or transmitted in any form or by any means, electronic or mechanical, including photocopying, recording, or by any information storage and retrieval system, without permission in writing from the publisher. The stories and characters depicted in this novel are entirely fictional. Printed in the United States of America.

Introduction

L'Homme fossile, aventures d'une expédition scientifique dans les mers australes, by Jules Gros (1829-1891), here translated as *The Fossil Man*, was published under that title as a book by Ernest Flammarion in 1892 and reprinted by Charavay, Mantoux, Martin under the imprint of the Librairie d'éducation de la jeunesse in 1898; the latter edition was reprinted at least twice. It had originally appeared as a 24-part feuilleton serial under the title "L'Age de pierre et l'homme fossile, aventures d'une expédition scientifique dans les mers australes" in the *Journal des Voyages* between 17 September 1882 and 25 February 1883. It was the fourth of the five feuilletons that the author published in the periodical in question between 1879 and 1891.

The story is a mildly satirical comedy describing the progress of an international scientific expedition to a fictitious island south-west of New Zealand, which sets off in 1876 to observe a transit of Mercury. In fact, there was no such transit, although there was one in May 1878, which was observable from the northern hemisphere and was, in consequence, tracked by several American astronomers. No sightings of the planet had been recorded in the previous sixteen years. Gros would, however, have been aware of the classic observations of transits of Mercury made from the southern hemisphere by Edmund Halley from the island of St. Helena in 1677 and by Charles Green and James Cook from New Zealand in 1769.

One of the principal sources on which Gros' story draws, and perhaps the most significant inspiration for its composition, was Henri Filhol's *Rapports géologiques et zoologiques de l'Île Campbell avec les terres australes avoisinantes*, published in February 1882, which was a report of one of six French expeditions sent to observe the transit of Venus in 1874. That expedition was unsuccessful in astronomical terms—bad weather ensured that very little was visible—and it was a much more limited operation than the one described by Gros, but the fictitious island described in *L'Homme fossile* is a clone of Campbell Island, situated at the same latitude a little way to the east, and the many of the details of its geology and natural history are appropriated from Filhol, whose explorations were the only substantial result of the 1874 expedition.

The modeling of the story on an actual expedition places *L'Homme fossile* at the "documentary" end of the spectrum of fiction routinely offered by the *Journal des Voyages*—the other extreme, of course, being provided by pure action-adventure stories set in far-flung locations. Jules Verne, whose works had provided the inspiration for the genre that the *Journal des Voyages* carried forward and helped to shape, had provided archetypes of the scientific expedition story-formula in such novels as *Aventures de trois Russes et trois Anglais dans l'Afrique australe* (1872; tr. under various titles, including *Measuring a Meridian*), but had usually added in narrative devices to add a melodramatic aspect to the kinds of low-key conflicts that a scientific expedition to remote parts might be expected to produce; in the example cited, the outbreak of the Crimean War heightens the tensions between the Russian and English members of the expedition.

Gros was one of the very few Vernian writers who was less inclined than his model to melodramatic devices, and *L'Homme fossile* reads for much of its narrative span as more akin to an exercise in the popularization of geographical science than a novel; some readers presumably got more than half way through the novel while still wondering whether it actually had a plot, and, if so, when the story was actually going to get around to its development. Contemporary readers can, however, be reassured; it does have a plot, albeit a rather contrived one, and it is, appropriately, the kind of plot that could only be deployed in a novel of this quasi-documentary format, with the kind of measured build-up employed in the story.

Unlike most tortuously-contrived plots, which calculate their complications purely for dramatic effect, and somewhat at odds with its breezy comedic tone. the plot of *L'Homme fossile* is contrived in order to construct an acute problem of a kind that could only arise in the context of an organized scientific endeavor, and although the solution provided by the narrative is artificial, the problem is sufficiently real to prompt the reader to wonder how much effect its analogues might have had on the development of the body of scientific knowledge. The novel is, in consequence, one of the purest examples of "scientific fiction."

Although the novel is bound to seem staid, and perhaps rather quaint, by today's standards, it is important to remember that its central motif, the existence of fossilized human remains, was still controversial in 1876, when the story is set, and 1882, when it was written, especially in Catholic France, where religious opposition to the idea of the great antiquity of the human species, implicitly making nonsense of Biblical chronology and the history of humankind in which Noah's Deluge played such a pivotal role, had been ardent and forceful for a long time. Geologists had been casting doubt on the chronology of *Genesis* for two centuries, the doubt in question increasing in intensity all the while, but that had only made the defenders of the Bible story, forced to concede that the six days of creation had to be considered metaphorical rather than literal, all the more determined to cling to their fallback position: that the Biblical account of the origins of humankind had to be taken seriously, the notion of original sin being a foundation stone of the entire dogmatic edifice. The idea that the human species had undergone a long, slow process of gradual evolution was therefore anathematized, and the gradual but enormous accumulation of evidence produced by excavations all over Europe, but particularly impressive in France itself, was thus a hot topic.

The topic was so hot that Jules Verne's pioneering dramatization of geological science, the magisterial *Voyage au centre de la Terre* (1864; rev. 1867; tr. as *Journey to the Center of the Earth*) initially treated the question of human remains very tentatively, and it was not until the revised version of 1867 that Verne inserted an actual sighting of a prehistoric human in his relic underworld, and he was careful even then to make the glimpse oblique and ambiguous, conserving the possibility that it might be hallucinatory. Verne was undoubtedly wholly convinced by the evidence relating to the slow and ancient development of Stone Age humans, but seems to have largely avoided the issue in his fiction in order to avoid upsetting devout members of his family. He did not tackle the question of the relevance of evolutionary science humankind in any elaborate fashion until 1901, when he published *Le Village aérien* (tr. as *The Village in the Treetops*), and retained a certain diplomacy even there.

The controversy in France regarding the antiquity of human life first became focused on physical evidence as a result of the accounts of flints and animal bones evidently shaped by human hands contained in *Antiquities celtiques et antédiluviennes* [Celtic and Antediluvian Antiquities] (1847) by Jacques Boucher de Crèvecoeur de Perthes, but the authenticity and significance of the discoveries was disputed for the next two decades. A crucial breakthrough seemed to have occurred in Boucher de Perthes' personal battle in 1863 when he found a human jaw in company with shaped flints in a gravel-pit, but it subsequently turned out that the jaw had been planted by a workman eager to claim a reward, and thus became a much-publicized setback rather than a step forward. Other finds, not so well-publicized, had already been made, however, and as the 1860s progressed, such discoveries came thick and fast.

Boucher de Perthes' most important contemporary in paleontological research, at least in terms of the volume of his data, was Édouard Lartet, who began rooting around in caves in the 1830s looking for ancient remains, and eventually found human remains together with those of extinct mammals in a cave in Aurignac, which he reported in 1861. His subsequent research in the Dordogne, which multiplied the number of finds vastly, was published in a series of papers between 1865 and 1870. He was a modest man—unlike Boucher de Perthes—and made less immediate impact on the public imagination, but his revelation of the extent and complexity of what came to be known as the Magdalenian culture of the Paleolithic Era cemented the notion of the Stone Age, and the image of "cave man" existence as it seemed to have developed in France after the last Ice Age. By the time Lartet died in 1871, the intellectual battle was effectively won, in the context of scientific orthodoxy—but the contest for the minds and imagination of the public was by no means over, and the pages of the *Journal des Voyages* provided one of the arenas in which that didactic project was engaged, from the periodical's foundation in 1877 throughout the early years, when Jules Gros was one of its most frequent contributors.

By the time Gros wrote *L'Homme fossile* in 1882, the scientific notion of Paleolithic culture had crystallized into a reasonably clear picture, and the finds of bone fragments made in the 1860s had been augmented by the discovery of entire human skeletons—a discovery carefully referenced in the story—but there was no way to date such remains with any degree of certainty, so the antiquity of such remains still remained open to challenge, in spite of their association with the remains of extinct animals. According to the Biblical chronologists, such animals had been wiped out by the Deluge, so their contemporaneity did, indeed, prove that the human remains were "antediluvian"—but nothing more than that. Nor was there any way to determine, at that point in time, how widespread paleolithic culture had been in geographical terms, and how its chronology related to the changes that had taken place in the physical surface of the earth, which were equally impossible to date accurately. That, too, is an important issue at stake in Gros' novel, and the discovery of quasi-Magdalenian remains in the southern seas would, indeed, have seemed as exciting and significant to real scientists in 1876 as it does to the fictitious ones in his story.

Jules Gros was one of the most prolific contributors of fiction to the *Journal des Voyages* in its first five years, along with Louis Boussenard (1847-1910). Like Boussenard, he had been an enthusiastic traveler himself, and was keenly interested in the progress of geographical science; he was the secretary of the Parisian Societé de géographie for some years. Whereas the much younger Boussenard was able to settle down once he became a popular writer via the periodical's pages, in order to devote himself to a substantial productive career as a fiction writer, Gros was nearing the end of his life when he began writing for the magazine, and the novels serialized there enjoyed their greatest popularity after his death, when they were repeatedly, if somewhat belatedly, reprinted in book form.

Gros' earlier books did include some fiction, including an extravagant Vernian account of the *Voyages extraordinaires du docteur Boldus* (1881), but those he published during his lifetime were predominantly nonfictional, including historical accounts of the exploration of Africa and the polar regions, and, perhaps most significantly, *Les Français en Guyane* (1887; all extant copies are identified as the "7th edition," but there is no evidence of the existence of the previous six). The last-named seems the most significant, at least in retrospect, because Gros involved himself intimately in Guyanese politics, under the influence of an old friend, the explorer Henri Coudreau, to the extent of accepting the presidency of an enclave on the country's disputed border with Brazil, where Coudreau had founded the supposedly-independent but universally-unrecognized République de Counani.

Gros moved his family from Paris to Counani in 1888, and although he returned to France before his death in 1891, he probably still considered himself to be the President of the Republic in question at that time, and was doubtless deeply disappointed by the fact that France had refused to recognize its existence. The episode was considered rather comical by many observers, but its consequences proved extensive, as other adventurers attempted to take up the slack once Coudreau and Gros had abandoned the cause, and diplomatic conflicts between France and Brazil continued for some years thereafter, eventually being settled following their referral to arbitration by the Swiss government.

In spite of his brief career as an unacknowledged head of state and the posthumous popularity of his novels and histories of exploration, Jules Gros faded almost completely from public view after the Great War, soon eclipsed by his namesake, the Breton writer Jules Gros (1890-1992). Even during his lifetime, he had a lower profile than another namesake, the politician Jules Gros (1838-1919), a long-serving député and the founder of the newspaper *Le Petit comtois*. He does, however, retain a significant niche as a writer of Vernian fiction, especially by virtue of occupying one of the extremes of the spectrum of that genre. He was by no means one of the most accomplished stylists active in the genre, and his frequent avoidance of melodrama in favor of attempted naturalism did not work entirely to his advantage, but he was a distinctive and thoughtful writer, who applied his light and politely satirical tone to serious questions with a certain deftness and charm, exhibited in all its quirkiness in *L'Homme fossile*.

This translation was made from a copy of an 1899 reprint of the Charavay, Mantoux, Martin edition. I have omitted the long summaries that appear at the head of each chapter, which serve no purpose except to function as "spoilers."

Brian Stableford

Chapter I

All the people in the world who are preoccupied with the great scientific movement of the present century are familiar with the name of Arthème Charmillon, a member of the Académie des Sciences. That knowledgeable professor had obtained an imperishable renown thanks to his studies in geology, meteorology and, above all on the natural history of the early ages of the world.

Paleontology, the marvelous science that is concerned with fossilized organisms—which is to say, those buried in the various layers that surround the composition of the terrestrial crust, has no secrets from him. His latest work, *The Absorption of Heat in Space*, although concerned with studies different from those that earned him his reputation, would have sufficed to classify him among the primary physicists of our era if that place had not already been acquired by his previous works.

On 8 July 1876 Monsieur Charmillon, of the Institut, occupied a modest apartment in Paris at no. 30, Rue de Fleurus, not far from the beautiful Luxembourg park.

He was sitting in his study in front of a blazing fire; his mind seemed to be absorbed by profound reflections. Suddenly, he pushed away the books and scientific journals open in front of him with an abrupt gesture, rose to his feet, paced back and forth briefly, and then, with an urgency that one would not have expected in a man of his age and knowledge, used his fist to strike polished steel bell placed on his desk.

"No, no," he exclaimed, responding to his internal thought, "it can't be! It shan't be! For myself, I'll oppose it so long as there's a breath of life in me."

A valet in livery answered the appeal and came with a grave and silent step to stand before the Academician, and then bowed, indicating that he was awaiting his master's orders.

"What is Mademoiselle Angèle, my niece, doing at this moment, Jean-Pierre?" asked Monsieur Charmillon.

"Mademoiselle Angèle," Jean-Pierre replied, "is in the dining room inspecting the linen that the laundress has brought."

"Tell her to come as soon as she can," commanded Monsieur Charmillon. "I have to talk to her."

"Very good," replied the valet, with comic emphasis. "Monsieur's orders will be followed punctually." And he left the room at a measured pace, striving to assume the compassed gravity that distinguishes the servants of aristocratic houses.

When Monsieur Charmillon was alone, he put his head in his hands and commenced a monologue in a low voice, as provincial actors do when rehearsing their roles as they march hastily through the streets.

"I'm crazy," he said, "To worry like this. There's nothing in Angèle's behavior to make me believe that she has ever had the fatal thought of marrying. The poor child is entirely absorbed by the cares of the household. Besides which, she loves me enough never to consent to causing me a voluntary chagrin. She knows what a profound horror I've professed throughout my life for what the majority of people call the sacred bond of marriage! It's all right! When she comes, I'll try to find out, adroitly, what her intimate thoughts are, and whether she's secretly nurturing any matrimonial tendency—which I shall hasten to combat with invincible arguments."

Reassured by his reflections, Monsieur Charmillon returned to his cherished work.

What Jean-Pierre had not mentioned to his master was that Angèle was not alone in the dining room.

Sitting next to her was a young man, who was watching her while she unfolded tablecloths and napkins, spread them out on the table, examined them minutely and then folded them up again. They were engaged in a very animated conversation, and they both appeared to be taking such a lively interest in it that they had not perceived either the ringing of the scientist's bell at the entrance into the dining room of the pompous Jean-Pierre.

"Oh, Mademoiselle," said the young man, "if you knew how painful it is for me to live so close to you in this state of perpetual embarrassment. I love you, and you have been kind enough to tell me that my sentiments do not offend you in the least. Like you, I belong to an honorable family; I have made my family party to my projects and my hopes. My father and my mother would be happy to see me marry the niece of the illustrious scientist who has been kind enough to facilitate my first steps in the world of scholarship, and to whom I owe the entirety of my first successes."

The young woman listened, while seemingly busy; it was easy to see that she was taking a very keen interest in what the young man was saying.

"I'm not exactly rich," the young man went on, "but the small inheritance that my Uncle Jolibois left me can now assure us a little comfort. You know, in any case, how much I like scientific work, and your uncle says himself to anyone who cares to listen that I have the right to count on a bright future. What serious objection can he have, then, to our marriage, since you consent to it? Come on, Mademoiselle, I'm asking you?"

The lovely Angèle raised her head, turned her beautiful eyes toward the young man, and smiled at him.

"If my uncle were to consult me," she said, in the most tender tone of voice, "I know what I would advise him to do and what reply I'd like him to make to you, but I've already told you several times that, unfortunately, he has never consented to acquire the habit of asking my opinion, and that he already has a fully-formed and very definite position on the subject in question."

"Personally, Mademoiselle, I believe that you're exaggerating the difficulties and that you ought to take your uncle to task for what is perhaps no more than a capricious whim on his part. Monsieur Charmillon has always shown me an almost paternal affection, and he professes an unequaled amity for you. If you would like to be amiable and follow my advice, you'll go to your uncle's study and, after having cajoled him with the grace of which no woman has ever possessed as much as you, you'll tell him our projects and dreams for the future frankly, and let him know that our entire happiness depends on a single word falling from his lips."

"Ta ta ta! That's your imagination taking flight. Have you forgotten, then, the profound horror that Monsieur Charmillon professes for marriage? If I say a single word to him about our hopes, he'll become crimson with anger and throw his secretary, Monsieur Émile Colin, out of the house without further ado, and all we'd have gained would be a separation that might perhaps be permanent, never to see one another again."

"Oh, this situation is unbearable!" cried the young man, whose eyes had filled with tears. "I dread that he'll make us renounce definitively the realization of our beautiful dreams of future happiness!"

"Come on, Monsieur Émile," said the young woman, in her most caressant voice. "Don't be dejected like that, for you'll take all my courage away. Do as I do, and arm yourself with patience. My uncle might change his opinion some day. In the meantime, we have the pleasure of living side by side, of seeing one another at any hour of the day. You tell me repeatedly that I please you. You can see that I'm not playing the coquette with you, and have never shown any sign of doubting your sincerity. For my part, I confess that your quest is not indifferent to me. If fate and my uncle's caprice permit me to marry, I don't want any husband but you; I'll even promise you, if it will give you any pleasure, that I'll never have anyone else."

"So, you refuse to talk to Monsieur Charmillon?" asked the unhappy young man, firmly.

"As to that, yes; I refuse absolutely, because I consider that step to be essentially imprudent."

"It will be me that does it, then, for I'd prefer anything to the false situation in which the two of us are obliged to live. I'll speak this very evening to the uncle you believe to be so terrible."

The quarrel between the two young people was perhaps about to take on new proportions, when the valet Jean-Pierre reappeared and said to Angèle: "Monsieur Charmillon would like to speak to Mademoiselle as soon as possible."

"Very well! I'll hurry," said the young woman. "*Au revoir*, Monsieur Émile—and no imprudence!"

"*Au revoir*, Mademoiselle. I repeat that I've decided to speak. I owe that to the loyalty with which your uncle has welcomed me into his home."

"Do as you wish, stubborn wretch," said Angèle sadly, "but may it please God that we don't have cause to regret your impatience."

She left the room as she was speaking.

When she went into her uncle's study, Monsieur Charmillon was sitting by the fire again. He indicated an armchair that he had placed next to his own. "Sit there, my dear," he said.

Angèle obeyed, sitting down beside the scientist without saying a word and looking at him with an interrogative expression.

"Angèle, I have something very serious to say to you," the Academician began, emphasizing his syllables, as he was accustomed to do in his teaching and in public lectures when he wanted to make a particular appeal to the attention of his listeners.

The young woman's heart began to beat violently, for it seemed to her that her terrible uncle must know something. She remained silent, however, and listened.

"I've just received a letter," Monsieur Charmillon went on, without seeing his niece's emotion. "It's a message from the Institut that threatens to bring considerable trouble into our peaceful dwelling."

Angèle sighed, and felt relieved. "I'm listening, Uncle," she said.

"You know—or rather, you don't know, because it's the lot of women to stagnate in ignorance—that a celestial phenomenon of great importance is to occur in a few months. The planet Mercury, which, with Venus, forms the group of interior planets, is to pass in front of the sun. That will be a scientific solemnity of all the more importance because it happens so rarely."[1]

Angèle opened her eyes wide and wondered what the planet Mercury could possibly have to do with a disruption of the family installed in the small apartment on the Rue de Fleurus.

The savant member of the Institut continued: "This interesting phenomenon will, unfortunately, only be visible from the southern hemisphere; all the scientists in the world have resolved nevertheless not to allow an event to pass unstudied that might permit the further rectification the calculations recently made in a similar circumstance. You know—or rather, you don't—that when Venus passed in front of the sun recently, the most illustrious scientists in all Europe went to distant seas to witness the spectacle, and brought back precious observations. Thanks to their studies, and the calculations made in consequence, we have been able to measure in a much more accurate fashion than had previously been possible the distance that separates us from the sun and the diameter of the star. You can therefore appreciate the importance of such an event. One shivers when one thinks that before the last transit of Venus an important error was committed on that subject, and that we would still be plunged in gross ignorance if valiant observers had not abandoned their hearths, their families and their cherished studies to travel thousands of leagues, in peril of their lives, to direct their gazes through powerful telescopes.

---

[1] In fact, transits of Mercury are more frequent than transits of Venus because Mercury is closer to the Sun; they occur approximately once every eight years, at irregular intervals.

"These details seem tedious to you, my niece, because you can't grasp heir importance, but don't be impatient—I'm getting to the mater that concerns us more directly, and you'll lose nothing by waiting."

The lovely Angèle uttered a sigh of relief, and redoubled her attention.

"A national expedition has been organized," Monsieur Charmillon continued. "It intends to go into the glacial southern seas to witness the fine spectacle that nature promises us. Special credit has been voted by various governments in order to facilitate the scientific mission. Each nation has nominated delegates from among its scientists who will take part in it. The expedition will not only consist of astronomers and mathematicians; all the branches of science will be represented in the unprecedented enterprise: naturalists, geographers, microscopists, physicists and geologists have been designated to take part and...."

"And?" said Angèle, on seeing her uncle hesitate.

"And it's your uncle, Arthème Charmillon, who will have the honor of representing France in that glorious enterprise; it's your uncle who is charged with making special studies of the geology and paleontology of the regions that we're going to visit."

"What, my dear Uncle! You've consented to expatriate yourself at your age? You're leaving your house, your pupils, your work, your cherished studies, and your unfortunate niece?"

"Stop there!" said the scientist. "That's why I summoned you, and what I want to talk to you about. You know what a great affection I have for you, but you also know what my well-determined ideas are about marriage. You'll be my heir—that goes without saying, since I have no other relatives but you in the world—but never, so long as I live, will I allow you to contract the ridiculous and odious contract that delivers a slave to a master. I'm a sworn enemy of the trade in Africans, and I have no more sympathy for the trading of white people. So long as I live, you'll remain a spinster."

"However, Uncle...," Angèle timidly ventured to say.

"No, no—no however!" the scientist interrupted, with a juvenile impetuosity. You'll coif Saint Catherine;[2] that will be better for you than making yourself the servant of some man before becoming his nurse. You'll remain a spinster—that's my wish!"

In his naïve egotism, the unfortunate scientist had no suspicion that the depiction of marriage and its defects that he painted with so much ardor to his niece was a faithful representation of the life that she was condemned to live with him.

As for the young woman, she understood that there was no way to tackle such an obstinate position head on; she contented herself with sighing, and said, resignedly: "Go on, Uncle; I'm listening."

"It's only the determined resolution I've made not to leave you for a moment that has made me hesitate to accept the glorious position that my colleagues at the Institut have offered me. I would never decide to leave you alone in Paris; you can't live apart from your uncle, who watches over you and loves you like a father."

---

[2] Young women in France were said to "coiffe Sainte Cathérine"—the virgin martyr adopted as the symbol of purity—when they reached the age of twenty-five, after which they were considered to be, as the English phrase puts it, "on the shelf" for good.

"So, my worthy uncle," said Angèle clapping her hands, "you've refused and you're staying!"

"No," retorted the Academician, swiftly. "I've accepted gladly, and we're going."

"What? *We*'re going? Oh, no—certainly not!" said the young woman, rebelling. "I can assure you, Uncle, that I have no vocation for distant peregrinations, and that, in spite of the keen chagrin that I'll feel in being separated from you, if you insist on going, I insist on staying."

"Come, come—calm down," said Monsieur Charmillon, who perceived, too late, that he had been unskillful, and that he was running the risk of colliding with a firm determination.

"But Uncle, it's an indignity that you're proposing to me!" cried the young woman, dissolving in tears.

"Good! Now she's crying! Come on, my dear Angèle," he added, softening his voice like a caress. "You mustn't get do upset. Nothing's happened yet, damn it! We haven't gone. If you persist in refusing to go with me, I'll stay, very regretfully, and I'll content myself with letting our poor Émile go, whom I can't honestly deprive of this unique opportunity to make a reputation in the world of science."

At these words, Angèle opened her ears wide; had she not been a daughter of Eve she would doubtless have given herself away; even so, she went as red as a cherry, and anyone else but the old scientist would have been struck by the sharp emotion that had just colored her florid cheeks. She succeeded, however, in mastering herself, wiped away her tears, and said, in a tone she tried to render indifferent:

"My poor Uncle, how good you are, and how unworthy I am to possess such affection! I'm going to deprive you of a pleasure, perhaps the greatest of your life."

"What do you expect? My dear child, it's not our fault that nature has made you a woman. To say 'woman' is to say weak, pusillanimous and cowardly."

On that subject, Monsieur Charmillon, who was not prone to gallantry, had an entire chaplet to tell. His niece, who would not have been hearing the diatribe against her sex for the first time, interrupted him.

"What grieves me, Uncle," she said, "is depriving you of the glory that you promised yourself, and would have crowned your brilliant career so well."

"It's a pity, no doubt," said the scientist, "but after all, the glory that escapes me will be collected by dear Émile. He'll become famous, and as no one is unaware that he's my pupil, the studies and observations that he'll have made will reflect well on me. He'll owe you a considerable illumination, my lovely niece, for after all, as my secretary, he would doubtless have been put in the light, but he'll be much more so when I've confided my own mission to him, and he won't be with his master, who would surely have collected the finest fruits of his endeavors."

"Even if you went, then," asked Angèle, "you'd take Monsieur Émile?"

"Of course! How could I do without him? Isn't he up to date with all my work? Who else could possibly replace him?"

The young woman reflected momentarily, and, increasingly convinced that she had just made a blunder, thought about operating a skillful reversal of direction.

"Uncle," she asked, "is it really very far away that your expedition is going?"

"Is it far? Nearly ten thousand leagues from our homeland, unless it's eleven, or even twelve."

"Is it a beautiful country where you'll be making your observations?"

"Some solitary rock in the middle of the sea, in a glacial climate, far from any inhabited land."

"It's singular, my dear Uncle, how much what you're saying excites my curiosity."

"Oh, the most difficult curiosity would have had plenty to satisfy it. First of all, there'll have been a long crossing during which all zones and all climates would have been visited. Moreover, we'd have had a magnificent ship, comfortably fitted out. On arrival, we'd have been able to study the disrupted terrains of volcanic islands, and the flora and fauna of the glacial seas—which is to say, mosses and lichens, all different from the vegetation of our country; no trees, almost no vegetation; seals and whales, and perhaps white bears. Everywhere, we have had before us solitude and the unknown!"

"Do you know, Uncle, that the picture you've jut painted is full of seductions? I almost regret having turned you away from making the voyage, and it wouldn't take much for me to decide to go with you. My dear Uncle's glory is dearer to my heart than I thought."

"My dear, dear child," murmured the old Academician, in a tender tone.

"You'll go, then—and you'll take me with you! Is it agreed?"

"No, no, my poor dear. It's only now that I understand how odiously egotistical my project was. No, I won't make you freeze amid the ice-sheets and the icebergs. No, I won't expose your beauty and youth to the perilous hazards of such a long voyage. My decision is made, my dear Angèle; you see me resigned, and we'll stay. Émile will depart alone. To him, the glory to be acquired! It's time I'd stepped side to make way for the younger generation."

The clever fly found herself caught in the web that she had spun herself, but she was woman enough not to abandon the game, and rapidly found a second string for her bow.

"I'd almost regret the decision you've made," she said, in the most ingenuous tone in the world, "if our dwelling hadn't become more agreeable since that English family came to live opposite. Have you noticed, Uncle, how pretty the young Misses are who play on the balcony? And their big brother is so funny that I can't think about him without dying laughing. From morning to evening he's behind a curtain watching my movements, and...."

"What! That young man has dared...?"

"Oh, Uncle, it's not as bad as that! Doubtless he finds me to his taste, and he's not obliged to be aware of the extraordinary ideas you have about marriage. Anyway, the English people belong to a great family, and I know that the young Monsieur will be very rich one day."

"And how do you know that, you little rogue?" said the scientist, all of whose blood had frozen in his veins.

"Oh, my God, it's quite simple," she replied, without showing the slightest emotion. "I asked the chambermaid." And she added, as if to herself: "All the same, it's a pity that you have such a profound aversion to marriage, for he's very good-looking, the young Englishman."

Uncle Arthème Charmillon pressed his bald head between his hands momentarily. He sensed the redoubtable abyss hollowing out beneath his feet. He reflected momentarily.

"On due reflection," he said, finally, "Since you'll consent to go with me, we'll go together to observe the passage of Mercury across the Sun." In a more caressant voice, he went on: "Angèle, go and tell dear Émile that I need to see him. Above all, don't tell him about our departure; I want to enjoy his pleasure and surprise when I announce that I've obtained an authorization to take him with me, and enable him to share the glory of my future discoveries."

The young woman did not need the request to be repeated, and departed with the agility of a frightened hind.

As soon as she was out of her uncle's sight. She said to herself, with a huge sigh of relief: "That was a narrow squeak!"

Chapter II

During the fortnight that followed the scenes that have served as an introduction to this story, the greatest disorder and incessant activity reigned over the scientist Arthème Charmillon's dwelling.

On the one hand, the Academician and his faithful secretary, Monsieur Émile Colin, piled volumes, journals, newspapers and manuscripts into crates, sorting out as best they could the precious documents from which they expected to extract the information useful to their work. On the other hand, Angèle, as a farsighted housekeeper, packed the trunks and filled them with clothing.

The valet, Jean-Pierre, like La Fontaine's coach-fly, ran from one room to another, offering his services in vain, and consoling himself for the refusals that usually greeted his proposals by increasing his air of self-importance.

When the initial preparatory work was done and everyone could read with satisfaction the carefully-written lists of objects set aside for the voyage, they set out on campaign to make the acquisitions that the projected long absence seemed to render necessary. Monsieur Charmillon made ample provision of all the instruments necessitated by geological research: forceps and steel hammers for breaking rocks; spades and pickaxes for digging in the ground; magnifying glasses and microscopes for examining the details and constituent parts of objects of study; boxes and filing-cabinets for putting them in order, etc., etc.

For his part, the young man, anticipating the necessities and leisure of a sojourn on a desert island, hastened to form a collection of books for his friend that he strove to render both attractive an instructive. Contemporary literary works took pride of place there. After having devoted his cares to preparations for the voyage for the person he considered as his fiancée, he thought about his own needs, and provided himself with everything that he supposed might be useful or agreeable to him for the duration of the voyage.

Born in the mountains of the département of the Isère, he had become accustomed in his youth, during his travels in the Alps, to physical fatigues, scorn for danger and a vulgar love of hunting. A visit to a prestigious armorer permitted him to equip himself with carbines and hunting rifles whose accuracy and quality were sufficiently guaranteed. Thus, he was soon furnished with rifles of various calibers and double-barreled shoguns; he added to that arsenal, for his personal safety, a pair of the rapid-fire pocket machine-guns that had just been invented by an already-famous French engineer, Abraham Martin.[3]

When the weapons had been carefully packed, the young scientist rubbed his hands and went to visit the Academician, who, doubtless also satisfied with his work, welcomed him with a smile.

"Well, where are we?" he asked.

"I'm ready, my dear Master, and we can set forth any time you please."

---

[3] Abraham Martin, born in 1834, was indeed the French engineer who invented a four-barreled handgun known as the "Martin Mitrailleuse" [Martin machine-gun], but the latter was manufactured in Birmingham in the 1880s because he was a notorious anarchist, who spend a lot of time in exile from his homeland. There is, therefore, a hint of irony in the reference.

"I too have put the finishing touches to my work, and if my dear niece doesn't hold us back under the pretext of having some dress to finish, we can leave tomorrow, if you wish, and head for the port where our ship is waiting for us."

Angèle appeared at that very moment; she had doubtless overheard the last words pronounced by her uncle, for she said, in the sweetest possible tone: "It isn't me, Messieurs Great Minds, who will hinder your noble ardor in any way; all my preparations are complete, my boxes sealed and my trunks carefully closed. You can give the signal for departure whenever you wish; I'm entirely ready to follow you."

"Bravo!" cried the old scientist, whose face was resplendent with joy. Come on, Émile, let's have our luggage transported to the Gare de Lyon without delay. That way, we'll be ready for the express to take us to Marseilles."

"It's Marseilles where we'll be embarking, then?" queried his secretary.

"Yes, my children," replied the member of the Institut, who, in his excitement, unconsciously enveloped the two young people in a common qualification, "we'll be in the open sea within a week; by then we'll have embarked on the *Glorieux*, a magnificent ship that the State has been kind enough to have fitted out especially for our expedition."

Émile did not need the old scientist's invitation to be repeated; a few hours later, thanks to the collaboration of the railway company's trucks, he had fulfilled his mission conscientiously. All the baggage was labeled and registered at the station.

The following evening, the three voyagers took the eight-thirty express.

Monsieur Charmillon had his reasons for departing thus, several days in advance; he had promised himself to give the two young people a surprise that he hoped would be agreeable to them. A few minutes away in the vicinity of Marseilles he had a friend whose country house, situated on a verdant hill, overlooked the blue horizons of the Mediterranean.

We'll stay with good old Margueron, he had said to himself, *and in that admirable location my niece and my secretary will have the time to make a few excursions to the beach, and a few fishing expeditions They'll be able to familiarize themselves thus with an element on which they'll be called upon to live for the first time, for God knows how long.*

One can see that except for his incurable fault—by which we mean his aversion to marriage—Monsieur Charmillon was the cream of men and the most amiable of scientists.

His plan was realized, point for point.

Thanks to a dispatch sent from the station on departure, Monsieur Margueron was notified in good time of the arrival of his guests, and came to meet them at Marseilles station with his carriage. The welcome could not have been more cordial.

Monsieur Margueron was not an ordinary man; after having spent fifteen fruitful years trading on the west coast of Africa, he had made a considerable fortune in the manufacture of soap and the exploitation of palm oil. From that moment on he had delivered himself without distraction to his vocation, which, since childhood, had led him to collect ancient objects and coins. He had not taken long to become a distinguished numismatist, and it was in that context that he had become linked in cordial amity, and also in fruitful studies with Monsieur Charmillon, the scholarly member of the Institut.

The grave and solemn Jean-Pierre, whom the Academician had decided, on his request, to take with him, was left in Marseilles with the responsibility of checking the arrival of the luggage confided to the slow train and to supervise its loading aboard the *Glorieux*. Then the three newcomers climbed into the carriage cheerfully, and accompanied their host to the superb Villa des Roches.

The days for which their sojourn in that charming place lasted were a series of enchantments for the young couple. Neither of them had yet seen the sea, and they could not take their eyes off the magnificent spectacle.

In the morning, taking advantage of the liberty that the rural existence gave them, they went down the step slopes of the hill on the summit of which Monsieur Margueron's house stood. While the two scientists indulged in interminable discussions devoted to the study of some Roman ruin or the classification of an ancient Italian faience, the young people went running over the sands of the shore, collecting crustaceans or shellfish from the rock-pools. Sometimes they embarked on a fishing-boat and, while the light vessel was pushed by the breeze, they allowed their reverie to wander at whim over the waves. They would both have gladly consented to spend the rest of their lives there.

Let is also say, in their praise, that by virtue of a kind of tacit convention, from the day when Angèle's uncle had pronounced so formally against any future marriage project, the two young folk had ceased to formulate any such hope. One thought was sufficient to fill heir hearts: they had nearly been separated, and the very hazard that had threatened to destroy their happiness forever had brought them even closer together. They were reunited; they could see one another every day; that was amply sufficient on its own to make them happy.

Finally, like everything down here, that interval of delight came to an end and it was necessary to think about taking the road back to Marseilles. Monsieur Margueron envied the lot of the voyagers and did not conceal the pleasure he would have had in accompanying them; it was, alas, a superfluous desire, for no one could be admitted aboard the *Glorieux* except the members of the mission. He was therefore obliged to content himself with harnessing his old nag to his country carriage and taking his dear visitors to the harbor where their beautiful ship was waiting for them, with all sails hoisted, and launching clouds of russet smoke from its funnel.

The *Glorieux* was a long, slender and graceful steam-frigate, slightly low-lying in the water, carrying sails suspended from her rigging as complex as if she had been a simple sailing-ship. Thanks to the elegance of her form and the surface of canvas she deployed, the *Glorieux* would have been a fast ship anyway, but she also concealed in her flanks an 850-horsepower steam engine, activating two propellers. Prior to the expedition that she was charged with conveying to distant seas, she had been fitted with sixty large-caliber cannons, and had more than once carried a crew of six hundred men.

The population of Marseilles, who know better than any other how to appreciate the naval qualities of a vessel, came every day to admire the *Glorieux* in the harbor, where she swayed nobly on her anchors. There, every connoisseur observed that the fine ship was no less than ten times as long as her master-beam, which is a certain condition for giving a ship a rapid speed as well as an excellent foundation. Although neither Monsieur Charmillon nor his secretary, let alone his niece, had the slightest pretention to naval expertise, they could not help gazing with pride at the superb vessel that was about to become their residence.

"Look," said the young man, addressing Angèle and pointing at the *Glorieux*, emerging in the midst of the boats of all kinds cluttering the harbor, "isn't she like a swan in the midst of a flock of geese and ducks?"

The young woman smiled, and observed that, if his comparison was flattering for the *Glorieux*, it was nevertheless humiliating for the other vessels surrounding her.

The ceremony of embarkation aboard a naval vessel is ordinarily rather awkward and difficult, but as we have said, the *Glorieux* had been fitted out in a very special fashion to receive the scientific elite of all Europe. The engineers charged with that delicate task had been careful not to forget to facilitate the access of men who were generally aged and whose habitual occupations did not dispose them to physical exercise and feats of agility. The rudimentary rope ladders that hang down from the sides of a ship and are amply sufficient to facilitate the ascension of skilled mariners had been replaced by a light and comfortable stairway. The three newcomers therefore went aboard without any difficulty or inconvenience.

In spite of all the precautions taken, the greatest disorder reigned on deck. A considerable number of the members of the expedition had neglected to comply with the sage instructions that had been given to them and had not sent their luggage and numerous packages aboard until the last moment. The result was that the entire upper surface of the ship was in chaos, further increased by the shouts of the sailors, the whistles of the petty officers, the comings and goings of the travelers and the friends who had come aboard with them, and the maneuvering of the steam-cranes responsible for bringing a little order to the various heaps, where one encountered, pell-mell, trunks, crates, instruments of various forms, containers, kitchen equipment, etc., etc.

Our three voyagers were advancing hesitantly, therefore, and with a very legitimate apprehension, through the midst of all the packages, the coiled or extended ropes and nameless objects when Jean-Pierre appeared before them.

"The master's orders have been scrupulously carried out," he said, bowing with a gravity that would have done honor to a chamberlain.

"But where the devil are we going?" asked Monsieur Charmillon.

"If Mademoiselle and the Messieurs would care to follow me, "Jean-Pierre continued, redoubling his politeness and solemnity, "I shall have the honor of conducting them to their apartment."

Angèle leaned toward the secretary and said to him in a low and slightly mocking tone: "Jean-Pierre is definitely losing his head at the thought of the honor of accompanying us. I'll wager that he already thinks of himself as a member of the scientific expedition."

Meanwhile, following the pompous valet, Monsieur Charmillon, his niece and his secretary arrived at a vast opening into the hull of the ship and went down a broad stairway covered by a thick carpet. It was the hatchway that would take them to their cabins and the part of the vessel designed to accommodate members of the expedition.

In renouncing her role as a warship in order to fulfill a peaceful mission, the *Glorieux* had changed appearance, especially in her interior fitments. Only eight large-caliber cannons had been embarked, four placed to starboard and showing their gaping maws through the gunports placed fore and aft of the funnel, and four more in similar situations to port. They were all solidly moored in armored redoubts. It was on that part of the first deck that the officers' quarters had been provisionally installed.

The entirety of the first deck beyond the main mast had been divided into lounges, libraries and workrooms for the members of the international scientific expedition. Only the Commandant had retained his private cabin, known as the "Commandant's corridor," toward the prow. He only occupied the small part of that deck placed against the extreme partition; he had renounced his office and dining-room, and had declared that he would eat at the same table as his illustrious passengers.

The cabin of the first mate had been relocated beneath that of the commandant, in the place normally occupied by the officers' ward-room. They had installed their table on the second deck, between the descending stairway and the mate's cabin.

Thanks to these dispositions, the upper deck at the rear was almost completely put at the disposal of the members of the expedition, whose cabins occupied the all of the free space of the corresponding part of the second deck.

By virtue of a flattering exception, two spacious cabins had been fitted out for Arthème Charmillon and his niece in the part of the upper deck backing on to the armored redoubt.

The midshipmen's quarters had not changed position, being, as usual, placed next to the mainmast between decks; it was feebly illuminated, like the other parts of that section, by circular portholes formed by thick lenticular glass. The section between decks is, in fact, placed between the artillery deck and the lower floor; only half of its height is above the flotation line, which necessitates those hermetic seals.

The young secretary was resigned to occupying a modest cabin set up next to the novices' quarters. He did not complain about that allocation, for his age and character was not too far removed from those of his new comrades, and he was allowed to share the table and studies of the members of the expedition, which was a great honor for him.

The whole of three travelers' first day aboard the *Glorieux* was spent arranging the most indispensable items as best they could in their respective cabins, and making themselves comfortable. When the bell announced the time of evening meal at five o'clock, they were still so far from finishing that task that they renounced going to the common dining-room and dispatched Jean-Pierre in search of some food, agreeing that they would eat as best they could in Monsieur Charmillon's cabin.

In the midst of the disorder that still reigned aboard the ship, it seemed unlikely that the negotiation in question would succeed, and Angèle was already talking about unpacking some of the tins and treats that she had embarked in anticipation of some such circumstance, but neither of them had taken sufficient account of the persistence and solemnity of their domestic.

They saw Jean-Pierre appear with a napkin over his arm like a perfect maître-d'hôtel, marching at a measured pace "like a rector followed by the four faculties"[4] and clutching a large round wicker basket. He placed the receptacle on the floor and, without losing his air of pomposity, removed a very white tablecloth and napkins, brilliant silver cutlery, and then warming-plates covered with silvery lids, on which delicate dishes were fuming.

When he had finished setting the table, he said: "Mademoiselle is served," and headed back to the door.

"Where are you going now?" asked the Academician.

"I'm going to fetch the basket of wines that I've had prepared for Monsieur," he replied.

He went out and came back with a basket filled with bottles of various forms and sizes; there were narrow ones sealed with long corks and sealed with pink transparent wax; there were wines from the great Bordeaux vintages, Château Lafitte or Château Laroze; other bottles of a more modest appearance but bearing large labels on their sides indicating that they belonged to vintages appreciated by gourmets, Clos-Vougeot and Chambertin. Alongside those were two bottles of Johannisberg, and two bottles of Champagne, one of them bearing the authentic brand of Madame Veuve Cliquot and the other than of Monsieur Soubeyran de Saint-Prix. You can imagine the amazement with which Monsieur Charmillon welcomed that master valet.

"What the devil do you expect us to do with all that?" he demanded, unable to dissimulate a broad smile.

"But that's not all, Monsieur. I still have to bring Monsieur the various desserts, coffee and liqueurs."

---

[4] The popular simile in question originated in the late 18th century in one of Nicolas Boileau's satires.

"Oh! Wretch, it's the dinner of the entire mission that you're bringing us."

"It's Mademoiselle's dinner," replied Jean-Pierre, imperturbably. "Monsieur knows very well that nothing is too good for Mademoiselle his niece, and the maître-d'hôtel asked me to give you his apologies; if the service leaves something to be desired, it's necessary to take into account the disturbances to which he's been subject all day."

Angèle burst into frank laughter. "Bravo!" she said, clapping her hands. "To judge by this prelude, it's evident that if we're going to die during the voyage it won't be of hunger or thirst. In the meantime, let's do honor to this feast of Sardanapalus."

The three travelers sat down at the table and unanimously declared that the ship's cook was an artiste worthy of exercising his talents at a royal table.

The wines were uncorked and declared exquisite. Angèle had only done mediocre honor to the savory dishes of game and fish that formed the basis of the succulent meal, but she made up for it in the delicacies of the second course and dessert.

After the coffee, Monsieur Charmillon was in a charming humor. His distraction was so great that he did not see the young people squeeze one another's hands cordially before separating.

Chapter III

Such an active day had fatigued our three explorers greatly, so, as soon as they had returned to their respective cabins, they did not take long to fall into a reparative slumber. The slept so profoundly that none of them heard the sound of the bell warning the last of the friends and curiosity-seekers who had come aboard to bid farewell to the voyagers to quit the ship without delay.

It was, in effect, the signal for departure.

Monsieur Charmillon, his nice and Émile were therefore unable to witness the moving scene. Everywhere, a numerous and sympathetic crowd had gathered to address its fond farewells to the explorers, crowding the jetties and the quays and waving pocket handkerchiefs.

Thanks to the first revolutions of her propellers, the *Glorieux* disengaged smoothly from the host of ships, great and small, that surrounded her, and then, in dark night, only illuminated by a profusion of Venetian lanterns forming capricious garlands on the poop deck, she went through the narrow entrance to the harbor. A few spectators perched on the rocks of Fort Saint-Jean and Saint-Nicolas waved farewell in their turn. Finally, the ship moved into the bay and followed her course in the direction of the open sea.

None of the noises without and within associated with the departure, any more than the monotonous sound produced by the spinning propellers, succeeded in waking the sleepers, who, when they went up on deck the following morning, were somewhat surprised not to be able to see anything but the sea and the sky.

"My friends," said Monsieur Charmillon, "the die is cast. Our great voyage has begun. Let us hope that it finishes without anything unfortunate happening to any of us, and without our having to deplore the loss of any of our companions."

The two young people looked at one another, addressing a mute interrogation by way of thought. Each of them wanted to know that no regret was concealed in some recess of the other's heart. Soon, they were seen to smile simultaneously, for they had both said to themselves that no care could arise in their hearts as long as they were together.

The sea, in any case, could not have been more conducive to navigation. A light northerly breeze inflated the deployed sails, pushing the ship from behind, adding its efforts to the rapidity of the propellers. The *Glorieux* was thus making between sixteen and twenty knots, which is a considerable speed. Everyone observed, moreover, with visible satisfaction, that they could not feel any pitching or rolling. Not a single passenger had yet been subject to the slightest affliction of the terrible sea-sickness whose terrible effects can only be appreciated by those who have suffered from it.

All the passengers on the deck were contemplating the sublime spectacle that extended before their eyes when the ship's bell rang to announce that it was time for the morning meal.

This time, Monsieur Charmillon, his niece and his secretary went to the dining room, where they found themselves confronted by a sumptuously-set table.

The Commandant of the *Glorieux*, an old sea-dog who had already been a ship's captain for ten years, did the honors of his ship that day. He was man of the world, in every sense of the term. It was to be assumed that during maneuvers and when issuing commands to his matelots, his language lost a little of its elegance, and that the most energetic oaths frequently replaced the flowers of his rhetoric, but thus far, that was only hearsay, which no one could verify. Then again, even had it been proven, there would have been no reason to disapprove, for everyone knows that it is necessary "to howl with the wolves" and that matelots are not timid schoolgirls with delicate ears.

At any rate, Commandant Beaudin showed himself so full of polite concern for everyone that they all declared him to be a charming man. They were all convinced that they would have the most pleasant relationship with him throughout the voyage.

He placed Angèle Charmillon to his left, so that she found herself between the Commandant and her uncle. She was the only woman on board; it was quite natural that every respect should be lavished on her, and everyone made it a duty to surround her with attention.

No aristocratic table anywhere had ever brought together so many illustrious scientists. Monsieur Charmillon, who was a corresponding member of a large number of scientific societies throughout the world, recognized many of his fellows. As for the Commandant, either because he could not remember everyone's names or because he did not think it indispensable, he contented himself with introducing the meal with a little speech in which he wished everyone welcome without designating anyone in particular. Only Angèle had the honor of a special compliment.

Monsieur Charmillon thought that he ought, for decency's sake, to shake the hands of the guests he knew personally. There were two Englishmen aboard: William Johnson, the well-known naturalist, and Mr. Wilson, a member of the Royal Geographical Society of London, a great mathematician with whom he had made a pact of friendship in Paris during the International Conference of Geography that had been held in the Tuileries in August 1875.

As the scientists gathered aboard the *Glorieux* not only did not know one another very well but did not all speak the same language, they were placed in national groups around the vast table on which a superb meal was served. In the group formed by the Russians Monsieur Charmillon recognized another two old friends whose hands he hastened to shake; they were Batschkoff, whose book on the history of the Slavic nations has been translated into all languages, and Pierre de Kolikoff, who had occupied himself with rare success with geodesics and geology. As colleagues, Kolikoff and the French scientist had been in correspondence for a long time.

Among the representatives of Germany Monsieur Charmillon recognized the celebrated naturalist Walter Müller of Berlin, whose collections are cited alongside those of the richest museums, and Dr. Franz Henrich, who was responsible for a theory as strange as it was personal regarding the formation of the terrestrial continents during the primordial age.

The Frenchman, who was unable, by virtue of a patriotic sentiment easier to imagine than to explain, to forgive Germany for its successes and our reverses,[5] was content to salute the two foreign scientists with a wave of his hand.

---

[5] In 1876, memories of the Prussian invasion of France in 1870 were still raw, and the consequent bitter resentment was still seething a long time thereafter.

He showed himself more expansive toward Otto Eliaison, Oscar Johannesen and Stuxberg, who represented Sweden and Denmark, to whom he went to present his amities effusively.

The Italian scientists Pietro Bono and Enrico della Maria did not wait for his visit and came to present their amities and respects to him, assuring him that his name was popular throughout Italy.

There was also a whole clan of foreign members belonging to Spain and Portugal, but Monsieur Charmillon, not being personally acquainted with any of the members of those two groups, thought it appropriate to wait for a favorable opportunity to present itself in order to enter into relations with them.

The meal was, as can be imagined, cold and rather ceremonious. Every guest observed his neighbors and was guarded in his conversation. It would have been desirable for that reserve to have remained the rule of the conduct of the mission throughout the crossing, but that was not the case, and a certain peevish antagonism son took the place of the ceremonious cordiality prevalent at that first meal.

The world of doctors of science is not always replete with indulgence; it is justly reproached for exclusivism and insupportable intolerance. A scientist, by the very fact of his serious studies, and the faith he brings to his theories, repudiates as so many gross and demonstrated errors the opinions and theories of colleagues who have followed a different path—hence the intemperance of language and occasional exchanges of wounding epithets that one is astonished to encounter in authorized mouths.

If, to those causes of dissent that one finds in the milieu of men belonging to the same scholarly body, one joins the rivalries between companies, cities and nations, it will be easily understandable that the benevolent understanding between the learned guests of the *Glorieux* was unlikely to last long. Nevertheless, during that first meal, it was untroubled by the slightest cloud.

Conversations initially began separately in the different groups, each of them maintaining one in low voices in its national language, but the generous wines that were circulating with a princely abundance did not take long to loosen tongues and give rise to expansion. During the second course, the neighboring groups began to address one another; those who knew other languages were pleased to show off their expertise, and gladly served as interpreters for their less fortunate friends.

When the dessert arrived, the conversations began in low tones had raised their volume, and someone passing by outside, on hearing that hubbub, in which all the languages of Europe were mingled, might have thought that they had been transported to the Tower of Babel at the moment when its constructors had been obliged to separate.

The rich and knowledgeable Kolikoff, who had been able to combine his specialist studies on the formation of the globe with a profound knowledge of all the languages presently spoken in the world, stood up and signaled that he desired to speak. It required nothing less than his uncontested authority to obtain silence, especially at the moment when the champagne was causing corks to pop and sparkling in crystal glasses. Nevertheless, silence fell, and the noble Russian was able to take the floor.

"My friends and colleagues," he said, "I desire to make you a simple proposition, and, for that reason, I ask you to grant me your attention for a moment."

From all directions there were cries of: "Listen! Listen!"

"The success of our enterprise is, I believe, dependent in large measure on the unity and mutual understanding that reigns among us.

"Hear hear!"

"How can we be united and understand one another if we persist in living in isolated groups, each speaking our national language? We can obtain a series of serious efforts in that way, but will lack the bond that could make it into a whole."

"Bravo!"

"Very good!

"*Très bien!*"

"I propose, in consequence, my dear colleagues, that we choose one special language that we will all speak, more or less correctly, during our meals. That will be the connection that will permit us to exchange our thoughts generally, instead of enclosing them in the restricted circles of our compatriots.

Mr. Wilson of the Royal Geographical Society of London stood up. "For my part," he said, "I agree completely with the idea suggested by our eminent colleague, Mr. Kolikoff, but which language should we adopt?"

"I've thought about that," said Kolikoff, "and I propose that it should be French, which the majority of us have studied, and which has already been chosen as the language of international diplomacy."

"We accept!" said the Italians, the Spanish and the Portuguese, with one voice.

"My English colleagues and I also accept, although we have some difficulty in expressing ourselves correctly in that language."

"Why not adopt English or German for preference?" said Walter Müller of Berlin, in an ill-humored tone.

The noble Russian rose to his feet again. "I cannot be accused of interested partiality," he said, in a conciliatory tone. "My old friend Walter Müller knows that, personally, I experience no difficulty in expressing myself in English or German, but it is not the same for all of us. A great poet—the greatest of our century, Victor Hugo—has said in a celebrated book that French is an admirable language, comprising sufficient consonants to be spoken by the men of the north, and sufficient vowels to be pronounced by the men of the south. I thus maintain my proposal, and ask that it should be put to a vote."

Oscar Johannesen of Stockholm asked to add a word. "I support Monsieur de Kolikoff's proposition," he said, "because I believe that all of us, inasmuch as we are here, understand French more or less, and that it would not be the same with any other language."

To that just observation was added that of Monsieur Picho-Baro: "Take note that we're aboard a French ship, and that it's a French crew who are conducting us; to choose a foreign language that would not be understood by all the honorable officers who are guiding us would, it seems to me be testifying a kind of suspicion toward them, by which they might be offended."

That argument seemed decisive to everyone, and by a unanimous vote, it was decided that French would be used exclusively, not only at table, but for the drafting of all the important documents written in the name of the entire mission.

After having consulted his three colleagues—the astronomer Chauvin, the chemist Guébard and the botanist Dr. Despierre, Monsieur Charmillon stood up in his turn and thanked the assembly on their behalf for the honor done to France.

"Messieurs," he said, "there is an argument that you have had the generosity not to put forward, but which it is my duty to mention, however sad the admission seems to me. You have all been initiated since childhood into the study of living foreign languages; we, on the contrary, have remained thus far in a very regrettable ignorance on that subject. You have done well to choose French to be spoken at meals because, had any other language been adopted, two or three of us would have been necessarily left out of the conversation. Thus, Messieurs, I thank you in the name of our worthy general staff, in the name of my savant colleagues, and in the name of race, my noble fatherland."

That perfect entente, that flattering choice, and the desire expressed by everyone to form a compact band, promised the expedition not only the success that the science of all the members composing it assured it, but also a cordial relationship, a pledge of goodwill and fraternity. It was, however, perhaps necessary to tribute to that decision to exclude any other language than French from general meetings the personal disagreements that were subsequently to divide certain members of the mission.

We shall not follow the scholarly company step by step and day by day in the long voyage that it had undertaken, and will content ourselves with citing the principal facts that characterized the progress of the enterprise.

The dissensions that we have mentioned burst forth in the early days between the French scientists and the Germans. The latter did not comprehend sufficiently the magnitude of the regrets left in the hearts of our compatriots by the memory of the disasters and misfortunes of

1870. They seemed to take a malign pleasure in twisting the knife in the wound, incessantly referring back to the events of that baneful epoch. Monsieur Charmillon finally found his patience running out, and reacted to some German boasting with a few sharp comments. War was thus declared, and the two enemy camps ceased to have the slightest communication.

The Commandant, while affecting a neutrality to which his official situation obliged him, did not neglect any opportunity to testify to our compatriot his amity and the high esteem in which he held him.

The petty perfidies in which our rivals from beyond the Rhine excel soon commenced; they affected to fall suddenly silent when Monsieur Charmillon entered, as if he had been the subject of the interrupted conversation and they did not want him to know what they had been saying.

The member of the Institut de France quickly perceived these persecutions, and, initially judging them to be insignificant, began by merely laughing at them, but soon, on seeing his adversaries' poor taste persist, lost his appetite for the various general meetings and resolved to live in his quarters, with his household, to the extent that it was possible. He expressed that desire to the Commandant, who welcomed his request with the greatest benevolence. Orders were given and Jean-Pierre was charged thereafter with going forth twice a day to fetch food for Monsieur Charmillon, his niece and his secretary.

The two young people were entirely happy with that change of circumstance; the new regime bought them back to the old family intimacy that the solemn existence of the common room had interrupted. From then on, they spent as little time as possible apart, and the voyage became private rather than being accomplished in the midst of a crowd.

We shall not insist on the joy that took its seat at the table of those three individuals, so worthy of mutual understanding and affection, and in order to arrive more rapidly at the events that are more particularly the object of this veridical narrative, we shall content ourselves with following in its broad lines the rapid voyage of the *Glorieux*, only interrupted from time to time by more or less prolonged sojourns at points designated in advance as ports of call, where certain members of the expedition had a few observations to make in passing.

The *Glorieux* left Marseilles on the first of August, passing the Balearic Islands on the third. Émile Colin, who had made special studies on the structure of the globe, had taken the young woman on to the deck, and both of them, leaning on the rail, were contemplating the immensity of the sea, whose intense blue merged with the blue of the sky on the horizon.

Suddenly, the watchman's cry of "Land ho!" was heard, and Émile, armed with a telescope, showed Angèle the large island of Majorca emerging in the distance, and then, further away in the mist, Ibiza.

"Where are the other three islands: Minorca, Formentera and Cabrera?" asked the young woman, who had not neglected in her turn to obtain a little geographical knowledge.

"Those, Mademoiselle, offer us their apologies; they're too far away, and we'll pass by without seeing them."

On the fourth of August the coast of Spain was signaled and they arrived at Gibraltar, where the *Glorieux* dropped anchor. Monsieur Charmillon and those he subconsciously called his children took advantage of it to go ashore.

This is not the place to talk about that redoubtable fortress of which the English are so proud and whose maintenance and protection are so costly for them.

Our three friends visited the citadel, entirely formed of bunkers hollowed out in the granite and lava of the rock. They were surprised by the immense deployment of forces that England maintains there, almost completely pointlessly. When they had gone back on board, Monsieur Charmillon demonstrated without difficulty to Émile that nothing is less exact than the epithet awarded to Gibraltar of "the key to the Mediterranean."

"See how broad the strait is," he said. "At its narrowest point between Ceuta and the tip of Europe, it's no less than twenty-two kilometers. How could the fire of Gibraltar stop a convoy of steamships desirous of forcing a passage? For that, it would require a numerous fleet protected by the batteries of the fort, which could blockade the strait. Even in that case victory would depend on a naval battle whose outcome might well be unfavorable to the guardians of the passage."

On leaving Gibraltar on the eighth of August the Glorieux headed at full steam for the large island of Madeira. The wind was contrary and it was necessary to lower the sails. Nevertheless, thanks to the double propeller of the steam engine, land was signaled in the distance on the tenth of August.

Émile, who had got up early and was parading his pensive gaze over the vast extent, was one of the first to sight land. First, he discovered to starboard the little island of Porto Santo, and then, ahead to port, a long series of desolate islets with bizarre silhouettes, which are marked on maritime charts as "desert."

Directly ahead of the ship, an enormous massif rose up abruptly, in the form of a truncated cone whose slightly undulating walls were tinted pink by the rising sun. Émile uttered a cry of joy. "There's Madeira!" he exclaimed. And, indeed, it was that superb island, which, ornamented and fresh, seemed to be emerging from the bosom of the waves.

The *Glorieux*, in whose itinerary it was marked as a port of call, passed to the south of the occidental tip of the island, went along a verdant coast serrated by gracious hills and picturesque valleys, and arrived at the entrance to a semicircular bay, into which it penetrated and dropped anchor. The expedition had arrived in the haven of Funchal, and all its members were invited to go ashore.

Émile, Monsieur Charmillon and his nice hastened to take advantage of the opportunity to visit the fatherland of a wine well-known but too often faked.

Chapter IV

For voyagers who are commencing a long peregrination, the slight incidents of the route seem interesting. When Monsieur Charmillon, Émile and Angèle went ashore the mode of disembarkation appeared to them to be very original and rather amusing.

The *Glorieux* was anchored in Funchal Bay, which is a calm and restful place rather than a cheerful one. The grave aspect of the high mountains there makes a striking contrast with the luxuriant verdure of the valleys descending therefrom.

As soon as the ship was moored, several launches came alongside, offering to sell fresh fish, vegetables and appetizing fruits, among which Angèle especially remarked superb grapes, which she declared more beautiful than pleasant to taste, and little figs that she found delicious. A host of small children with bronzed skins had thrown themselves into the water like a swarm of frogs and, soliciting alms from the crew, dived repeatedly to search the sea-bed for the coins that were thrown over the side. That is customary, with an audacity and an unusual skill, to the young natives who live on the entire African coast, on the east as well as the west.

The bay is generally very placid; nevertheless, a sea breeze easily enters into it, and as there is no quay in front of the city, the launches usually employed for disembarkation cannot, more often than not, deposit their passengers on land dry-footed. Thus, use is made of local craft that are flat-bottomed. When one of them presents itself for landing, all the mariners and people of the port who are there go to meet it, some placing themselves at the sides and others harnessing themselves by means of a rope to the prow, and they drag the boat as far as they can on to the shingle. That was how Monsieur Charmillon and his companions were able to disembark without getting their feet wet.

We shall not describe Madeira at length, the enchanting aspect of which moved the voyagers profoundly. Let it suffice to say that what astonished and charmed them the most was to find the crops of hot countries and those of the temperate zones growing side by side. In a geological excursion ventured by the old scientist and his pupil, on which Angèle insisted on accompanying them, she noticed that the cacti, banana trees, palm trees and oleanders ornamenting the lower reaches of the island were succeeded as they went higher by aloes, sugar cane, and the by the wild brambles and ivy of Europe. Higher still, they encountered plane trees, elms and oaks. Everywhere there were flowers in profusion: sunflowers, wisteria, enormous fuchsias Cape lilies, myrtle, amaryllis, magnolias and magnificent blue hortensias.

The hills were covered with thick woods beneath which isolated houses were scattered, making bright patches amid the intense verdure. If Angèle was struck primarily by the splendors of the picturesque landscape, the two scientists, for their part, found ample gleanings in the tormented terrains of volcanic origin. When they returned aboard the *Glorieux*, each of them was laden by the harvest they had gathered. While her companions were weighed down by specimens of rock of various forms and colors, the young woman was carrying an enormous and admirably bouquet containing samples of all the flowers she had encountered in her excursion.

After Madeira they visited Tenerife, and the *Glorieux* anchored in Santa Cruz Bay. After having traveled through the three districts making up the island—Laguna, Oratava and Quarachico—the visitors were impressed by the prodigious fertility of the soil. The hills were covered in vines all the way to the summit. Orange trees, lemon trees, myrtles, cypresses, palm trees, date-palms, peach trees, banana trees, sugar cane, oaks, and even pines were growing in the valleys.

If Madeira has its justly renowned wines, so unfortunately counterfeited in Sète and elsewhere, Tenerife has the Malvoisie wines produced by the Greek grapes of the same name.

The *Glorieux*'s sojourn in Santa Cruz Bay lasted a week, and several scientists, members of the expedition, took advantage of it to make an ascent of the peak of Tenerife. Monsieur Charmillon and his niece, one by reason of his age and the other because of the fatigues of the enterprise, were unable to take part, but Émile, who had the good fortune to reach the summit, recounted its marvels when he returned.

It is always a great event on the island when a French warship arrives, but the advent of the commission of scientists representing all the peoples of Europe was almost the subject of a revolution. A thousand courtesies were extended to the newcomers. A great ball was held for them. Angèle, with her graces and French dresses, had a veritable triumph there. As for Émile, he had the honor of dancing with a charming Spanish lady who spoke a little French. He told his fiancée the next day that it had been a chore for him rather than a pleasure.

"You wouldn't believe," he said, "how disagreeable it is to dance with these beautiful Spaniards; on looking at them, one thinks involuntarily of fairground booths where wax figures are displayed. It's impossible to say anything to them without them looking at you with expressions of amazement."

When she quit Santa Cruz Bay the *Glorieux* set a course for Rio de Janeiro. It was the first long crossing that she was to accomplish without encountering any land. In spite of the speed of the vessel and the continuing favorable weather, the voyage undertaken would last some ten days before reaching the American coast. They made what arrangements they could to pass the time with the least possible tedium.

The naturalists and the geologists of the expedition began to sort out the scientific treasures that they had amassed at Madeira and Tenerife. In those islands one not only finds admirable specimens of tropical flora on land, but the depths of the seas that surrounds them are also incredibly rich.

As soon as his leisure permitted him to do so, young Émile hastened to rejoin Monsieur Charmillon's niece, and augmented by means of interesting conversations the sum of the knowledge that his lovely fiancée already possessed.

Sometimes, they watched the groups of flying fish pursued by the dorados that gave chase to them eternally, seeing them suddenly rise up out of the water, like a flight of arrows. Gliding like swallows at the approach of rain, the unfortunate fugitives scarcely skimmed the waves, and suddenly sank back into them like falling stones.

"See how their vibrant wings sparkle with azure reflections!" said the young woman. "How transparent their little bodies are! How reminiscent their indecisive flight is of the first steps of little children!"

One day, an entire flock of those scatterbrains, with a maladroit twitch of the wings, fell on to the deck. The sailors fell upon the unexpected prey, which they were not long in handing over to the cook, passing from the great sea into the frying pan.

Passengers and crew alike declared that they tasted delicious.

In order to distract Angèle one day, Émile went hunting dorados, the born enemies of the flying fish. A strong hook at the end of a solid line was garnished with a piece of cloth vaguely representing the form of the graceful little fish, and a dorado, perhaps myopic or blinded by the ardor of its pursuit, threw itself upon the gross bait and fell victim to the young geologist.

While Angèle admired the large and beautiful fish with a body like a blade, with its innumerable thin oblong scales, her friend, after having pointed out its color, silver above, with dark blue patches on the back and brighter ones underneath, with yellow fins variegated with leaden or black spots, told her about the impetuous speed with which the beautiful fish followed the fastest ships in numerous bands, avidly pouncing on anything that was allowed to fall overboard.

"I thought until now," the young woman said, "that pursuits of that sort were the work of the famous sharks."

"That's an error all the more serious," the young scientist replied, "because a shark is incapable of swimming as fast as the *Glorieux*; one hardly ever encounters them except near coasts, and if, by chance they're found in the open sea it's because they've been drawn there, either by currents or their insatiable appetite, which has made them forget themselves in pursuit of a school of fish they desire to prey upon."

On the twenty-fifth of August, in the evening, the navigators perceived, for the first time, the Southern

Cross: the principal constellation of the southern hemisphere, with plays a similar role there to the Great Bear in the part of the sky visible from Europe. Angèle observed, sagely, that the group of stars in question, although quite bright, would hardly be noticed in our hemisphere, where the constellations are much more numerous than in the other.

Sometimes, the scientists met on the bridge of the ship, in the part of the aft section reserved for them, strolling or lounging on wicker chaise-longues, gazing out at the immensity of the Atlantic Ocean and admiring the powerful fight of seabirds describing circles around the *Glorieux*. Those masters of the air, driven by hunger sometimes came very close to the ship in order to glean in her wake. Idle matelots sometimes extended perfidious nets in which fiches or Cape pigeons entangled their wings. Frigate-birds came of their own accord by night to get caught up in the rigging.

One day, Angèle, leaning on the rail, pointed at a white dot on the horizon. like a vessel deploying its sails over the foam of the waves.

Émile clapped his hands. "Finally," he said, "there's an albatross."

Soon, in fact, the young couple saw the giant bird drawing closer. Gradually, its large body and its long snow-white wings stood out more distinctly; it came so close that they could make out its two pink eyes and the collar of the same hue that nature has traced around its neck.

That first arrival as soon followed by others, and all the passengers took pleasure in seeing their strange hungry troop, sometimes describing immense and eternal circles, and sometimes flying over the ship.

The albatross is the largest bird in the world in our epoch, which has seen such immense birds as the epiornis and dinornis disappear.[6]

One day, thanks to his skill and the long range of his rifle, the young scientist succeeded in bring down one of those princes of the air, which came to fall inertly on the deck. The young woman was able to admire at close range its beautiful silky plumage, and the ship's sailors hastened to make long pipe-stems with the bones of its feet and wings, while the skin of the feet was converted into tobacco pouches.

While his masters utilized the forces leisure of the long crossing in that fashion, Jean-Pierre, for his part, had made numerous friends—or rather, found an audience—among the sailors in the fore section. His gravity and marvelous aplomb had not taken long to impress the crewmen, who were not far from seeing him as one of the luminaries of the scientific expedition. He was so proud of being in the service of Monsieur Charmillon that he almost believed himself to be a superior individual; at least he liked other people to think of him in that way, and he never neglected an opportunity to give birth to the idea or maintain it in their minds.

Every time that his occupations permitted him to do so, he went forth at the grave and magisterial pace familiar to him, mingled with the troop of matelots awaiting the orders of their petty officers at the front of the ship. As they knew him to be an orator and saw him as a well of science, a profound and respectful silence greeted

___

[6] The epiornis, more commonly known as *Aepyornis*, and the *Dinornis*, or giant Moa, were both flightless, like modern ostriches—which are, of course, bigger than albatrosses—so the comparison is illegitimate.

him. He sat down and spoke with the aplomb of a perfect imbecile about anything that came to mind. The crewmen, simple and naïve folk, listened to him religiously, and swooned with ecstasy as they listened to him.

One evening, Émile Colin, leaving the young woman in the society of her worthy uncle, had gone up on deck in order to breathe a little cool nocturnal air and savor at his ease the perfumes of an excellent panatella. He was wandering back and forth along the deck when, as he approached the fore section, he was struck by the familiar voice of the solemn Jean-Pierre.

Taking advantage of the darkness and hiding as best he could behind the tackle and pulley-blocks heaped up there, he drew nearer to the orator.

Seated on a coil of rope, holding forth in the middle of an attentive crowd, and bringing to his discourse all the unction of a renowned preacher praising the Lenten fast before an elite audience, he said:

"My friends, my master Monsieur Charmillon, the most knowledgeable man in France, the entire world and Paris, would not have departed for such a long voyage if he could not bring his darling niece and his secretary, Monsieur Colin, who would be in the Académie as soon as there's an empty seat if he did not have extremely important things to do."

A respectful silence welcomed this speech, and, in order to make use of an expression as energetic as it is popular, Jean-Pierre's listeners seemed to be drinking his words.

After having paraded a satisfied glance over the circle surrounding him, the orator continued: "Certainly, I too, you understand, have my share of education, and Monsieur Charmillon would not have taken just anyone into his service; however, I must confess," he continued, in a modest tone, "that I don't know absolutely everything."

The matelots looked at one another—not without astonishment, because that confession surprised them a little.

Without losing his gravity, Jean-Pierre continued: "Don't be astonished by that, my friends; the life of a man is too short for him to have the time to learn everything, even if he studies from dawn to dusk, and from dusk to dawn. That's why everyone applies himself most particularly to a single science, which is what is known as an especialty.

"Like my master, like each of the scientists composing the expedition that you have the honor of conveying, I have my especialty, about which I can speak to you as and when it gives you pleasure."

A unanimous murmur of approval greeted that statement.

The orator continued: "Our company is made up of several kinds of scientists having various especialties. Some, the astrologers, are going to the southern hemisphere to make a passage of the sun by Mercury; as it's not our especialty I haven't yet taken account of that operation, or the manner in which it has to be carried out. All that I know is that they're bringing enormous telescopes with windows that the call lenses, although they're perfectly round and as big as the full moon.[7] They also have photographic instruments for taking por-

---

[7] Jean-Pierre might be slightly confused by the double meaning of the French *lentille*, which means "lentil" as well as "lens." The fact that the text sometimes renders Mercure [Mercury] with a capital letter and sometimes without suggests that he is also confusing the planet with the liquid metal.

traits of the sun at the moment when its face is covered with mercury in order to be able to examine the results of the operation at close range. In any case, we'll all the able to watch them do it, and when we come back, we'll know a much as they do."

The orator paused momentarily to draw breath; his encourage lavished marks of approval on him. After a brief silence, untroubled by any indiscreet comment, he resumed.

"While the astrologers pass their mercury over the sun, other scientists will go to pick herbs in the country-side, or those that grow on the sea bed, These herbs, of which they know all the names, because it's their especialty, will be taken back to Paris, where they'll make them into remedies for a pharmacy far superior to the one manufactured with the plants of France. They're the precious medicines that make rich people live to be very old, because poor people don't have enough money to pay the price. Those are called bottlists, because they mix their herbs in jars, but that's another especialty that I don't have.

"I won't talk to you at length about the naturalistes either, who call themselves that for reasons I don't know. I'd find it more natural, since their especialty con-sists of stuffing birds and beasts, if they simply called themselves stuffers. I advise you never to let yourselves be tempted by their prey, because I know pertinently that to protect them against cockroaches, mice, rats and jok-ers who want to put them in a casserole, they stuff their bellies with poison."

There was a shiver of horror in the audience, and the matelots engraved that nasty habit of naturalists pro-foundly in their minds.

"Monsieur Charmillon, Monsieur Émile Colin and I," said Jean-Pierre, only citing his own name in last place by virtue of a praiseworthy modesty, "have an especialty much more difficult. We've been sent to the other hemisphere to determine the age of stones."[8]

"What, the age of stones?" demanded Petty Officer Grand-Victor, a fine mariner from St. Malo, known throughout the fleet as a topman without equal.

"Yes," Jean-Pierre replied, with conviction. "We divine it just by looking at them, the age of stones. It's to divine their age that Monsieur Charmillon and Monsieur Émile go to pick up loads of pebbles in the fields and on the highest mountains."

"But what's the use of that?" interrogated Grand-Victor, in whom the eccentricity of that specialty seemed to have given rise to doubts.

"What's the use of it?" the valet went on impetuously. "Ask me instead what's the use of you having learned the ABC, or what's the use of knowing the four rules![9] Tell me, Monsieur Grand-Victor, what use is it to you to know the names of the masts, the yardarms and the rigging? How could you command a maneuver if you didn't know? Do you understand now what use it is?"

---

[8] In French, *"L'Age des pierres"* [the age of stones], is not as far removed from *"L'Age de pierre"* [The Stone Age] as the alteration of the word order in English obliges the equivalent phrases to be.

[9] The "four rules" to which Jean-Pierre is referring are those suggested by Descartes in his *Discours de la méthode* as the fundamental principles of rational analysis, although one is strongly inclined to doubt that he knows what they are.

The petty officer was so stunned by that energetic reply that he believed that he did indeed, understand. "That makes it clear," he said.

At that moment, Émile, who had remained hidden throughout the valet's long speech, could not suppress a burst of laughter. He went toward the group, ready to unmask the fake savant and charlatan who was abusing the candor of so many worthy men, but he was utterly disarmed when Jean-Pierre, taking him for a witness, pointed him out to his listeners and said: "Look, my friends, here's Monsieur Émile Colin, the great scientist I was talking about. Ask him, who has sacrificed his life to it, whether there's any use in knowing the age of stones."

The young geologists doubtless understood that he would be wasting his time is he attempted to disabuse the worthy fellows. How, in any case, could they comprehend the truth? What difference was there, for them, between true science and false? Would it be any easier to demonstrate to them the utility of knowing the species and origin of stones than to make them believe that it was important to know their age?[10]

Those reflections, the advanced hour, the difficulty of the goal to be attained and perhaps also the eulogies that the fake scientist had heaped upon him arrested the critique on the edge of his lips. He hastened to return to Monsieur Charmillon and his niece and to recount to

---

[10] The geologists of 1876 would have to wait thirty years before the first publication of a radiometric method for dating rocks, but that hardly excuses Émile from not being able to explain why it would be very useful to be able to make such calculations, or, of course, from being so patronizing in his consideration of the sailors.

them what he had just overheard. The young woman and hr uncle laughed so wholeheartedly that none of them dreamed of reproaching Jean-Pierre for his ridiculous lessons.

Chapter V

The elements of dissension that had become manifest in the early days of the voyage between the members of the international scientific expedition had continued to develop during the forced leisure of the crossing. Thanks to his wise retreat, Arthème Charmillon had virtually withdrawn from the conflict, but his French colleagues and the delegates of the foreign powers had not followed his example and had continued not only to take their meals in common but also to meet in the morning and evening in the main lounge and to engage in scientific discussions that often terminated in arguments.

One day, William Johnston and Walter Müller, the two naturalists, one representing England and the other Germany, commenced a courteous contest on a question of the greatest interest, which concerned determining the limitations of the geography of giraffes.

That requires a few lines of explanation.

Every animal, like each item of flora, occupies a determined area of the globe outside of which it cannot survive. Naturalists have striven to draw up planispheres in which the limits of the habitat of each species are traced as precisely as possible.

It is thus that special maps have been drawn up to indicate the limits between which wheat can be grown, others designating the areas where rice, sugar-cane, palm trees, oranges, etc., etc., can grow.

After long and difficult voyages undertaken in the Africa continent, William Johnston of London had carefully drawn up a map bearing in pale yellow the points at which other explorers from his country had observed the existence of giraffes.

Walter Müller of Berlin had devoted himself to a similar study, but relying uniquely on data furnished by German explorers. On his map, conscientiously drawn up at the Geographical Institute of Gotha, he had chosen an orange-yellow hue to designate the habitat of giraffes.

By reason of the different sources on which the two scientists had drawn, a few evident differences were encountered on the two maps, with regard to the regions designated as inhabited by the long-necked animals.

Mr. Johnston had dined copiously and drunk a few glasses of an excellent Bordeaux, which, following the English tradition, he had baptized with the name of "claret." Encountering his Prussian colleague in the saloon, he had found himself in a humor to address a few benevolent criticisms to him on the subject of his map.

The moment could not have been more ill-chosen. The dinner, which had seemed excellent to the Englishman because it had consisted almost entirely of roast meat and had been crowned at dessert by a superb plum pudding, had seemed inedible to the German, who had not found therein any jugged hare with redcurrant jelly, nor sauerkraut, nor garlic sausage.

Walter Müller was therefore in a very bad mood when Mr. Johnston addressed him in these terms:

"I've jut been looking attentively at your map of the giraffe, my dear colleague, and I give you my sincere compliments for the erudition that you've deployed herein. But for God's sake, my dear colleague, tell my why you've tinted the regions inhabited by that animal orange-yellow? I've always seen giraffes of a pale yellow color, and never encountered one exhibiting the garish color that you give their habitats."

The German, although umbrageous, did not lack wit. "If you wanted to give those seen on your map the exact color of the giraffe's coat," he riposted, "why haven't you dappled your tint with white patches?"[11]

The Englishman sensed the justice of the observation, and changed his line of attack.

"We generally find ourselves in agreement," he said, still sarcastically, "with regard to the points of the Africa continent where one encounters the giraffe, but tell me, my dear colleague, where you have found that those animals lived in the region of Sudan between Bilma and Lake Chad?"

"If my colleague had taken the trouble to read the account of the voyage that Herr Rholffs has just published, he would know that the explorer in question encountered a domesticated giraffe there, which was part of a caravan traveling toward Timbuktu."

"I notice," observed the Englishman, laughing, "that you said a *domesticated* giraffe. On that count, you can tint Paris, London, Berlin and Vienna orange-yellow, as well as all the other cities in the world that have giraffes in their zoological gardens."

Al the scientists present at the discussion thought the English naturalist's argument so amusing that they burst out laughing—which brought the anger of his opponent to a peak.

---

[11] Any reader who has seen a giraffe might be slightly puzzled by this remark, although it is not entirely out of keeping with the somewhat surreal discussion. The German cannot be assumed to be arguing that black is white, given that a giraffe's spots are not really black, any more than the rest of its coat is pale yellow, no matter what Johnston and certain children's picture books might allege.

"Monsieur," he said, dryly, "we leave the habit of responding to an argument with a joke to the French. Since it pleases you to do as they do, permit me to cut the conversation short."

As he said these words he turned his back on Mr. Johnston and went to sit down some distance away, on a large divan that circled the room. That impoliteness caused the face of the English scientist to turn red.

"You're a pedant, Mr. Müller," he said, clenching his teeth.

"You're an imbecile, Monsieur Müller," added, like an echo, the Parisian chemist Guébard, who had listened to the conversation and did not want to allow the attack of which the French had been the object to pass without protest.

"If Prussians fought other than *en masse* and ten against one," said the astronomer Chauvin, "I'd send you witnesses, Monsieur Müller, Monsieur Impertinent."

The Berliner naturalist went pale, and darted a glance of savage hatred at his adversaries, but did not say a word.

"That's right—cowardly and stupid," said the English naturalist, loudly.

The rest is understandable; war had been declared, and it was to be a war without truce or respite until the end of the expedition.

Commandant Beaudin, however, thought it appropriate to intervene. He was the most amiable and conciliating man in the world. The French and English scientists willingly promised him not to take the scene any further, and, if necessary, to forget anything that had been said that might have wounded them. As for the German, he swore hypocritically that he had not taken offense, and that he bore his colleagues no grudge for the slightly sharp words that had been addressed to him.

Those protestations were lies, and Walter Müller was only waiting for a favorable opportunity to get his revenge.

A few days later, Monsieur Charmillon, who had not witnessed that scene, leaving his secretary and his niece to take a stroll on the deck, went into the common lounge after the morning meal and engaged in an amicable conservation with the Italian geographer Pietro Bono. The Frenchman put forward his favorite subject—by which we mean his antipathy to marriage—and the amiable Italian, while refuting his arguments, took a malign pleasure in listening to him develop his theories and launching diatribes, sometimes against the weakness of the female sex and sometimes against the tyranny of married men.

The two Germans, Walter Müller and Franz Henrich, were sitting nearby, silently smoking two immense pipes with huge porcelain bowls.

Taking advantage of a pause in the conversation, Müller said in a low voice, but loud enough to be overheard: "It's odd that there are people whose practical life is so far away from their theory. One doesn't like marriage, but one allows one's niece to spend her life in the company of a young man."

Monsieur Charmillon was a timid man, an absolute enemy of any ardent polemic, and could not bar anything resembling an argument. He felt directly insulted, but dared not reply. Pale and unsteady, he rose to his feet, bowed amicably to Pietro Bono, and, going past the two Prussians without looking at them, went to his cabin, prey to a violent anger.

"Jean-Pierre," he called.

Jean-Pierre, ever alert, came in "What does Monsieur desire?" he asked.

"Go up on deck without delay, find Monsieur Colin and my niece, and tell them I want to see them immediately."

The valet bowed and disappeared.

A few minutes later, the young couple appeared in the doorway.

"Sit down," said Monsieur Charmillon, designating two chairs.

He took an armchair himself, and came to sit down solemnly in front of the fiancés, surprises and tremulous before his sudden change of expression.

"I've heard nasty things said about you two," said the scientist, abruptly, anger and emotion making his voiced tremble. "Monsieur Colin, we'll be arriving in Rio de Janeiro in two days' time; you'll disembark there and go back to Paris to await my return."

The young man went frightfully pale, but he was able to dissimulate his emotion. "Monsieur Charmillon," he said, "Would you care to tell me the reason for this sudden resolution?"

"I needn't tell you anything, Monsieur, but I'll speak nevertheless, because I think it only just that an accused individual has the right to defend himself.

"You say accused, Monsieur? Of what have I been accused, pray?"

"You have been accused, Monsieur, of abusing my generosity in order to aspire secretly to the hand of my niece."

Émile was so honest and so sincere that he was paralyzed by that accusation, which he felt to be fundamentally just. He lowered his eyes and remained silent. All was about to be lost when the young woman came to his aid.

"Well, Uncle," she said, in an authoritarian tone, "you're going to tell us, without delay, the names of those who have told you this fine tale! Come on, look at poor Émile—he's fallen from the clouds, he's so bewildered by it."

"My dear Angèle," said the old scientist, in his most caressant tone of voice, "I know full well that they might be calumnies, but after all, it's necessary to take account of the opinion of people with whom one is required to live. Today, just now, in the lounge, I heard that insinuation formulated by Walter Müller, the naturalist from Berlin."

The young man had had time to recover his composure. "In that case, Monsieur," he said, "if it's only from there that this ridiculous insinuation emanates, it's absolutely nothing, and you won't take long to see for yourself that it's nothing but a simple calumny gratuitously launched by an enemy of our fatherland with the objective of personal vengeance."

Émile told Angèle's uncle the about the scene that had taken place in the saloon a few days earlier—the impertinence of the German and his cowardice before the aggressive words of his adversaries

On hearing that story, Monsieur Charmillon was completely reassured. He realized that Müller had wanted to take revenge on him for that attacks he had received from Chauvin and Guérard.

"What dos it matter to me, after all, what those sauerkraut-munchers think?" he exclaimed, full of irritation. "My children, I know now what stance to adopt, and people can gossip as much as they like about you. I'm glad that you're friends. You can't marry without my consent, damn it! As I'm determined never to give it, so much the worse for you if you get any conjugal whim into your heads. That said, you can go and resume your strolls on the deck. *Honni soit qui mal y pense!*"

The *Glorieux* came within view of Rio de Janeiro on the first of September.

The mooring at the city, as soon as one has recognized the location, is facilitated by an islet situated outside the entrance to the bay, to which there is a lighthouse visible from a long distance. The ship headed straight toward the light on Raza Island, and eventually penetrated into the haven. During the three-day sojourn that she spent there, the passengers were able to visit the city and its surroundings.

The richness of the country struck them with admiration. Brazil is, in fact, a veritable Eldorado.[12] Its forests produce inexhaustible quantities of all kinds of precious our useful wood, known or unknown—wood for construction, cabinet-making and paneling; resinous wood, trees producing oil, butter, gum and textile fibers; fruit trees and bread-trees—as well as medicinal plants, tapioca, cocoa, colza, sugar-cane, tobacco, pepper, vanilla, tea, wheat and almost all other cereals. Add to that the mountainous regions where, one finds a profusion of mines of precious or useful metals—gold, silver, mercury, iron and lead—and also, in the dry beds of torrents, precious stones—diamond, emerald, topaz, sapphire, ruby and cornelian—and you will have a faint idea of the

---

[12] This mistaken conviction seems to have played some part in the author's subsequent decision to accept the Presidency of the ostensible Republic of Counani.

immense riches contained in that vast empire, so little known, traversed by the greatest rivers in the world.

The *Glorieux* left Rio de Janeiro and the American shore on the morning of the fifth of September.

Taking advantage of the trade winds and her renewed coal supplies, she headed in a straight line for the Cape of Good Hope, where she made another stopover. There, Monsieur Charmillon and the couple he called his children were able to visit the diamond-bearing terrains and the parks in which modern industry confines and raise ostriches with sought-after feathers. The old scientist, who, as we have said, had a weakness for delicate dishes and god wines, took care not to miss the opportunity to taste the famous Constantia wine whose reputation extends over the two hemispheres.

"My friend," he said to his secretary, "remember that if ever the vines perish in our beautiful land of France, it's in Africa, the north as well as the south, that they are called upon to reflourish, and, if possible, cause our noble vintages of Bordeaux and Bourgogne to be forgotten."[13]

The itinerary of the expedition included landfalls in the two volcanic desert islands of Saint Paul and Amsterdam, but bad weather that held them back at the Cape for three more days than had been anticipated caused the Commandant to opt for another route. Leaving the two small islands to port, the *Glorieux* headed directly for

---

[13] When this line was written the vines of France were, indeed, perishing in vast quantities under the ravages of *Phylloxera*, but the substitute stocks that were eventually employed to rescue the industry mostly came from *Phylloxera*-resistant American vines.

Australia, stopping first at Melbourne and then at Sydney.

If the purpose of this story was geographical education, we would not fail to follow our heroes into those marvelous cities, which seemed to have surged forth suddenly from the earth, so rapid and immense had their growth been. After passing through Melbourne we would have gone into the interior and would have gone with Angèle, her uncle and her inamorata to visit the gold mines of Ballarat at the foot of the Australian Pyrenees, and even further, to Majorca, Maryborough or Avoca.

Later, we would have gone to see the squatters in the outback and gone with them to hunt the platypus, the opossum, the beautiful talking multicolored parrots, wild turkeys, black swans, lyre-birds, ducks, kiwis,[14] blue cranes with red crests, gray ostriches or cassowaries, green sparrows, whistling crows, honeysuckers, the mockingbirds that the Australians call "laughing jackasses," the gray and black mynahs that chirp in the trees and the sulfur-crested cockatoos.

Émile was able to devote himself in moderation to the pleasures of hunting. His rifles fired marvelously, and it was due to his expert eye that the English naturalist, who had become their ally, was able to bring away an admirable collection of al the birds of the island and specimens of almost al the animals making up the strange family of marsupials: mice, opossums and kan-

---

[14] The hunters would have been highly unlikely to find any kiwis, which are exclusively native to New Zealand, and one or two of the other creatures on the list might well have proved elusive—fortunately for them.

garoos of all sizes. Even today, they are still talking in the colony about the young scientist's skill and accuracy.

The sojourn at Sydney, or rather at Port Jackson, was no less agreeable for the foreign scientists. The entry into the bay is a marvelous spectacle in itself.

Two days after the departure from Melbourne they perceived, at dawn, that they were following the sinuosities of the coast very closely, alongside dark brown rocks, not very high, which were sometimes entirely covered in verdure. The wind, which had been rather violent on departure, had dropped; nevertheless, the ship continued to perform a veritable *danse macabre* on the heavy sea. Let us say, however, that none of our friends was afflicted by the horrible sea-sickness so redoubted even by some navigators. The waves broke with an unparalleled fury against the strand beneath the rocks, forming a kind of ribbon of silvery foam.

After crossing Botany Bay, the former penitentiary colony that forms the first point of New South Wales, they soon arrived opposite the two rocks that guard the entrance to Port Jackson. Eventually, they penetrated into the port, which is perhaps the most beautiful in the world. Angèle, her uncle and her intended could not weary of admiring the magical spectacle that unfolded before their eyes.

The agitated sea precipitated itself furiously against the two high rocks forming the entry to the port, and the waves, hurtling blindly to assault the obstacles placed by nature to render their power impotent, climbed all the way to the white Fort Macquarie, situated at the summit of the southern point.

As soon as they had passed the points, the water became completely calm and the decoration changed as if by theatrical trickery. At the entrance Angèle pointed out to her uncle a pretty village with white houses, and then, a few minutes later, the ship turned a corner; the open sea disappeared and gave way to a delightful small bay surrounded by magnificent woods with a background of hills forming and amphitheater and gradually rising up to the center of the little bay.

The frame of this book does not permit depicting at greater length the emotions of every sort that the travelers were to experienced in the locale; everything is made to astonish and seduce in that singular country where everything seems to have been created at cross-purposes with the spirit that presided over the formation of beings and things in the other parts of the globe.

The immense Australia is, in fact, a singular land, part of which is composed by endless plains formed by pebbles, devoid of vegetable life, vast deserts with no shade and without a blade of grass, and others no les huge covered with thick grass, in which it would be impossible to find a pebble; a singular land in which enormous trees grow, gum-trees or eucalyptus, which cast no shadow and allow the ardent light of the day star to pass through their leaves, in the form of lancets; a singular land in which one encounters birds devoid of wings or feathers, quadrupeds with a beak, laying and brooding eggs and then providing their progeniture with milk— such is the platypus, the paradoxical animal whose existence the scientists of Europe only consented to recognize after seeing multiple specimens; a singular land in which animals sit on their tails and possess belly-pouches in order to transport their young, which take refuge there are the slightest danger—such are the marsupials, of which the Australian continent has the entire series, from mice and rats through minuscule wallabies, which constitute a delicate dish when braised, to the great kangaroo, which the English call "old man" and measures nearly three meters in length from nose to tail.

Chapter VI

The *Glorieux* finally left Sydney and the Australian continent. The open sea had become calm again and the wind favorable. Commandant Beaudin announced to his passengers that there would be no more stopovers until they reached Seal Island. That was another crossing that lasted several days. It was, in fact, a matter of following a known route, setting a course directly eastwards and advancing, passing to the north of New Zealand, to the 180th degree of longitude east of the Paris meridian and then steering southwards to Seal Island, a deserted volcanic mass not on the route of any ship. Only the illustrious Lapérouse visited it in 1788 in his ship *Astrolabe*, and later, in 1791, Entrecasteaux, while searching for the celebrated French navigator, determined its exact position.[15]

The passengers of the *Glorieux* resumed their shipboard habits, and Monsieur Charmillon, in particular,

---

[15] The *Astrolabe*, carrying the great French navigator the Comte de Lapérouse, was lost in the spring of 1788 after setting forth eastwards from Botany Bay. Antoine Bruny d'Entrecasteaux was sent by the post-Revolutionary government to search for him in 1791. The only "île des phoques" [Seal Island] he encountered in the region was the one in the vicinity of Tasmania still known by the English name; the one featured in the present story is subsequently revealed to lie south of Antipodes Island, nowhere near the actual routes followed by Lapérouse and Entrecasteaux, and is evidently a fictitious substitute for Campbell Island, the seal-hunting and whaling base visited in 1874 by the French scientific expedition sent there to observe the transit of Venus.

began to live in his apartment with his niece and his secretary.

Angèle seemed to be acquiring a taste for study that was increasing by the day; not only did she listen avidly to the lessons that Émile Colin gave her, but when she found herself alone with her uncle she bombarded him with questions and paid admirable attention to the explanations that the aged scientists always took pleasure in giving her.

One day, the conversation turned to the goal of the expedition and the particular scientific study that Monsieur Charmillon intended to carry out.

"Explain to me, Uncle," the young woman asked, why the *Glorieux* didn't take the shortest route to reach Seal Island" Examining a terrestrial globe placed on her uncle's work table, she added: "It seems to me that we would have reached the expedition's proposed goal more rapidly if, after leaving Marseilles, the *Glorieux* had gone to Port Said, gone through the Suez Canal, the Read Sea and the point of Aden. Having arrived in the Indian Ocean we could have touched at Point de Galle in Ceylon, headed directly for Australia and abridged our journey by at least two thirds."

The old scientist smiled, and, doubtless satisfied by the young woman's observations, replied with his usual complaisance: "Your reflections are very judicious, my dear Angèle, but you're losing sight of the object of our voyage."

"Isn't it primarily," Angèle said, "to observe the passage of Mercury across the Sun?"

"Undoubtedly," said Monsieur Charmillon, "but if that had been the only goal of the expedition I would certainly not have been given the honor of taking part in it. The European nations and their governments, in making the very considerable pecuniary sacrifices that such a voyage entails, thought of making as much use of it as possible.

"A large number of very interesting problems are still pending, among them that of determining the respective ages of the various continents. It's for that reason that the *Glorieux* has visited in rapid succession Madeira, Tenerife, and then the eastern coast of South America. From there we went to study the soil of the African continent sat the Cape of Good Hope, and that of Australia at Melbourne and Sydney."

"But tell me, my dear Uncle, how the appearance of a land can tell you the epoch of its formation."

"That, my girl, is an entire science, very complicated, which involves several others. The science in question is geology, with which I am particularly occupied, whose objective is to study the various layers of terrain, rocks and sedimentary deposits. Paleontology, which is a branch of geology, is occupied with animate organic beings that once lived on our globes in the epochs of various terrestrial revolutions."

"What I'd like to understand most of all," the young woman continued, "or, at least, what I want to obtain a clearer idea of, is precisely what you call terrestrial revolutions. So the earth wasn't created as we see it, and has undergone important transformations?"

"Undoubtedly," replied the scientist, with indulgent bonhomie. "Give me a few minutes of attention, and I'll summarize as best I can a few general facts that are now certain and indisputable, and which will enable you to obtain a fruitful understanding of the observations that you'll be able to see us making."

"I'm all ears, Uncle," said the young woman, sitting down in a chair facing the obliging professor.

"Our globe," aid the latter, "was originally a fiery fluid mass; all the parts making it up—rock, earth, metals—were reduced to vapor by an enormous heat, accomplishing their movement through space as comets do today, trailing their long gaseous tails behind them.

"How long did that period of incandescence last? No one knows exactly, but it was at least several million years. Gradually, however, by virtue of a relative cooling, the metals and minerals in a gaseous state, whose density nevertheless formed the nucleus of the planet, passed into a liquid state. Around that burning mass, the light of which must have been as bright as that of the sun, the masses of water that now occupy at least two-thirds of the surface of the globe formed an atmosphere of vapors, confused with the atmosphere of gases in the midst of which we live today."

"I understand perfectly," said Angèle. "Continue, please, for this seems as interesting to me as a fairy tale."

"As the cooling continued," Monsieur Charmillon went on, glad to find his niece attentive, "the incandescent liquid mass was gradually covered by a kind of crust, half mineral and half metallic. That crust, passing gradually from white hot to red hot, must have changed the luminous color of our globe, while still conserving its glow for a long time."

"How could life be life manifest on our globe then, at such a temperature?" Angèle put in, seriously interested.

"It goes without saying," the scientist continued, "that then, and for a long time afterwards, perhaps for millions of years, all life was impossible, for you, like everyone else, know that one of the essential conditions of any living organism is the existence of water and humidity. It was therefore necessary to wait until the terres-

83

trial mass cooled sufficiently for the vapors suspended in the atmosphere to be able to condense, fall as water and form vast oceans."

"I'm beginning to understand," said the young woman, "that such a result couldn't have taken place in a single period. Undoubtedly, it must have happened more than once that the mass of liquid matter enclosed in the light enveloped formed by the terrestrial crust produced boiling, vapors seeking an issue, and in consequence, unexpected deformations and upheavals of the entire globe."

"Your remark, my dear Angèle," Monsieur Charmillon went on, "is so just that even today, those revolutions of which you speak still take place only too frequently, although on a much smaller scale. They're called earthquakes; volcanoes are the mouths opened for the subterranean fires that are still burning inside the planet, and which play the role, so to speak, of safety valves, by allowing the subterranean gases that are trying to break the envelope escape."

After a momentary pause, the old scientist said: "I'll continue my demonstration. People are not overly preoccupied with the duration necessary to arrive at that cooling; one day, doubtless, the question will be resolved, but it's of slight importance thus far, since the existence of organic beings is entirely foreign to that period. When the surface of the globe had cooled sufficiently to permit the sea to form, the first seeds of life were able to develop.

"Did the waters deposited in vast extents over all the scarcely-cooled depressions of the globe already contain, when they were in the gaseous state, the principal salts and alkalis that characterize sea water today, or did they encounter those salts in the terrestrial crust, ready to be dissolved therein? Everything suggests that one or other hypothesis must be true, for no one doubts that the first animate beings and the first vegetables that appeared on the globe in that epoch were aquatic and marine."

"In that case, fish and algae must be anterior to quadrupeds and trees?" queried Angèle.

"There's not a shadow of a doubt about it, and paleontological science has demonstrated it conclusively."

"Go on, then my dear Uncle," said the young woman.

"The internal heat of the globe, communicating with its surface," the scientist went on, "must then have facilitated the existence of immense creatures and monstrous vegetables. At the same time, the waters, sometimes sent forth in vapors and sometimes falling back on the ground in compact masses, began to alter or decompose the metallic rocks forming that envelope of sorts, drawing away the softer pats in their courses and wearing them away by their contact while leaving others intact. That's how science explains the stratified sedimentary layers of which traces are found everywhere on the globe."

"My dear Uncle," said Angèle, "has it been possible to explain why the part of the terrestrial crust that emerges from the waters, which we call land, has taken such strange and various forms, so uneven almost everywhere."

"That's undoubtedly one of the most seductive aspects of geological science—but it's a separate question, which, if you don't mind, we'll consider another time. I'll conclude this little lesson, to which you've listened with an attention for which you have my sincere compliments, by telling you briefly about what are known as the geological ages." With a benevolent smile, he added: "It's necessary that Dr. Charmillon's niece shouldn't think, like Master Jean-Pierre, that her uncle studies the age of stones.

"Four principal ages are distinguished: the Primordial, the Secondary, the Tertiary and the Quaternary.

"The Primordial age is the long period during with the earth was part of the series of luminous heavenly bodies.

"In the Secondary age the earth ceased to be the exclusive theater of mineral action. The Ocean appeared and covered the globe. The projecting parts, disseminated here and there, formed islands, perhaps continents. It's the era in which the first organic beings made their appearance. When you want to study the beautiful science of paleontology, you'll see that the first plants that grew were of the family of the acotyledons, which includes all the algae and those of the *Equisetaceae*, which includes all kinds of ferns. In the same way, the first animals were the most elementary, those that we now call the inferior animals: the zoophytes, the mollusks and the trilobites.

"During the second period of the Secondary age, these rudimentary beings were succeeded by plants that now characterize tropical vegetation and large species of saurian reptiles that have now disappeared.

"In the Tertiary age, the continents began to take shape with their principal outlines, climates were distinguished in accordance with zones; every place had its temperature and its seasons. The great class of mammals appeared and populated the lands; traces of monstrous ones can still be found. It was the epoch of giant pachyderms that have long ceased to exist.

"Until the Quaternary age, the solid layer of the terrestrial globe was not thick enough to prevent the external radiation of internal heat. In the Quaternary, the temperature of the earth's surface ceased to decrease, climates were fixed; the generations succeeding one another in the same location always found the same environment there, and the human species, which had just appeared, rapidly established its empire over the globe."

At that point of the savant professor's lesson, Émile came into Monsieur Charmillion's room. As usual, he was going to present his compliments to the Academician, his master, and to Angèle, when the latter put an indicative finger over her lips, signaling to him to be quiet. The young man understood the instruction, and sat down silently in a corner of the cabin.

"Tell me, finally, Uncle, about what you call the Stone Age. So far, you've only pronounced the phrase in order to make fun of poor Jean-Pierre."

"That expression," said Monsieur Charmillon, belongs more to the domain of archeological science than that of geology. When one studies the history of humankind, by inspecting the instruments and weapons of which usage was made during the various periods of its existence, we find that primitive people were unaware of the usage of any metal. For instruments of work, attack and defense, they only employed stone and flint for a long time. It's that period that we call the Stone Age.

"Copper is found fairly commonly in its native state even on the surface of the ground; humans later learned to exploit and use it; then, finding the metal too soft for the majority of the uses for which it was applied, they discovered the art of alloying it and making bronze. That second period of humankind acquired the name of the Bronze Age. Finally, iron, the most precious metal of all, by virtue of its abundance, its hardness and its solidity, was added to the imperfect instruments of the primitive ages. Then was born the Iron Age, to which we belong ourselves."

As he concluded that sentence, the old scientist stood up. "It seems to me," he said, "that that's enough for one day. It's a veritable lecture that this curious girl has made me give there. That's all right—I confess that my audience, although not numerous, was nonetheless attentive. I award a merit point to Mademoiselle Angèle, and her professor remains at her disposal."

Since the departure from Sydney, fortune had greatly favored the scientific navigators making up the expedition embarked on the *Glorieux*. The strong winds blowing from the west or the south-west, so common in those regions, where they are sometimes very redoubtable, did not make themselves felt. Favored at first by an easterly wind, and then by a northerly—which is to say, having the wind incessantly behind them, they left the large islands of New Ireland, Ika-na-Mawi and Tawai-Ponumamo to the west.[16] Passing through the group of the Chatham Islands, they continued their southerly course and, without stopping at Antipodes Island—so-called because it is located almost at the antipodes of Paris—they did not take long to perceive in the distant mists of the horizon the Seal Island that was to be their future dwelling.

---

[16] New Ireland is in Papua-New Guinea. Ika a Maui and Te Wapounanu are the Maori names for the north and south islands of New Zealand. The first-named island is therefore north of Australia, whereas the others lie to the south-east.

Since the ship, after quitting the latitude of Sydney, had been sailing southwards, the temperature had been dropping incessantly, without having acquired an unbearable intensity of cold. When the watchman, crying "Land ho!" signaled the appearance of the island they desired to reach, the weather was overcast, as on the previous day, and the wind was beginning to feel icy. The thermometer indicated zero in the air and sea alike.

The calmness of the sea and the atmosphere, and the clement temperature, if one considers that Seal Island is situated on the 52nd degree of latitude and the 180th degree of longitude, presaged that the landing would be achieved in the most favorable conditions: no fog, no wind, and, above all, none of the monstrous waves that are so frequently prevalent in that region, entirely covered in water.

Angèle, her uncle and the man she privately called her fiancé were on deck, attentively considering the coasts of the island where they would be called upon to live for several months.

The appearance of the land was dismal. It was not yellow and desolate, like some parts of the coast of Australia that the *Glorieux* had skirted on the journey from Melbourne to Sydney, but the sadness of its aspect came from the uniform hue that enveloped it. Everything was gray, on the land, in the sky and on the sea, all the way to the extreme limits of the horizon.

"Look, Messieurs," said Angèle, shivering, "wouldn't one think that we were in the empire of death and silence here? Look over thereat those waves, which the coast causes to elongate and them rear up, to fall back in white cascades. Look at those gray rocks that puncture the waves with their dark points. Wouldn't one think that all that movement has something slow and sleepy about it? Listen—all of that doesn't produce the slightest sound; everything is mute and silent."

Émile smiled. "Permit me to observe, Mademoiselle," he said, "that the somber and fantastic scene that you think you see and describe so well offers nothing that isn't perfectly natural. The waves only seem to you to be advancing more slowly than usual; you don't hear their roar as they make their assault on the rocks and cliffs solely because we're still too far away for the sound to reach us."

In the northern part of the island, which was most clearly visible, they could not see any trace of a tree. A great plateau with sheer cliffs: such was the general aspect of Seal Island, seen from the ship.

In those cliffs, composed of gray strata that could be attributed to volcanic eruptions, the eye was arrested involuntarily by other red-brown strata, which the waters had eroded and thus formed hollow moldings of a sort extending horizontally along the sheer coasts. The gray parts, by contrast, formed vast ledges overhanging the sea.

To the south of the island rose a large islet with a triple summit, whose form was involuntarily reminiscent of a monstrous shark's tooth. Further away there was a large high mountain with a majestically rounded head, and then, finally, a partly-crumbled peninsula.

Monsieur Charmillon pointed out that grandiose landslide to his companions, who were gripped by admiration.

"There's no denying it," exclaimed Émile, "half that enormous mountain has collapsed into the waves! What colossal force could have produced that cataclysm?"

Meanwhile, the *Glorieux* continued to advance. It traversed a series of currents that might have been taken for shallows; then, after having crossed the tumultuous stretch without even seeming to perceive it, she found calm water near the entrance to a bay that appeared in the north of the island, not far from the huge rock planted there like a remote sentinel.

Commandant Beaudin was on deck, multiplying his orders. The member of the Parisian Académie des Sciences approached him in order to speak to him.

"Commandant," he said, "Have you been to these parts before? Do you know that island?"

"No, my dear scientist," the Commandant replied, "but we'll soon make its acquaintance."

"Your intention is to land immediately?"

"To land, no—but to drop anchor in that bay, which seems to me to be a port as safe as it's comfortable. I'll disembark you by means of launches, and you'll have the leisure to choose the location on the island that suits you best for the foundation of your settlement and the construction of your observatory."

Those words did not take long to be followed by the fact. The sails of the *Glorieux* were lowered, and she entered the haven driven by her two propellers.

That operation, which was watched with keen attention by all the members of the scientific expedition, frightened a large whale that was playing close to land, and which made its escape rapidly enough to have nothing to fear from the hunter Émile and his terrible carbine.

In any case, the young man and his fiancée were plunged in an ocean of mute contemplation, which scarcely permitted the murderous instincts of the young scientist to awaken.

Chapter VII

The operation of the disembarkation did not take long. Above the rocks that enveloped the waters of the bay like a belt, a vast plateau extended covered with heather about two meters high. It was in the middle of that dense vegetation, ready to flower, that the scientists had initially hoped to be able to pitch their tents and live during their sojourn of several months.

The place did, in fact, seem propitious for an establishment; the high rocks that formed a kind of advance sentinel at the entrance to the bay sheltered it completely from high winds coming from the west or north, while the high mountains of the interior protected it from any storm coming from the south or the east. It remained, however, to know the opinion of the astronomers, for it was necessary not to forget that the principal aim of their long voyage was to study a celestial phenomenon. It was expressly to seek a favorable location for astronomical observations that the exploration of that part of the island was undertaken.

When one looked down at the verdant ground of the plateau at a distance, from a more elevated position, the heathland resembled a stand of pines, some seven or eight years old. Monsieur Charmillon made that remark soon after they landed.

"We'll do admirably well here," he said. "The ground is soft underfoot, and he verdant mosses that garnish the old branches and coil around the young shoots produce spring hues of a superb effect."

"In truth, Uncle," replied Angèle "it seems to me, as it does to you, that it will be a pleasure to walk across these as-yet-unexplored terrains. Agree with me, however, that there's a little breeze blowing that chills the fingers and the tip of the nose."

The uncle and niece set out lightly en route, followed by the faithful Émile, but they had scarcely taken a few steps when they found their feel entangled by an inextricable network of stems and creepers. Further on, they found the ground beneath them hidden, and their feet sinking into invisible holes. The moss that they had admired so much clung to their shoes and seemed to want to attach them to the ground.

When they had covered fifty meters in that fashion, they were exhausted, and sat down to get their breath back. Alas, they were not yet at the end of their difficulties; Angèle uttered an exclamation and stood up as if moved by a spring.

"But we're in the water!" she cried.

And indeed, the unfortunate strollers perceived, too late, that in spite of the steep slope they were crossing, everything was wet, and formed a veritable marsh.

Such was Seal Island: green on the surface and reminiscent of a cheerful meadow, but in reality covered in water.

Having been tempted to moisten his lips with that water, which seemed clear and limpid, Émile spat it out swiftly. It was absolutely undrinkable, so much was it impregnated with organic matter in dissolution or formation.

While all of them made heroic efforts to get out as best they could from that difficult situation, the Russian scientist Batschkoff pointed out to his traveling companions several points situated on the top of the mountain from which swirls of smoke were escaping. Everyone wondered what the cause of the phenomenon might be.

Mr. Wilson of the Royal Geographical Society of London expressed the thought that they might be distress signals made by one or more unfortunate shipwreck victims.

The prospect of being able to assist unfortunates rendered young Émile all his vigor. Forgetting his fatigues and the difficulties of the route, he launched an assault on the high mountain. His hunting-rifle and game-bag were his sole companions.

Angèle perhaps thought, deep down, that to venture forth alone into an unknown land was not absolutely prudent, but she dared not express her fears in case she allowed the sentiment that gave birth to them to show. On the other hand, she felt proud to see so much masculine courage and chivalric devotion in the man she had chosen and whom she had promised herself to make her husband and master one day.

While Émile disappeared into the folds in the ground, the rest of the expedition arrived on the plateau and began to study the terrain.

The north-eastern bay was unanimously condemned from the astronomical viewpoint; the same factors that would have ensured its security against bad weather rendered it inappropriate for the establishment of an observatory. The northern horizon was non-existent, and so was the southern; it was in a trench.

With regard to communication with the sea, Commandant Beaudin judged, for his part, that the security of his ship might by compromised in that location by north-easterly winds, against which there was no protection.

Everyone, after mature deliberation, was therefore in agreement as to the necessity of finding another point of disembarkation, and they were about to return to the

Glorieux when they saw the valiant Émile returning from his mission, wet, ragged and exhausted, but satisfied to have given proof of his devotion and courage. After three hours of the most fatiguing march, he had returned completely edified as to the nature of the fires perceived on the mountain. The smoke that was escaping from various points was produced by miniature craters rising above the soil in little cones that might have been mistaken at a distance for the huts of savages or ant-hills.

When evening came and night fell, the travelers, on returning to the ship, were able to perceive flames escaping from the summit of the mountain in more than twenty separate places and rising up to a prodigious height. They concluded without difficulty from that observation that Seal Island was full of volcanic nuclei.

When the *Glorieux* quit the north-west bay—which they had named Station Bay—the following morning, however, they regretted the perfect shelter that it had provided against the westerly and northerly winds. They set out to make a circuit of the island, in search of a better mooring.

Following the current that it had crossed without difficulty thanks to the power of its propeller, the ship did not take long to find another inlet, to which they gave the name Mercury Bay, in honor of the planet that the expedition had come to observe. It took less than an hour and a half of sailing under full steam to reach it,

The appearance of the coast between the two bays was the same as in the north. A broad plateau, high and bare, extended throughout the journey; above it rose basaltic rocks, and the horizon was closed by escarpments a hundred meters high, formed of strata of lava and pozzolan.

Monsieur Charmillon and his secretary did not fail to point out to their young companion how everything about the island demonstrated its volcanic origin.

"This land," said the old scientist, "appears to me to be recent in its origin. Everything thus far demonstrates superabundantly that it must have emerged from the waters in a submarine eruption. That was, moreover, the opinion clearly affirmed by Entrecasteaux, who visited it during his great voyage in search of the unfortunate Lapérouse."

At the foot of the escarpments forming the sharp ridges of the carcass emerging from the bosom of the waves, narrow fissures were visible at intervals, penetrating into the interior like long corridors, and caverns with dark mouths in which the waves were engulfed with muffled detonations.

"My dear Uncle," said the lovely Angèle, "I assure you that this land, in spite of its somber and dismal aspect, excites my curiosity to the highest degree. The little specimen that we have been allowed to see has given me a guarantee that nothing here resembles what I've been able to see in my excursions in the vicinity of Paris. Only one thing frightens me, and that's the cold that menaces us at this latitude.

"My dear girl," the scientist replied, "the dread that you express would be entirely rational if we weren't arriving here in October—which is to say, the middle of spring. The snows have already disappeared from the summits they crowned; the thermometer almost obtains the zero of melting ice at its maximum. Every day we'll see the warmth returning, and we'll soon be in the middle of summer."

"What! Summer in November and December!" exclaimed the young woman, unable to suppress the marks of her astonishment."

"My God, yes!" replied her uncle, smiling. "You mustn't forget, my child, that we've passed the antipodes of Paris, and when it's winter at home it's summer in this hemisphere."

Mercury Bay suddenly appeared to the travelers in a grandiose fashion, and none of the spectators doubted at first glance that it was the promised land.

This time, there was not, as in Station Bay, a plateau—or, rather, a valley enclosed between two mountains—but a gigantic cutting leading to an arc, on the coasts of which conical pylons and hillocks of bizarre form loomed up.

The bay, seen as a whole, resembled a colossal seal, its lateral inlets representing the arms and flippers fairly accurately.

Monsieur Charmillon, armed with an excellent telescope, studied the ground with incessantly increasing attention. To begin with, everything there that was not rock or stratifications appeared to his eyes to be masses of ash furnished by the extinct crater of the primitive volcano, but the water had cooled them so well that they had been cold for a long time and, in mingling with the detritus of heather and mosses, they had metamorphosed into vegetal earth.

"Perhaps I was too hasty," he said to his pupil, "in affirming just now the recent appearance of this island above the waves. The nature of the soil I'm looking at indicates instead that the last major eruption of the formative volcano goes back to the Upper Cretaceous."

"What do you mean by the Upper Cretaceous, Uncle?" asked Angèle, who was decidedly getting a taste for science.

"Cretaceous," replied the obliging professor, "means 'of the nature of chalk.' Cretaceous terrains form the uppermost layer of Secondary terrains. The period in the life of the planet when those terrains were formed is called the Cretaceous period."

On the southern coast of the entrance to the bay a basaltic flow had crystallized into prisms, which a second eruption had raised up irregularly, and then set them down again like voussures of a gigantic arch. The savant Academician, pointing out that disposition to his listeners, also showed them the base of those rocks.

"Look at those natural bases," he said, "those narrow corridors, those cyclopean arcades. Nothing is simpler than explaining their formation. The sea alone, mining those inferior bases, has eaten them away at the least resistant points; it has only made use for that of its natural waves, that marvelous and irresistible battering-ram."

At midday, the *Glorieux* had penetrated into the bay and moored at a point that permitted putting a long kedge into the water, where she was in perfect security.

In the month of October in those regions it gets dark at seven o'clock; that gave the members of the expedition time to go ashore to make a summary inspection of the coast that was doubtless going to be the site of their sojourn. Monsieur Charmillon, Émile and Angèle took care not to miss out on that pleasure trip.

At the very back of the bay, the geologist discovered a location that seemed to him entirely suitable for setting up an establishment. On the edge of a stream there was a flat terrain formed of fine sand, where a large number of plants with ornamental leaves similar to large acanthias were growing, vigorously and splendidly.

They were admiring that superb vegetation when the young woman's eyes were suddenly attracted to a part of the field where a large area had been ravaged and disrupted as if a stone roller had passed over it. A few stems of the large-leafed plants, stripped of all their verdure and leaning over in a melancholy fashion, were the only vestiges of the luxuriant vegetation that had previously covered the soil.

Angèle pointed out the disaster, which seemed quite recent, to her fiancé. Émile paraded around an investigative gaze, and was soon able to observe that the compressing roller that had caused the damage was not far away.

An enormous seal of a particular species, known as an elephant seal, four meters long and as large as a cow, was sleeping peacefully not far away on the edge of the beach. It was, moreover, an exceedingly ugly beast with black teeth, rotten or broken, and a grim appearance. On perceiving it, the young woman could not repress an exclamation of terror and disgust.

When it saw the unexpected visitors, the frightened animal started to make hectic efforts to flee, crawling away. Sometimes it threw itself to the right, sometimes to the left, with the most awkward movements, and, in sum, made so little progress that the sailors in the launch that had landed the voyagers perceived it before it was able to get back to the sea, its true element, and killed it without difficulty. Émile, who was never without his carbine, had taken pity on the poor beast and had not deigned to honor it with a rifle shot.

He approached the cadaver and, in consideration of the limited vigor deployed by the animal before its death, was easily able to suppose that it had come up on to the beach in order to yield its last sigh, as its fellows often do. The crewmen had therefore merely abridged the monster's existence slightly.

One fact subsequently observed, however, weighed against that hypothesis, which is that the expedition, during its various explorations of the island, did not find any of the sorts of deposits that form the basis of guano on certain islets, and are composed of bones in various stages of decomposition. They are the cemeteries in which seals have the custom of coming to end their existence. One encounters them often enough in the polar regions, just as one finds large elephant cemeteries in the heart of the African continent.

Monsieur Charmillon and his traveling companions thought the site they had just visited charming, and resolved, for their own account, to establish their private dwelling there, without worrying about the location hat might be chosen for the establishment of the expedition in general. We shall see that sage precautions had been taken by Commandant Beaudin, which rendered the execution of that project possible.

They had arrived on October the tenth. The weather continued to be very tolerable. The thermometer marked two or three degrees above zero. The high mountains surrounding the bay only had snow in the fissures with a southern exposure.

The most important thing of all was to find a favorable spot to construct the observatory. The astronomers of the expedition came together and set off at an early hour for he definitive search for the position where they were going to establish themselves. The conditions that had to be met were numerous. It had to be spacious, with views to the north, south and west, with firm ground, a shield against the wind and—an almost contradictory condition—they did not want to be under the protection of a high mountain.

Finding nothing to the north of the bay, the scholarly investigators passed on to the south; a little inlet presented itself, limited to the south-west by contorted rocks. A basaltic eruption emerging from a cliff terminated the western point, forming a kind of natural jetty. Afterwards came a volcanic overflow that seemed to spring up from the heather in order to plunge into the sea.

It was there that the majority of the expedition decided to stop. On leaping to shore from the launch that had brought them, Pierre de Kolikoff and Otto Eliaison fell to their hands and knees.

"That's a bad omen," said the German Dr. Franz Henrich.

"No," replied William Johnston, "those gentleman have just imitated William the Conqueror when he disembarked in England. Thanks to them, our taking possession of this ground has become effective."

Five minutes later, everyone, chiefs and ordinary seamen, engineers, scientists and mariners, each with a meter rule, a hatchet, or even a saber, in hand, set to work.

The plan of the observatory to be founded had been drawn up a long time ago. The dimension of the sections had been carefully regulated, as well as their interior distribution and their reciprocal dependencies.

Thanks to these preparatory studies and works, they were able to divide the active personnel into three crews and begin the work in three places simultaneously.

Ten sailors had been especially attached to the expedition, aided by three carpenters embarked at Sydney for that specialist labor; they set to work. In the evening, a detachment of sixteen crewmen joined them, which brought the number of workers on the improvised building-site to twenty-nine.

The work made rapid progress; to protect the sections destined to serve as storerooms and kitchens against squalls, they were dug into the hill. That increased the amount of rubble to be shifted; the turf was attacked and carried away in large blocks. They were separated from the mass by cutting them out along their length, width and height.

After a few hours of hard labor, they knew what held together that turf, composed of mosses, leaves and half-composed heather branches. No air or light circulated in the undergrowth where that vegetable debris piled up; the undecomposed layer increased in height every year and caused the level to rise of the new growth, which was reminiscent of a hemp-field or an assemblage of broomsticks. That deposit of leaves, branches and mosses was subsequently felted by the entanglement of stems and twigs, the roots traversing it in all directions and the damp decomposing it.

At a depth of fifty centimeters making use of a heavy saber, square blocks could be cut, so resistant that they could be used to construct walls, used as if they were bricks. At a depth of a meter the material became unctuous, at two meters it was a mud mixed with compost, lower still, a residue that was indescribable, as much because of its appearance as its odor.

In the heathlands of Brittany one finds similar layers of soil and vegetal detritus, which are cut in the form of briquettes and dried out in the sun in order to make use of them as fuel in winter.

Arthème Charmillon, who had followed the works with a keen interest, while waiting for the construction of his own residence to begin, put forward the hypothesis that a spring must be bringing sulfates there, which decomposed on contact with organic substances, and that, on the other hand, the rocks of volcanic origin doubtless contained iron sulfide crystals. All the members of the expedition, struck by the characteristic nauseating odor that was escaping from the rubble, agreed with that opinion.

When the kitchens were comfortably established, a kind of jetty was sketched opposite and the commencement of a quay. The sailors of the *Glorieux* gave proof in that circumstance of marvelous skill and expertise. Let us say that there were Bretons among them who were veritably Herculean, capable of constructing works of art using their menhirs as bricks.

The volcano had hurled enormous stones into the inlet and "cannonballs" of iron oxide blackened by fire. They were used as the foundations of works designed to survive the expedition for a long time. Those endeavors would have done honor to a company of engineers and tradesmen.

On the evening of the first day, when they went back aboard for dinner, the small bay, which the matelots had baptized Robinson Bay, had already changed its appearance. The seagulls, astonished by the unexpected upheaval, soared over the works emitting loud screeches.

While those sudden transformations were accomplished, a small scientific excursion was organized. William Johnston, the English naturalist, and Dr. Despierre, the botanist well known in Parisian society, had taken the initiative. Émile Colin, in his capacity as a meritorious hunter, easily obtained the favor of taking part in the expedition. As for Angèle, she had asked her uncle to let her spend the day on board, because the previous day's excursion had tired her out and she felt a veritable need to rest.

That desire, which could only please Monsieur Charmillon, who was exhausted, was greeted with favor, and the excursionists departed, accompanied by the good wishes of their companions whose occupations retained them on the ship or the shore.

Chapter VIII

The following evening, when the excursionists came back aboard, they were laden with rich booty. It was in a tone half-delighted and half-modest that the indefatigable Émile received the congratulations of all the members of the expedition, and his female friend in particular.

He had left, as we said, accompanying the two naturalists and escorted by two of the *Glorieux*'s sailors.

Under the murderous lead of his Lepage rifle, two enormous albatrosses had fallen. His travelling companions had also collected eagle eggs and an armful of mosses off various species.

The aspect of the island, during that first exploration, had appeared less frightful than they had thought at first and Entrecasteaux had recorded in the course of his voyage. The spring vegetation was fairly active there, but very specialized. In particular, they had encountered bizarre clumps of grass, of which they had brought back very curious collections. Species of couch-grass and sorghum covered enormous areas of the plain and the mountain-sides above the region of the briars with their feathery tufts.

The clods of earth protected by the root-networks of the plants in question remained at a certain level, while the rain hollowed out profound furrows all around them.

Angèle could not weary of interrogating the young man and listening to his description of the desert island that would soon become their common residence.

"Didn't you encounter any quadrupeds grazing those meadows?" she asked.

"No cow has ever set foot on their primitive soil," the young hunter replied. "They'd find poor provender here, in any case. Only sheep and goats could eke out a living here, but it would be necessary to import them."

Dr. Despierre, who overhead that conversation, interrupted Émile. "We'll certainly never encounter sheep," he said, "but it's necessary not to swear with regard to goats. Entrecasteaux affirms that he left a pair here during his voyage. Lapérouse, for his part, never landed on a desert island without depositing goats and pigs there. If the rigorous cold hasn't destroyed that breeding stock, you might expect, Monsieur expert hunter, to encounter prey worthy of your skill at any moment."

"For want of wild goats or boars," the young man replied, laughing, "We've encountered legions of rats, whose grandparents undoubtedly escaped from the ships of one of our great navigators. We'll have serious enemies to combat there, when we're established on land."

"What other plants have you noticed?" asked the young woman, ever avid for information.

"At intervals," the young man replied, "we found very large cabbages about a meter high: Macquarie Island cabbages, like thick-leaved burdocks, which, if I'm not mistaken, might well constitute an alimentary plant.[17] We also encountered a large number of those plants with large ornamental leaves that we've already

---

[17] The Macquarie Island "cabbage" (*Stilbocarpa polaris*) was found on Campbell Island by the 1874 expedition; it is, indeed, edible and was often used by sailors to ward off scurvy, although the original population on Macquarie Island was almost wiped out by accidentally-introduced rats and rabbits.

noticed on the strand. William Johnston made a singular observation on that subject, which is that the plants are distributed in the soil with such perfect symmetry that one could swear that they had been planted by a skilful gardener. What also contributes to that illusion is that everywhere in the plants' surroundings the earth is clean, deprived of all vegetation, as if the hoe and rake had passed that way.

That exploration earned its authors the unanimous congratulations of all the members of the expedition. The resolution was made not to wait until they were definitively installed on the land in order to carry out further expeditions, and groups formed in order to visit every part of the island while the works were ongoing on the shores of Robinson Bay.

This time, Monsieur Charmillon's niece did not want to stay aboard, and it was decided that a geological excursion would take place under the guidance of her uncle, in which she would be allowed to take part.

The project was put into execution on Saturday the twelfth of October. A caravan was formed, composed of Monsieur Charmillon, the two English scientists Johnston and Wilson, Pierre Guérard, Pierre de Kolikoff, Dr. Despierre, the Swede Oscar Johannesen and his friend Stuxberg, from Copenhagen. Young Émile Colin, the expedition leader's secretary, and Angèle, his niece, were accepted as traveling companions. Finally, four robust matelots from the *Glorieux* completed the little column, which, taking advantage of a beautiful sunny day, was taken by a launch toward the shore opposite the vessel's mooring.

As they approached the shore, a magnificent spectacle struck their gazes and compensated them in advance for the trouble they were about to take. Near the bank where they were about to land there was a perfect calm and everyone was able to judge the marvelous effects produced by the wind in the interior of the bay. Angèle was particularly impressed by the curious aspects of the sight. She never wearied of contemplating the meteorological phenomena that had been manifest over the agitated waves of the bay. Sheets of wind passed between the summits that protected it, following the depressions of the soil as they descended and extending over the surface of the sea. There, by reason of different wind velocities, series of eddies were produced, which the pressure of rising waters rendered very evident.

The waves foamed under that powerful impulsion and a procession of miniature whirlpools moved across the bay, all the way to the southern point, which had been named Horror Point.

The explorers carried by the launch moved alongside the coast where they were to land. The port oars were dipping curtly into the algae that they were picking up. Snow blown off he high summits by the wind and sea spray whipped the voyagers' faces, but they advanced nevertheless.

Suddenly they perceived a vast crevice opening in the flanks of a vast rock that they had baptized the Sphinx by reason of its heraldic form, into which the launch moved, in response to Monsieur Charmillon's order, without any difficulty. They landed, after a quarter of an hour of that navigation under vaults where semi-obscurity reigned, alongside a bank of rocks that formed a kind of jetty.

The leader of the expedition, who had already observed the structure of Seal Island attentively, had been looking forward to an exploration of one of its numerous grottoes, the gaping mouths of which opened at regular intervals. In order to determine the nature of the rocks and soils, he had equipped himself with a provision of lanterns and candles. Everyone armed himself with a light-source, and they were able from then on to continue penetrating the cavern on foot.

The walked for about a quarter of an hour over the rocky jetty on which they had landed, and then arrived at a point of the grotto where the sea ceased to penetrate, even at the highest tides. There, the ground offered the footsteps of the excursionists a bed of fine sand, on which they could advance without difficulty.

"Here we've reached my veritable domain," said Monsieur Charmillon.

Johnston, who was parading his lantern over damp walls encrusted with saltpeter made no reply, but nodded his head energetically.

"Now," the French scientist went on, "I can affirm without fear of contradiction by anyone, that this island belongs to the Upper Cretaceous formation. Everything here proves it superabundantly."

"Uncle," Angèle hazarded to say, "doubtless all these Messieurs, who are erudite men, understand your implication, but don't forget that you've permitted an ignorant person to follow you, and that I'd be very glad to profit from your instruction."

"I excuse you, my niece," replied Monsieur Charmillon, "in your capacity as a woman, for your ignorance and your curiosity. I'll try to explain myself, then, for your benefit. Everyone knows, and I've already told you, that the Cretaceous terrains form the upper layer of the terrains of the Secondary epoch, and that they play an important role in the constitution of the soil of Europe, particularly France.

"Before being covered by the substances that constitute the Tertiary terrain, their surface presented depressions and protrusions that formed hills, valleys and buttes there. Those inequalities, as you've been able to observe many a time, and as you can still see here, are indicated by islands and promontories of chalk that are exposed at certain points through more modern foundations. One can also observe them by making excavations, thanks to which one can find chalk at very variable depths."

The professor shot his niece an interrogative glance, as if to ask whether she had understood, and continued: "The sands on which we're walking are reminiscent of those of Hastings; like them, they must be ferruginous, and I hope to encounter here, by digging in them, a few remains of vertebrate animals, which will give us a precise idea of the ancient fauna of this land.

"Modern science believes, and it's probable, that this isolated land is attached to Campbell Island, the Auckland Islands,[18] New Zealand and Australia, Perhaps it even forms part of a land-mass serving as a connection between this oceanic continent and Tierra de Fuego.

"It was in the epoch when these combined lands formed a vast part of the globe that the singular primitive

---

[18] We now know that the Auckland Islands, which were produced by two Miocene volcanoes, subsequently accumulated fossil-bearing sedimentary rocks, so the author's hypothesis is not as far-fetched as it might seem, in spite of being based on a primitive geological understanding. The hypothesis regarding the one-time linkage of the various landmasses cited was subsequently confirmed by the identification of the mostly-sunken subcontinent of "Zealandia," although Campbell Island is on its eastern rim, which might have placed the fictitious Seal Island some distance off its original shore.

birds and animals lived whose fossil bones are found today in all the emergent points, and of which we might, I hope, reap an ample harvest here."

Monsieur Charmillon paused to draw breath, scanned his listeners with his gaze, and, finding them still attentive, continued his interesting lecture.

"You have doubtless seen, as I did, during our passage through Melbourne, in that city's rich cabinet of natural history, the colossal foot of a *Dinornis*. That grandiose and majestic foot, nearly two meters long, belonged to a bird whose stride must have competed with the seven league boots of our popular tales. It's thanks to that gigantic pylon that we've been able to reproduce, in theory, the entire body of the animal, for thus far, it's the only specimen that we've been able to find of that giant fowl.[19] How do we know that we might not be able to find here, in this cavern, other parts of the *Dinornis*, and that we might not be able to confirm or refute the scientific hypotheses according to which we ought to have reconstituted it?"

An approving murmur greeted those words from the scientist, who became animated, as if giving a public lecture, and continued: "After the Cretaceous epoch,

---

[19] In fact, numerous specimens of the bones of Moas were found in New Zealand from 1839 onwards, and must have numbered in the hundreds by 1876, but very few of them would have found their way to Melbourne—the three species of Moa were all limited to New Zealand—and it is possible that some confusion might have arisen. Robert Owen's original naming of the *Dinornis* species, on the basis of a single femur shipped to England, was greeted with widespread skepticism, but a photograph of him exists showing him standing triumphantly beside a complete skeleton, which proved him right.

whose origin is lost in the night of time, a great volcanic upheaval took place. Immense torrents of lava covered everything; then the ground of this part of the world collapsed and sank beneath the sea during the Miocene period. Only the summits remained above water, and the archipelagos of Oceania were born."

"Since my uncle is an in amiable vein," Angèle put in, in a pert tone, "I'd be grateful to him to tell me what he means by the Miocene period."

"You ought to know, although you don't," Monsieur Charmillon, "that the name Miocene is given to the median formation of the Tertiary terrains. I've already explained what is meant by the Tertiary period.

"In France the sands and marine sandstones that constitute the base of the median formation in the Paris basin are subdivisible into two varieties. Some are yellow and micaceous—which is to say, strewn with mica—in the lower part; in the upper part they're composed of sandstone impregnated with limestone. The others are reddish. You can see, Messieurs, that we find the same phenomena here.

"In the parts that compose this terrain and the rocks that you can see forming the vault we shall doubtless find, if we search sufficiently, large crocodiles, marine and terrestrial chelonians and bizarre mammals. In the epoch in which these terrains formed pachyderms analogous to tapirs lived, which have been named *Anaplotherium* and *Palaeotherium*. The existence of a certain number of carnivores resembling dogs is also observed, and other animals that we shall classify as and when we find traces of them."

"That seems all the more important to me," said Dr. Despierre, speaking in his turn, "because the impossibility of these animals crossing the immense seas that separate the continental coasts and establish a barrier between them will evidently demonstrate that, since the lands nourished the same species, they only formed a single continent in primitive times."

The valet Jean-Pierre had received orders from his master to follow the little caravan and take charge of the food. As we have said, the expedition had set forth early in the morning, and, in order not to be obliged to return to the ship for the first meal of the day the explorers had taken care to embark provisions, so as to be able to prolong their absence until the evening.

Jean-Pierre was a frightful braggart but, if he never tired of lies and boasts when he found himself facing an ignorant audience, he was able to keep quiet when confronted with educated people, and had qualities capable of making them forget his faults. He was a faithful servant; furthermore, he was not lacking in intelligence, initiative or practical knowledge of the quotidian necessities of life. He was a valet but, if necessary, he could acquit himself honorably as a cook.

Monsieur Charmillon instructed him to return to the launch and prepare the meal, with the aid of two sailors who had stayed to guard the boat.

"If the Messieurs don't want to disturb themselves," Jean-Pierre said, imperturbably, "I could serve their meal here, on the fine dry sand."

"Good idea," said the scientist. "What do my colleagues think?"

"So far as we're concerned, it would be a pleasure," replied Johannesen, "but it's necessary not to lose sight of the fact that we have a lady with us, and that it doubtless wouldn't be pleasant for her to sit down on the sand, even if it were drier and softer."

"On, Messieurs, I beg you not to disturb yourselves on my account," the young woman replied, swiftly. "I'll gladly do whatever you do, and if you put yourselves out, you'll deprive me in future of the pleasure I obtain from accompanying you."

"In that case," said Wilson, "We'll eat here, by torchlight, and it will constitute for us, when we return to Europe, a picturesque memory that we can recount to our friends by the fireside during long winter nights."

Jean-Pierre, bearing a lantern, did not take long to disappear into the depths of the grotto.

On the orders of the French geologist, two sailors who had accompanied the explorers began digging in the sandy soil of the cavern with mattocks. Monsieur Charmillon, Johnston and the celebrated Otto Eliaison followed the workers closely, sieving the removed sand through their fingers, and did not let any of it pass without having examined it attentively.

The other members of the expedition, leaving their colleagues to devote themselves to their specialty, moved deeper into the meanders of the subterranean grotto, torches in hand, desirous of knowing how far it penetrated into the island. They did not take long to disappear round a corner of the oblique corridor.

It goes without saying that Émile Colin and Angèle remained with Monsieur Charmillon.

The geologists had been occupied with their scrupulous search for a quarter of an hour when Johnston saw a few fragments of broken and more of less deformed bones emerge beneath the tools of the laborers. He threw himself avidly on to that prey, which he showed to his colleagues triumphantly.

The poor state of conservation of the bones did not prevent Monsieur Charmillon from recognizing their nature immediately. He took the gray fragments in is hand and placed them in the lantern-light.

"This," he said, without hesitation, "is a fraction of the fourth molar tooth of *Bos primigenius*, or primitive ox, which is an extinct species."

Carefully, he examined another fragment, slightly larger and contorted in form. "This," he affirmed, is the humerus of a *Lepus cuniculus*, which is nothing but an ordinary rabbit."

The lovely Angèle could not get over it; her astonishment was extreme at finding her uncle's judgment so knowledgeable and so sure.

A third fragment, however—very tiny, to be sire—seemed to embarrass the aged scientist somewhat. He went to Johnston and presented the specimen to him. The English geologist set about examining it methodically, but dared not pronounce a verdict.

Otto Eliaison seized the little fragment and smiled. "What, Messieurs," he said, in a god-humored tone that had nothing aggressive about it, "you don't recognize a milk tooth of a *Sus scrofa*, which the vulgar call a wild boar? I have more than a hundred fossil and modern specimens in my collection in Stockholm."

Monsieur Charmillon and Johnston bowed their heads, as befits modest scientists who recognize the justice of a solution they have not found.

The young secretary of the French Academician had taken the little bone in his turn and was examining it. He wanted to hazard an observation, which he would have refrained from doing if the proffered opinion had come from his dear professor.

"Monsieur Eliaison," he said, "might not this tooth, for it incontestably is one, have come from the jaw of a *Sus vulgaris*, or common pig?"

"You're very young, Monsieur," replied the Swedish scientist, acidically, "to bring your voice into the counsel of men of our age and experience. Having said that, I admit that your observation doesn't lack sagacity. I would have offered the same diagnosis as you if the tooth had presented on its external face the grooves characteristic of an adult pig, but you can see for yourself that the superior face is rounded instead of being flat and grooved."

The young secretary, doubtless convinced by that irrefutable evidence, bowed his head as a sign of concession and remained silent.

During these scientific discussions the mariners had not remained idle. They had already set aside several further fragments when a matelot named Le Dall, who was digging furiously, plunged his instrument into a veritable nest of shells. They were very well preserved, covered by a bed of sand thirty centimeters deep.

The scientists fell upon this new prey, which was about to furnish their investigations with interesting objects of study.

The new treasure contained a quantity of shells, among which the English scientist, who was the first to look at the specimens brought into the light had no difficulty recognizing *Ostea vulgaris*, the common oyster, *Patella vulgata*, the common limpet, and *Mitylus edulis*, which ignorant individuals and fishermen are content to call the mussel.

Monsieur Charmillon picked up among those empty shells a few fragments of *Pecten jacobaeus*, or marine scallop.

These wrecks of another age formed a collective mass such as one sometimes encounters in large cities at the doors of restaurants. They were not of a nature to astonish anyone who has seen quarries in the vicinity of Paris, notably at Gentilly, with layers of rock entirely formed from accumulations of fossil shells. Those layers conserve within an infinite perimeter a thickness that varies between one and a half and two meters.

Even Angèle noticed that analogy, while making the remark that the shells in the banks of Paris are fossilized and petrified, whereas those in the Grotto of the Sphinx were conserved as if the animals they contained had been eaten recently

Monsieur Charmillon had no difficulty in explaining to her that the state of perfect conservation was doubtless due to the envelope of fine sand that had kept them constantly out of contact with the air.

These interesting investigations had taken rather a long time, but the indefatigable geologists had not yet thought of interrupting themselves when their colleagues appeared in the depths of the grotto, returning from their subterranean excursion.

The young woman was struck by the splendor of the spectacle produced by the distant appearance of all those torches shining like glow-worms. The glimmers that were almost imperceptible to begin with grew as the explorers came closer. Sometimes the somber vaults of the cavern were illuminated, and millions of fragments of mica incrusted in the rocks could be seen sparkling like diamonds; sometimes the huge shadows of the travelers, projected along the sheer walls, seemed to be gigantic and fantastic phantoms.

The arrival of the excursionists was greeted with enthusiasm; for their part, they were dazzled by the marvelous discoveries that the geologists set before their eyes.

When they had admired the bones and shells extracted from the ground sufficiently, they told their own story.

Chapter IX

After a quarter of an hour or twenty minutes of walking, always following an upward slope, they had arrived at a point in the grotto where the broad corridor they had been following divided into three narrower branches. Each of those openings led in a different direction; they were equal in width, and nothing initially designated one more than any other as the first choice of the excursionists.

After a few seconds of hesitation, however, the chemist Guébard, who had thus far only seemed to be taking an interest in the efflorescences of saltpeter that formed large white patches on the grotto walls, indicated that he wanted to speak.

"In my opinion," he said, "We ought to take the right-hand tunnel, which will bring us closer to the sea. Who knows whether we might not find another exit from the little cave?"

This advice found no contradiction, and they engaged in the indicated corridor without further delay.

When they had covered a few hundred meters in that direction, progress became more difficult. Sometimes the two side walls came so close together that only one man could squeeze through; sometimes the tunnel widened but the rock forming the ceiling gradually sloped downwards, coming close enough to the floor to oblige the explorers to crouch down, or even to crawl.

No matter how many difficulties of that sort they encountered, they did not hesitate to continue going forward; nothing, thus far, prevented their return as soon as the whim took the to return to their point of departure.

The geographer Wilson, who was equipped with an aneroid barometer, observed that from the moment that they had entered the branch, the floor had been descending incessantly.

"We're now almost at sea level," he said. "If the tunnel we're in leads to the Ocean, we won't take long to find salt water."

Just as he said that, Guébard, who was at the head of the column, suddenly stopped and uttered an exclamation of surprise.

His friends, seeing his torch disappear, along with the shadow of his body projected backwards, thought that he had suddenly been swallowed up by some pit, and they moved forward in the hope of bringing him help if there was still time. However, in spite of the desire they had to make themselves useful, they only advanced with the hesitation that prudence recommended to them. They walked slowly, only putting their feet down when they had assured themselves by lowering their torches that the ground was solid.

Suddenly, a magical spectacle was offered to their gaze.

The corridor along which they had been advancing was abruptly terminated, and an immense chamber opened up in front of them. It was entirely surrounded by a colonnade that seemed to be the work of human hands, so regular and architectural was it.

What drew an exclamation of admiration from all of them, however, was that each of the equally-spaced columns seemed to be composed of a mosaic of diamonds launching dazzling reflections in all directions. The light of the torches, candles and lanterns was caught by millions of luminous points forming accumulations of minuscule tremulous stars, which reminded the visitors of showers of sparks escaping from a firebrand and tracing a luminous route through a dark chimney.

When they had recovered from their initial astonishment and reassured themselves regarding the fate of their colleague, who was striding back and forth in the huge subterranean hall, the explorers set about inspecting the marvels that were unfolding before their eyes in detail.

Behind the natural gallery formed by the brilliant colonnade, the walls offered smooth and polished surfaces, as if made of marble. Like the pillars of the colonnade, the walls were glittering.

Who, then, had created these architectural marvels? The members of the commission were too knowledgeable to ask themselves that elementary question. Each of the columns had been formed very simply by the meeting of a stalactite and a stalagmite.

Imperceptible crevices in the vault had allowed the passage of water heavily infused with chalk and other salts that it had dissolved while passing through the superior layers of soil and rock. That water had fallen drop by drop on to the floor of the cavern and evaporated, depositing the salts that it held in solution. The deposits thus formed were constantly superimposed and had ended up forming a kind of incessantly-growing pyramid. Such is a stalagmite. At the same time as that deposit firmed on the floor, however, a symmetrical deposit was created on the ceiling; the successive drops, as they fell, remained suspended long enough for a part of the salt-saturated water that composed them to evaporate and leave behind a sedimentary deposit known as a stalactite.

As the stalagmite departing from the ground rises up perpendicularly, the stalactite hanging from the ceiling descends in the same way, until the two of them meet half way, fuse and form a single column.

The visitors, charmed and dazzled by the brilliant reflections of the calcareous salts, wanted to prolong their inspection. When they arrived at the opposite extremity of the huge space, they encountered an opening that led them into a smaller chamber, which caused them no less astonishment. There, the infiltrations had given birth not to regular columns but to an infinity of objects of the most various and bizarre forms.

Everyone thought that he could see all kings of natural and artificial things there: suspended icicles, suddenly-congealed fountains or waterfalls, flowers, fruits, yew-trees, palm-trees, cabbage-flowers and mushrooms of every form and species, from the twisted chanterelle to the proud boletus and the elegant poisonous agaric. True and fantastic animals could also be seen there, human forms imitated with varying degrees of exactitude, mummies, phantoms and draped statues, as well as vases chandeliers, candelabras, pyramids, columns, altars, pulpits, fonts and organ-pipes: a immense and fantastic bazaar of bric-à-brac.

In one corner, in a recess, fantastic nature had formed, unmistakably, a butcher's shop with the merchant at his counter. It was marvelous to see suspended from the ceiling and along the walls chaplets of sausages, black-puddings and saveloys, and, further away, hams, ribs, smoked tongues and shelves laden with plates carrying assortments of salted pork, etc.

Those who have visited the natural grottos of France—at Balme, for example—will not be astonished by these fantasies of nature, which one encounters there heaped up in profusion.

The explorers would have liked to push their investigations further, but, on the other hand, they feared causing anxiety to the colleagues they had left behind by too long an absence. Then too, time was passing and their stomachs were beginning to announce that it was time to eat.

They retraced their steps, therefore, while reserving the intention of coming back another time to complete their subterranean journey and extract any scientific conclusions that they might encounter therein.

The tale of their adventure was greeted with the keenest interest by the geologists, who promised firmly to assist them in their next excursion—but they perceived in their turn that the time had flown by. They all turned their attention to the cavern entrance, not daring to express too loudly the astonishment caused by the absence of Jean-Pierre and the two sailors who had accompanied him.

Monsieur Charmillon was the first to say something.

"Jean-Pierre's taking a long time," he said. "I think it might be a good idea to make our way back to the exit and give up on the idea of eating here."

"With your permission, Monsieur Charmillon," said Émile, "I'll go look for the laggards, and bring them back dead or alive."

He was just about to leave when they saw a light appear some distance away, seemingly emerging from one of the side walls of the tunnel. A human form vaguely designed behind the light approached rapidly. They did not take long to recognize the silhouette of the valet, who, baring his head ceremoniously before his master, bowed deeply and aid: "Monsieur is served!"

Everyone looked around inquisitively, and, not perceiving any trace of a meal, began to believe that it was a joke.

"What is this nonsense?" demanded Monsieur Charmillon, severely.

"Monsieur knows that I do not permit myself to jest with him," replied the domestic, humbly. "If Monsieur, Mademoiselle and these Messieurs would care to follow me, I will indicate, a few steps away, the dining room that I have discovered and on which, I hope, they might like to compliment me."

Convinced that a surprise awaited them, the members of the expedition set out to follow Jean-Pierre, who set of at a solemn pace.

When they arrived about a hundred meters from the place where the excavation had been carried out, they saw the valet-cum-cook turn right, and perceived, not without astonishment, that a smaller tunnel that they had not noticed on the way in opened in the wall of the principal cave. It was into that corridor that Jean-Pierre went; the scientific explorers followed him without hesitation.

They had scarcely taken thirty paces when a bright light struck their gaze, They advanced further and penetrated into a kind of square clamber that the valet had illuminated for the occasion, in the middle of which a long table stood, covered by a white table-cloth. All around it, folding seats had been set up, fabricated with pieces of cloth and bamboo poles, like those used by painters and tourists who have the habit of taking them on their excursions. Enthusiastic bravoes greeted the unexpected spectacle.

On examining the improvised décor more closely, they were soon able to take account of the ingenious methods employed by Jean-Pierre to realize the miracle.

The opening of the tunnel had not escaped the inquisitive gaze of the valet. When, accompanied by the two matelots similarly charged with the food provisions, he had returned to the place where the launch was moored, he had ventured into the tunnel and when the square chamber had appeared he had said to his companions: "Here's an admirable dining room."

Immediately, an entire plan had taken form in his mind. As soon as everyone had set down the provisions he was carrying he said: "My friends, it's not a matter of going to sleep; quickly, let's go back to the ship and bring back everything necessary to give these Messieurs an agreeable surprise."

Thus, planks, trestles, folding chairs, the cloth, napkins and even a pile of plates had been brought, which had permitted the superb table to be set up. Add in a provision of lanterns and candles with which Monsieur Charmillon had provided himself, just in case, and there was nothing surprising about the bright illumination in the empire of darkness.

Jean-Pierre had not contented himself with those tricks—which were, he said, in sum, merely a treat for the eyes. With the aid of a few bundles of firewood ferried by a third trip, he had lit a blazing fire in another compartment of the subterranean corridor and, improvising a spit in front of a respectable heap of incandescent embers, had roasted eight superb ducks that Émile had killed that morning on the way, in order not to get rusty.

All those comings and goings had remained unknown to the savant professors, too occupied with their research to pay attention to external matters.

They therefore made a superb meal under the profound vaults, which doubtless had not received the visit of a human being since their creation. Generous wines were poured in profusion and tinned food made up the bulk of the meal, but the principal honor reverted to the magician Jean-Pierre, who had been able to bring a genuine comfort to a meal in which everyone had been resigned in advance to his share of abnegation.

When they thought about getting up from the table, the session having lasted longer than anticipated, they realized that there was no time to undertake further research, and postponed until another day an exploration that would complete the first.

The return of the expedition to the *Glorieux* was a veritable ovation. The discoveries made by both parties keenly interested all those who had not been part of the little caravan, and it was unanimously agreed that all the members of the expedition would select a day to continue the investigations commenced in common. An exploration had already been planned for the next day, and everyone had been invited to take part in it, but the astronomers, very preoccupied at the moment with the construction of their observatory, renounced that pleasure.

Monsieur Charmillon and his two colleagues, William Johnston and Otto Eliaison, desirous of filing the specimens they had collected the day before and beginning their scientific report, declared in their turn that they would stay on board. That decision seemed to cause considerable chagrin to Angèle, for it might perhaps have been a unique opportunity or her to visit Seal Island in company with the celebrated naturalists of the expedition. Alas, she understood very well that she had to resign herself to remaining aboard, for Émile, as Monsieur

Charmillon's secretary, would inevitably have to assist him in his work.

The pleasure trip, the mere thought of which had spread joy throughout the guests of the *Glorieux*, thus left her profoundly sad.

Her excellent uncle perceived that state of mind and had no difficulty deducing the reason for it. That evening while the three friends were eating their communal mal, as usual, the amiable French scientist said: "I see that her uncle's glory is insufficient to full Mademoiselle Angèle's heart. She's chagrined by not taking part in tomorrow's planned expedition."

"My dear Uncle," the young woman put in, "I would doubtless have liked to make that excursion, but I'm certainly not complaining about remaining with you, since you don't think it appropriate to go with the Messieurs."

"For me it's another matter," the Academician replied. "I know my duties and I fulfill them. Besides which, between us, I wouldn't trade the smallest bone I found yesterday for the entire harvest that will be collected tomorrow. But after all, you're not obliged to espouse my triumphs, and you can't be of any assistance to me here. I've therefore arranged things for the best."

Angèle pricked up her ears, understanding that she was about to hear something agreeable.

"Doubtless Émile would be very useful to me, but why the devil can't the fellow cultivate hunting and geology at the same time? All my colleagues, the naturalists, are asking for the collaboration of his carbine tomorrow. I'd certainly like to send them packing, but they'd be bound to make me a reputation as a tyrant and a bad companion."

"So, my dear Uncle?" Angèle asked.

"So, my dear niece, I've authorized Émile to join tomorrow's expedition and, as he'll be there to look after you, I don't see any strong objection to your taking part in it too, if the Messieurs are willing to take you."

Reddening with joy, the young woman leapt to her feet and threw her arms around Monsieur Charmillon's neck. "Thank you, thank you, Uncle! You're the best of men!"

It was thus that Angele and her fiancé took their places in the caravan from which it had seemed that they would be left out.

They were ashore early in the morning, and were able to observe, by examining the advancement of the work, that the matelots of the *Glorieux* had not been idle during the previous day's excursion. Thanks to their zeal since the previous evening, the edge of the quay constructed as a dry landing and the jetty constructed to facilitate the disembarkation of materials were beginning to take shape. The jetty was to project into the sea for a length of twenty meters; it was to be two meters wide and it had to be possible to reach the extremity in a launch at any hour of the day. Behind the jetty there was to be a shelter in which the boat could be placed and kept in complete security.

Soon, the young couple saw several launches disembark, successively, Mr. Wilson of London; Batschkoff and Kolikoff, the representatives of the Russian Empire' Oscar Johannesen; Enrico della Maria; and then their compatriots Despierre and Guébard. Other members of the expedition, with whom they had only had relations of the strictest politeness throughout the voyage, came to join the caravan, with consisted of seventeen people.

Seeing the gathering complete, Émile asked Wilson what they were waiting for before departing.

"I think we're only waiting for our German colleagues, Walter Müller and Henrich, who put their names down yesterday."

At that moment, however, a stout individual with a red face and flaxen hair disembarked from a launch. It was Peter Hartmann, Dr Henrich's valet. He handed a sealed letter to Pierre de Kolikoff, who had been unanimously appointed as the leader of the expedition they were about to undertake.

Kolikoff opened the letter and read aloud: "*My honored colleague, we decided yesterday to join you when we thought that the French would not be taking part. Today, since it is otherwise, we shall abstain. Accept our regrets with our salutations. Franz Henrich and Walter Müller.*"

A long silence followed the reading of the impertinent lecture.

Eventually, Dr. Despierre said: "On behalf of my French colleagues, I protest with all my might against this rudeness."

After having consulted his colleagues, Kolikoff spoke in his turn: "In the name of all our colleagues, I supplement Dr. Despierre's protest, and declare that Messieurs Henrich and Müller are ill-educated individuals."

The incident was thus closed, and the little troop got ready to depart.

Six matelots from the ship had been attached to them, some carrying food supplies and others baskets of wine. One was carrying a ladder, a knotted rope with a hook, and a gaffe designed to facilitate the climbing of any sheer rocks, if a more convenient route could not be found.

The caravan set off cheerfully, and soon engaged in the foothills of a high mountain that they had decided to climb. The march was fatiguing to begin with, because of the entanglement of the vegetation and the kind of felting that we have mentioned, formed by networks of mosses, plants and briars. When they reached the top of the first hill, however, those difficulties disappeared, and they were able to advance with no more difficulty than a walk in mountainous country in Europe.

With his rifle slung over his shoulder and his game-bag on his back, Émile did not lose sight of his lovely fiancée for a moment. At every difficult point of the route the young woman was certain to encounter a friendly arm on which she could lean, which diminished the obstacles considerably.

The morning's journey did not pass not without a few incidents, but they were fortunately restricted to the comical spectrum.

One stout gentleman from Vienna, a professor of natural science, following Émile's example, had armed himself with a hunting rifle, and, is not infrequently the case with individuals of considerable corpulence, prided himself on being more agile than the young. He obtained a certain self-respect from remaining at the head of the column, and was climbing a slope, rifle in hand, that was not very steep but encumbered by heather when he turned round with a triumphant expression and shouted: "Come on, come on, slowcoaches—follow me!"

At the very moment when he pronounced those words, he disappeared as if through a trapdoor, and cries of distress were heard.

Émile ran forward and found the unfortunate hunter plunged into a hole entirely covered by rushes.

Fortunately, the rifle that the scientist was carrying had placed itself across the opening of the shaft, which was filled with water to the brim, and he had been able to retain himself and spare himself a more serious and perhaps mortal plunge by not letting go of his weapon.

The young man lent the stout scientist a helping hand, and their combined efforts succeeded in getting him out of a situation that was disagreeable, to say the least. Fortunately for the victim of a shipwreck on dry land, Commandant Beaudin, who thought of everything, had included three spare matelot's uniforms in the baggage. The brave Austrian was therefore able to change his clothes while waiting for his own clothes to dry out sufficiently to be put on again without the risk of catching a chill.

Chapter X

Thanks to the presence of mind of the victim and the intervention of Monsieur Charmillon's secretary, that incident had no grave consequences, and inspired the explorers to be more prudent and circumspect. To the great satisfaction of Angèle, whom the rapid march of the caravan was beginning to tire, the pace was moderated and they continued the ascent of the mountain while placing two mariners at the head of the column, who only went forward after prudently sounding out the terrain.

The precaution was not unnecessary. In that singular country, wherever a furrow began to form in the turf, springs that emerged continually, bringing forth more or less considerable trickles of water, cut vertically through the solid terrain, sometimes very deeply. Sorghum, saxifrage and ferns then masked the upper part of the narrow but deep fissure. If they were not suspicious of vegetation that was usually more luxuriant than elsewhere, they risked disappearing into the hole, as had happened to the unfortunate Austrian naturalist.

Those channels sometimes broadened out as they descended toward the sea, and were able to function as pathways extending all the way to the sand and shingle of the beaches when the quantity of water they contained was not too considerable.

To conclude this depiction of the terrain of Seal Island, let us say that on the higher slopes, by reason of the limited thickness of their layer of humus, those perfidious ditches were shallow, whereas in the bottom of the valleys, the clumps of grass were separated quite considerably by large numbers of those channels, deep and filled with black water. Those ditches, deployed for some unknown reason in quincunxes, made a simple stroll into a violent gymnastic exercise, which frequently concluded with a plunge when it did not begin with one.

A rather singular phenomenon of hygiene ensured that in the numerous excursions that were to take place during the duration of the expedition's sojourn on the island, everyone returned soaked to the skin. Nevertheless, in spite of the relative coldness of the climate, even during the summer, no one caught a cold. It is necessary to add that they maintained an incessantly active existence and never went to warm themselves up in front of a fire. We recommend that hygienic observation, which has been made by all the voyagers who have visited the polar regions, to our readers.

The caravan had chosen a route for its excursion overland that ought to lead to Station Bay, which the navigators had already visited with the ship. It made good progress when it arrived at a certain elevation, the mach seeming easier on the western slopes of the volcano.

That ancient hearth, which had ended up as nothing more than a series of fumaroles, was linked by a pass to the great upheaval that formed the northern part of the bay, and which, by virtue of a pious memory of Europe, the voyagers named the Jungfrau. The route presented no particular difficulties.

After traversing long expanses of heather, they found themselves in a belt of dense brushwood that attacked trousers but, more particularly, did not take long to rip up the Parisienne's skirts. Further on, the grasses and large-leaved plants grew.

Snow then began to fill all the holes; the weather was cold, but as the air was calm, the march could only gain by that. It was at that height that the explorers discovered albatross nests. It was Émile who had the honor of discovering the first. He ran to take the hand of his lovely fiancée in order to show her the rudimentary dwelling of the largest bird in creation.

The nest that he had just discovered consisted of a small mound of earth, sufficiently hollowed out in its center to accommodate the abdomen of its proprietor, while its feet stuck out to either side.

Angèle would have been very glad to contemplate the beautiful bird on its nest, but alas, although the season was already somewhat advanced, the dwellings were empty.

When they studied the soil round the nest attentively, however, they saw that it was covered with feathers and the debris of eggshells, doubtless the birds that had been born there the previous year were not far away, for when they looked up in the sky, they could see a number of dots describing enormous circles.

"What are those," asked the curious demoiselle.

"They," replied Dr. Despierre, "are father albatrosses, who watch over their previous year's progeniture, already emerged from the nest but as yet incapable of flight, from the celestial heights. The emancipated young are doubtless hiding in some depression in the ground."

Meanwhile, the members of the expedition had continued their research, and a large number of other nests had been discovered, all as empty as the first.

Skeletons of young birds that remained in the green grass informed the walkers that, in spite of the vigilance of the parents, voracious eagles had left traces of their depredations.

Émile strove to furnish his fiancée with all the details of natural history that he possessed related to the masters of the air, which cross the oceans as the swallows of our land fly over our narrow valleys. He told her that young albatrosses, although out of the nest, can only take flight two or three months later, when the thick white down covering them to begin with has given way to solid and resistant feathers.

He was at that point in his amicable lesson when a matelot ran up as if to provide a material demonstration of the theory. He was holding in his arms one of the enormous chicks, whose down, dazzlingly white, made it resemble a snowball.

Glad of the attention that his companion was giving him, Émile took his role of professor seriously.

"Notice how wisely calculating nature is" he said, "and how all the beings in creation are endowed with the spirit of conservation of their species and concern for the future. Once on the ground, if it is flat, the albatross finds it impossible to take off again. Occasionally, when sailors aboard a ship succeed in capturing one in flight with the aid of a lure, once the unfortunate bird is on the deck it runs around in all directions, vainly replying its vast wings, but it is impotent to resume its flight and remain captive on the deck without there being any need to attach it. In order to launch itself into the air it's necessary that it allow itself to fall from a high rock, and its wings are only sufficient to sustain it when it can extend and maneuver them during its fall. Look at these nests: all of them are placed in locations from which the bird can easily launch itself into space."

Angèle contemplated the beautiful captive, and would gladly have run a caressant hand over the white duvet that served it as a vestment, if it were not for the fear of receiving a peck from the beak that the young bird clicked in a threatening manner at anyone who tried to approach it.

"If that beautiful chick was born last year," she said, "how has it been able to live for such a long time, especially when it was still too weak to quit its nest, and thus unable to search for nourishment?"

"The father and mother provided for its existence," Émile replied, "for it's sufficient to look at our captive and the protuberance that it has beneath its neck to be assured that it's stuffed with nourishment." He smiled as he added: "However, several fantasizing voyagers have affirmed that the young birds fast completely throughout the winter and that the food they take in during the autumn has to suffice for six months."

The little caravan reached the pass that its members desired to reach, and which they baptized the Nordenskiold, in honor of the great Swedish navigator who discovered the North-East Passage. There, the valiant voyagers were amply rewarded for their troubles. The panorama that unfolded before them was magnificent. The inlets of the great bay extended at their feet with a clarity that the transparency of the air rendered perfect.

The English geographer made a sketch of the whole island, and in the meantime, thy named its principal features. They observed that the great Jungfrau crater was limited to the north by Mount Levasseur, which was attached by the summit of the Nordenskiold Pass to Mount Petermann, and to the south by the great Franklin Massif and Mount Élisée Reclus.

All these mountains presented hundred-meter scars on all their faces: basaltic cuttings whose scaling was, at first glance, if not impossible, at least extremely difficult. They put off that exploration until later, if a favorable occasion should present itself.

To he north-west they could see the sea, which was breaking around a large islet; then, in the north, Mount Azimuth, which would be baptized later by the expedition's astronomers, because it was almost due north of their observatory.

From the point where the expeditionaries were positioned, the physiognomy of the island was clearly outlined. Beneath them, the valley that would have taken them to Station Bay seemed to be obstructed by a dark green massif that resembled a pine forest when seen from above.

That view of the ensemble demonstrated to the scientists that the place designated by the astronomers for the establishment of their observatory could not have been better chosen. It would, for instance, have been absolutely impossible take the instruments and food supplies up to the plateaux of Mount Petermann. An ascent of six hundred meters, without traced paths, is impracticable, when it is a matter of dragging five thousand kilograms after you. They observed, in addition, that it would have been impossible to keep anything standing at that height. Even in the place they had reached, nearly half way to the summit, the grass was torn out of the ground by the wind. Large bare patches appeared from which he tempest had rolled away aggregations of uprooted grass, as it would have done a sheet of cloth laid on the ground.

The splendor of the view, the tranquility of the air, the lateness of the hour and the appetite that was beginning to make itself felt persuaded the explorers to extend their sojourn in that delightful spot and eat their meal there. The food was set out as best they could on the carpet of moss, and everyone set about consuming the cold provisions carried by the valiant seamen of the *Glorieux*.

The modest meal—during which the guests, cheered up by a few glasses of the foamy liquid manufactured in Champagne, were swapping amusing stories—had not yet terminated when Angèle, without saying anything, started wandering around the surrounding area. She had been one for some time, and Émile was looking around vainly, not without anxiety, when a cry of anguish was heard.

The young man was on his feet in the blink of an eye and, outdistancing his companions on the way, he sprinted in the direction from which the familiar voice had come.

He arrived thus on the edge of a broad and deep fissure hollowed out in the volcanic terrain; it seemed to him that he could hear a muted moaning emerging from the abyss open beneath his feet. He leaned over, and could not retain a cry of terror.

The ground on which he was standing showed evidence of a recent collapse, and his eyes, sounding the depths of the precipice, had just glimpsed, in the midst of a massif of heather suspended along the sheer wall, a floating piece of cloth that he recognized as part of Angèle's dress.

The sailors of the little caravan came running in response to his desperate cries, and started organizing he rescue without wasting any time.

The accident to which the young woman had been the victim had left traces so visible that everyone had quickly reconstructed what had happened mentally.

Doubtless, on arriving here, she had wanted to fathom the fissure with her gaze, and had been unable to refrain from advancing a little too far. The soil, disaggregated by the first thaw, had given way beneath her weight, and she had been precipitated into the abyss with the landslide.

The bottom of the precipice disappeared in the gloom, but the plaintive moans that reached the rescuers' ears periodically proved hat the unfortunate demoiselle had not reached the extreme depths of the gulf, where she would inevitably have broken bones, but had been providentially arrested by the clumps of heather in the midst of which a piece of her dress was floating. That, therefore, was the goal that it was necessary to reach, but, by reason of the depth of the place to be attained and the complete absence of a point of support, the problem seemed insoluble at first glance.

The matelots were discussing the problem when Émile approached them.

"Do you have ropes?" he asked.

One of the matelots dropped a packet of solid ropes at his feet, brought in the hope of facilitating the ascension of steep slopes.

"That's good. Plant this steel-tipped alpenstock as deeply as possible in the ground."

The young man's order as carried out with a marvelous rapidity.

He noticed that one of the sailors had a broad and solid belt around his waist, of the kind habitually used in gymnastic exercises.

"Will you lend me your belt?" he asked.

When it was solidly fixed around his own waist, by means of a triple leather thong, he passed the end of the tope through the external ring with which it was fitted and knotted it securely.

One of the sailors, understanding that he young scientist wanted to attempt the descent along the wall of the abyss, tried in vain to oppose that reckless action. "Let one of us do it, Monsieur," he said. "Climbing up and down is our métier; where you have every chance of dying, we're almost sure of success."

"Thank you," relied the young scientist. "I appreciate your generosity, but it's impossible for me to take advantage of it. I've decided to go to Mademoiselle Angèle's aid myself and I shall, even if you refuse me your collaboration. I'd a thousand times rather perish at the foot of that precipice than reappear before Monsieur Charmillon without bringing back his niece personally."

Seeing that the young man's decision was firm, the mariners ceased to put up the slightest objection, and got ready to help him as best they could.

Émile's cane, which he had picked up in France on one of the high plateaus of the Dauphinois Alps, was a long and stout piece of holly capable of supporting an almost indeterminate weight. It was plunged profoundly into the ground in such a way as only to leave about fifty centimeters of its length protruding. After having wound the solid rope twice around that improvised axis, he told them to let it out as slowly as they could, in spite of the weight of his body, which they were obliged to sustain.

When everyone was ready, Émile let himself slide down the perpendicular wall of the precipice, and soon found himself hanging in the void, He had to use his arms and feet to hold himself away from the wall and avoid painful impacts.

The descent was effected without a hitch, and he soon found himself in the midst of the heather in which he assumed that Angèle must have been arrested in her fall.

All noise of moaning, had ceased some time previously. Without letting go of the safety rope that had facilitated his descent, the young man took a firm grip on the ferns that formed a kind of undergrowth suspended over the abyss, and started fathoming the depths of that redoubt with his gaze.

From the first glance he was guided in his search by the broken branches that marked the passage of the unfortunate young woman's body had left. He followed that track, and soon saw the poor demoiselle lying sideways, retained by solid branches that had withstood the impact. That body was completely motionless, as rigid as a cadaver.

Émile drew closer to it and lifted away a piece of fabric that was hiding the face. That poor face, formerly so pink and youthful, was wan and pale.

"Heavens!" exclaimed the unfortunate young man. "She's dead!"

He placed his hand on her ribs, but he could not feel any heartbeat. His alarm was so great, his dejection so complete that, as he had said before and had believed it, that his last hour had come. How would he have the energy to undo his belt, place it around the young woman's waist, stay where he was, solidly attached by his clenched fists to the to the busy ferns, and shout to the mariners above to hoist up the unfortunate woman's body?

Interrogated about events subsequently, he confessed that he only retained a vague memory of them, and it had all seemed to him as if it were happening in a dream.

At any rate, the matelots set about hoisting up the body on the end of the rope, while moving in perfect coordination and with calculated slowness, in order to avoid the precious burden impacting with the sheer and icy wall.

While two of them slid the rope around the piece of holly stuck in the ground, the others lay down on the ground and leaned over the abyss, guiding the rise of the poor breathless body, devoid of any sign of life.

Finally, the precious burden reached the upper rim of the abyss. The rescuers, with a reserve and piety that it would have been difficult to anticipate from uneducated men, set the young woman down on a bed of ferns and moss that they had improvised.

When they saw her, whiter than marble, voiceless and breathless, they too thought that she was dead and heir eyes let loose a furtive tear.

Then they thought about Émile, who, half-mad with grief, only remained clinging to the frail supports by the human instinct of self-preservation that subsists and resists peril in the most terrible moments. They threw him the safety-belt at the end of the rope. Mechanically, he put everything back in place, and then, when he felt the rope stiffen under the effort of his companions, He moved upwards by means of the strength of his arms. Thanks to his legs, which helped him to remain away from the perpendicular wall, he arrived without having needed much help from the seamen at the rim of the abyss and surged over it. He ran to the body of his fiancée, lying on its bed of moss.

Kneeling beside her, he was paralyzed by dolor, and did not even think about lavishing the cares on his fiancée's body capable of brining her round, if there was still time. At that moment, however, the members of the expedition arrived, having become anxious because of the young man's long absence. On seeing the inert body of the young woman lying on the ground, Dr. Despierre ran forwards, cut the laces of her dress and hastened to place a bottle of smelling salts, which he took from his pocket, beneath her nostrils.

All gazes were anxious fixed on the physician, everyone was seeking to read in his eyes the definitive verdict, but the old doctor remained impassive. Several minutes, which seemed to be centuries, went by in that fashion, while the scientist too Angèle's cold hands in his and rubbed them vigorously.

Leaning over his fiancée's face, Émile seemed to be watching out for her return to life, but anyone looking at him attentively might have wondered whether he was not on the brink of the tomb himself.

Finally, the doctor stood up. "She not dead!" he proclaimed

An immense sigh of relief emerged from every mouth, and they thought about organizing the caravan so as to carry the precious burden on its return journey. The mariners quickly constructed a stretcher of sorts, on which they placed a thick bed of foliage and moss. While they devoted themselves to that important work, the young woman came round completely and was able to reply to a few questions that her physician addressed to her.

By a fortunate chance, she did not feel any sharp localized pain. Her entire body was aching, but the doctor did not take long to ascertain that she had not broken any bones

"Come on!" he said, smiling, "I'm beginning to hope that we've been more frightened than hurt, and that in a few days, no evidence will remain of an accident that might have been mortal."

The young woman was laid on the stretcher as comfortably as possible. Two sailors each took one end of the improvised bed in their callused hands, and the little caravan moved off in silence along the path that would taken them back to the *Glorieux*.

The enterprise was still replete with difficulties, given the unevenness of the terrain, continually examined for any trap that it might conceal.

Émile, who could not conceal his joy, took the head of the column. Like one of the faithful hunting dogs that precede their master, ferreting to the left and the right, he did not let any clump of grass or crack in the ground pass without inspecting it carefully. The porters of the demoiselle's stretcher had no more to do than set down their feet boldly in the places indicated to them by the young man.

One significant fact will say more than we can about the attention that the intrepid hunter put into his task. One of the sailors, who was scouting the route as he was and coming back to help his comrades who were carrying the stretcher during difficult passages, came to him and pointed out a goat that was standing on a rock well within rifle range, which seemed to be watching curiously as the newcomers passed by. Émile, who still had his precious carbine slung over his shoulder did not deign to make use of it. He shook his head as a sign of refusal, and—this time, at least—the fortunate beast was not obliged to make the acquaintance of the European's murderous devices.

The return journey was a long one, as can easily be imagined, but it was completed without further incident.

Angèle got better and better. In the middle of the journey she even insisted on getting down from the stretcher and trying to continue on foot. It required a formal prohibition from Dr. Despierre to convince her not to risk such an imprudence.

Chapter XI

While these dramatic events had been unfolding in the interior of the island, the expedition's geologists and astronomers has not remained idle. The latter, pressing the workmen, had the end of their preliminary troubles in sight. The observatory was ready to receive the instruments that were to be installed there. Furthermore, a comfortable house destined to become the residence of the members of the expedition was being constructed facing Mercury Bay, beside the dyke that was to facilitate the use of the dinghies and launches.

A few more days of effort and the construction work would be completed.

The ill-will shown in his regard by his German colleagues had hurt Monsieur Charmillon deeply, and occupied his mind more than he wanted to admit to himself. He sensed that some Germanic perfidy was lurking beneath the surreptitious persecution and calculated impoliteness. He went over in his memory all the more or less important events that had manifest the malevolence of his colleagues from beyond the Rhine since the beginning of the voyage.

What struck him most was the affected indifference that that two men as knowledgeable as Walter Müller and Franz Henrich had shown the day before when he had reported in their presence the significant discoveries he had made in the cavern of the Sphinx.

It's not possible, he said to himself, silently, *that facts as curious as the ones we observed yesterday left men cold whose lives have been devoted to the study of problems of which my discoveries might perhaps lead to a definitive solution. It's certain that our excavations, as they go on, will furnish us with irrefutable arguments relating to oceanic formations. We'll know, without a doubt, whether the thousands of islands that make up this fifth part of the world are of recent formation, and owe their origin, as some people claim, to volcanic eruptions or to accumulations of coral; we'll also know whether, as other scientists have suggested, the islands are the summits, still emerging, of an immense continent once linking Asia and America, which sank, making way for a new ocean. Whatever order of ideas those gentlemen profess, that's certainly a capital question so far as they're concerned, as it is for me—so their indifference is only simulated, and must conceal a trap.*

These ideas took on such consistency in the French scientist's mind that he went to the apartment reserved for the Commandant of the *Glorieux*.

"Commandant Beaudin," he said to him, "I'm going to submit ideas to you that I can only express under the seal of secrecy. I beg you, therefore, before I speak, to give me our word of honor only to talk about my suspicions in the case that they have been realized, or I am able to bring you a material proof of accusations that I dare not make formally."

The Commandant held out his hand to the French scientist.

"Have no fear," he said, smiling benevolently. "Speak—you can count on my discretion."

Monsieur Charmillon then listed not only the grievances that he had against his Prussian colleagues, but admitted frankly the suspicions that the recent conduct of Müller and Henrich had provoked in him.

"I'll wager," he said, as he finished, "that those fellows are thinking of nothing less than robbing me of the

147

glory of my discoveries and attributing to themselves the initiative of the research that I've begun and which has already been crowned by success."

"Well, well!" said the captain, pensively. "That almost explains why those Messieurs, after having refused to go with the exploratory mission that departed this morning for the island's interior, asked me to put a boat and four crewmen at their disposal." After a momentary silence, he added: "Don't worry, Monsieur Charmillon; it will be easy for me to find out whether there's any truth in your suspicions, because when they return, I'll be able to find out where they went from my sailors."

Having returned to his quarters, Monsieur Charmillon was sad and morose, like a man menaced by some black treason, when the members of the expedition came back aboard. Émile Colin immediately appeared before him, his expression somber and preoccupied. Although his head full of his ideas, the old scientist nevertheless recognized that there was something unusual about his secretary's face—but such is the empire that science exercises over those who cultivate it that there might have been some misfortune outside of his personal preoccupations.

"I can see," he exclaimed, addressing the young man, "that you're bringing me bad news! Have you discovered something, and is the treason I fear an accomplished fact?"

"I don't know what treason you're talking about," said Émile. "On the other hand, I'm pleased to inform you that, although the news I'm brining you is far from cheerful, it is, thank God, far from constituting a disaster."

"What is it, then?" interrogated Monsieur Charmillon, pulling himself together. "Speak, speak! You're keeping me in suspense."

"I fear," said the young man, slowly, "that Mademoiselle Angèle, your niece, has just been in frightful danger, but fortunately, she and all of us escaped with a scare."

He was about to tell the story of the terrible event that had almost thrown the little colony into mourning, when the young woman appeared, still carried by the four matelots. Monsieur Charmillon ran to her."

"Injured!" he cried. "Perhaps dangerously!"

"No, no, my dear Uncle," Angèle hastened to reply. "I have no injury and I'm not hurt. But for the strict instruction of Dr. Despierre, who was kind enough to care for me, I'd be on my feet and I wouldn't have given these worthy men the trouble they've had in carrying me." As she spoke she slipped off the stretcher—but as she set foot on the ground she could not help uttering a cry of pain.

Her uncle caught her in his arms. "What is it?" he demanded. "Are you hurt?"

"Yes—my ankle gave me a horrible twinge when I put my weight on it."

At that moment Dr. Despierre came in. "It's nothing," he said. "A slight sprain, nothing more. A few days' rest and she'll no longer give it a thought." He moved closer to Monsieur Charmillon. "Be glad, my good friend," he said, with his best smile, "for no one ever came closer to death than the one we've just brought back safe and sound."

When the young woman had been carried into her cabin and her uncle had poured a few glasses of excellent rum for the sailors who had brought back their precious burden, Émile told the story of the day's events.

When he learned that the young man had risked his life a hundred times to save the poor girl's, the aged scientist felt his eyes well up with tears. "My young friend," he said, "I shall never forget the service you've rendered me. I want Angèle to be eternally grateful to you to." He fell silent for a few seconds, and then added: "Truly, if I hadn't sworn that my niece would never be the wife of any man while I'm alive, I wouldn't hesitate to offer you her hand and confide her happiness to you. But that isn't possible. It can't be." Getting carried away, he added: "Let no one mention it to me, unless they want me to die suddenly of chagrin!"

Without saying another word, Émile Colin bowed gravely to his master, and was already on the threshold of the cabin, about to leave, when Jean-Pierre—ordinarily so calm and compassed—arrived breathlessly, his face distraught. He came into the cabin almost at a run, without even noticing that he had just jostle the young scientist rather violently.

"It's a horror, an abomination!" he cried, as soon as he was face to face with his master. "I never would have believed those squareheads, those straw-munchers, capable of such a thing!"

"Come on, my friend, calm down," said Monsieur Charmillon, more emotional than he wanted to appear. "What's put you in this state?"

"Go ask Peter Hartmann, that brigand Müller's domestic!" replied Jean-Pierre. "Or rather, don't go and ask him anything, because I believe that he knows what's what now and will never give anything away again."

"Come, come, my dear Jean-Pierre—get your thoughts in order and answer my question. What's the matter with my German colleague's servant?"

"Monsieur, the Prussian Müller isn't your colleague; he's a dirty Prusco, Bismarck's hireling, a cabbage-muncher, a capon, a traitor!"

"All right, all right! Calm down and tell me: where is Peter Hartmann?"

"Lying on the deck, doubtless trying to get his breath back."

"Why is he having difficulty breathing?"

"Begging your pardon, Monsieur, I strangled him."

"Damn!" murmured Émile Colin, retained on the threshold by the domestic's invasion. "This seems to be getting complicated."

Seeing that he would not get anything out of Jean-Pierre while he was in such a state of excitement, Monsieur Charmillon made an effort to moderate his own impatience and waited until the poor fellow had regained a little composure.

He learned then that Jean-Pierre, who, like his master, did not profess a boundless confidence in the German scientists, had heard about their departure and had remained on deck as a sentinel, watching out for their return. That return had taken place without any indication of what the goal of their expedition had been, neither of them carrying any kind of package. Even Peter Hartmann, Müller's valet, had come back aboard with his hands in his pockets.

Rather disconcerted, Jean-Pierre had been about to retire when he saw the German domestic retrace his steps and go back down a rope-ladder to the boat that had brought them back, and which remained moored to the side of the ship.

Uh oh! he had thought. *My nose didn't deceive me. Those scoundrels are trying to hide something.*

He his himself behind some bales and waited for the Prussian to return. He saw the other climb up again and, as soon as his head emerge over the rail, look around as if to make sure that no one could see him.

"Good, good!" Jean-Pierre murmured, between his teeth. "You want to hide something from Papa, but Papa is watching. Get on with it, my lad!"

As soon as Hartmann, reassured by seeing the deck deserted, had climbed over the rail, Jean-Pierre, observing that he had a large bag slung over his shoulder, wet with sea-water and full of objects that it was impossible to define, leapt forward and appeared like a specter in front of the fearful Prussian.

"Vot you vant?" murmured the latter, with a frightful accent.

"I want to see what's in there," said Jean-Pierre, in a commanding tone not calculated to reassure Hartmann.

"Nodding in dere," the other replied.

Jean-Pierre leapt upon the sack, tore it from the German's hands, and cut the cord that bound the neck. A quantity of fossil seashells and bone fragments similar to those his master had collected in the cavern of the Sphinx tumbled out on to the deck of the ship.

"Triple rogue!" exclaimed Jean-Pierre. "Ah! You want to study the age of stones too, and go into competition with my master! Well, I'll give you some competition!" So saying, he had delivered two or three punches to Peter Hartmann's abdomen. The latter, stupefied and open-mouthed, had not tried to hit back, or even to ward off the blows."

"Prute!" he said finally.

"And that's for calling me a brute!" Jean-Pierre had replied, repeating the dose.

"Rapid!"

"And that's for 'rabid'!"

"A low plow!

Jean-Pierre continued his assault while his opponent sought for a further epithet with which to humiliate him.

He doubtless thought he had found it, for he said, after a silenced broken only be the sound produced by the incessant rain of blows: "You're no petter than your master Charmillon."

That insult, not being addressed to him alone, exasperated the Frenchman, who put his hands around Hartmann's throat, and would have strangled him if the matelots attracted by the noise of the scuffle, who were laughing heartily, had not judged that the moment had finally come to intervene. They snatched the victim from his executioner's grip, and the former ran off to tell his master about the ill-treatment of which he had been the victim.

As can be imagined, that adventure caused a great deal of talk aboard the *Glorieux*. Monsieur Charmillon made a detailed report to Commandant Beaudin, who thought the charge leveled against the German scientists sufficient to call a general meeting of the expedition's scientists.

Walter Müller and Franz Henrich were summoned, and did not deny that that they had gone in secret to carry out excavations in the Grotto of the Sphinx in the absence of Monsieur Charmillon, its legitimate discoverer. Disdaining any self-justification, they declared that, having been charged by their government to study Seal Island, they were studying it, without paying any attention to any research that might be carried out by their colleagues.

These arrogant assertions met with unanimous disapproval. All the members present, whatever their nationality, drafted a protest, which they all signed and put in the hands of Commandant Beaudin.

The latter spoke in his turn. "Messieurs," he said, "if you had not unanimously made appeal to my authority in the question raised by two among you, I would have abstained from any involvement. Like you, I consider as dishonest the research carried out in the Grotto of the Sphinx by Messieurs Müller and Henrich. Those Messieurs had the choice of following the work commenced by Monsieur Charmillon and a number of his colleagues or of conducting their personal investigations in another direction. I shall say no more about the decision they made. Let it suffice, Messieurs, for me to say to you that, by virtue of the full powers conferred upon me as commandant of the ship and head of the expedition, I order the aforementioned Messieurs Müller and Henrich to abstain from going into the Grotto of the Sphinx outside of the hours when Monsieur Charmillon and his colleagues are carrying out excavations there, and declare that, if they do not accept that condition, I shall confine them aboard ship with sentinels at their cabin door until we return to Europe."

This thoroughly military and authoritarian speech was greeted by a profound silence. It seemed to each of the members of the expedition, to whom that sentence had just been revealed, that the terms of the order formulated by Commandant Beaudin would necessarily meet with resistance on the part of the two German scientists.

They consulted one another in low voices. Then, Walter Müller approached the naval officer.

"Monsieur," he said, "We incline before your decision. Henceforth, neither he nor I will set foot in Monsieur Charmillon's grotto, but without disinteresting ourselves in the discoveries that might be made there. We shall content ourselves with taking note of them as they are presented to the general assembly."

Thus concluded an incident that had threatened momentarily to sow disturbance and dissent among the members of the great international scientific expedition for the observation of the transit of Mercury.

Important new research was not long delayed in being carried out, not only by the naturalists, but by the mathematicians and astronomers, whose installation was rapidly completed and who were condemned to inaction until the moment came when their serious astronomical observations would commence. The Grotto of the Sphinx thus became the daily rendezvous of all the scientists; the mattocks of the matelots, skillfully plied, dug down into the virgin soil of the cavern in twenty places at once.

Let us hasten to say that no vain hope deceived the investigators, who were generously compensated for their efforts from the outset. The fragments of bone and seashells encountered to begin with were soon supplemented by a series of precious specimens, which were carefully sorted and further enriched the expedition's collections on a daily basis.

Among the bones encountered, let us indicate, in the order of mammals, a large quantity of debris originating from the *Mus domesticus* or common rat. Those bones were generally broken and scattered; there was only one almost-entire skeleton. Various parts were also found of *Chiroptera*, known to the vulgar as bats, among which the English naturalist William Johnston affirmed that he recognized the remains of *Galeopithecus*, also known as "flying cats" or "flying monkeys."[20]

A little further on, at a point where the soil of the grotto formed a kind of slight tumulus, the scientists observed the presence of an accumulation of bones scarcely covered by a thin layer of sand, which came from animals of the family of *Phocacea*, which, as the name indicates, comprises various species of seals.[21] Among the detritus they distinguished with certainty *Orthocephales*, *Calocephales* and *Halicheres*.

Pierre de Kolikoff, the Russian geologist, discovered a well-preserved skull of a calocephalous seal that Dr. Despierre recognized as having belonged to a white-tailed seal. The skull was flattened on top with bulges at the sides. The occipital crests, as Oscar Johannesen observed, were reduced to slight bumps.

That fossil head conserved its thirty-four teeth, to wit, six incisors in the upper jaw and four in the lowers,

---

[20] *Galeopithecus* was an early designation given to the animals nowadays allocated to the order *Dermoptera* and usually called colugos, although many other similes were ventured in addition to the ones cited as zoologists tried to figure out where they fitted into the scheme of things—certainly not, at any rate into the category of the *Chiroptera*.

[21] The term *Phocacea* has also been dropped from the lexicon of classification, having been replaced by three genera, in which the "true seals"—as opposed to "fur seals" and the walrus—are now identified as the *Phocidae*. The primitive name sounds indicative to French readers because the French term for seal, derived from the sane root, is *phoque*. The subsequent classificatory terms for different kinds of seal, which I have reproduced directly from the original, are all similarly obsolete.

five molars to each side in each jaw, with pairs of larger, pointed teeth in front and smaller ones behind.

"These distinctive characteristics demonstrate irrefutably," said Monsieur Charmillon, "that this skull belonged to the smallest species of seal living in the glacial Ocean, which is also found in the Atlantic, from which they often come to visit the shores of France."

Numerous debris of fur-seals was also found mixed in with the heap, but their presence was not astonishing to the scientists, since those aquatic mammals are among the few that still frequent the region today.

One object, however, put the entire scientific colony in turmoil. It was the matelot Le Gall who discovered it beneath his mattock. It was a piece carefully carved at both ends, flattened on the interior surface and retaining its natural unevenness on the outer surface. Two little round holes had been pierced at each of the extremities of that curious specimen of a lost world.

That specimen, incontrovertibly the most precious of all those found so far, certain originated from the anther of a red deer, *Cervus elaphus*. William Johnston, who examined it carefully, was the first to make that observation.

"I think this discovery all the more fortunate," he added, "because the presence of the animal that produced it has never, so far as I know, been identified in the polar regions, whereas it is one of the most common in the temperate zone. We can already conclude from this discovery that, in the same way that the Arctic polar regions are covered in the debris of mammoths and elephants—animals that can only live in tropical regions—the seas that cover the south polar region today must once have been situated in a temperate zone."

"Perfectly reasoned!" exclaimed Monsieur Charmillon. "But the revelations brought by this little fragment of antler don't stop there. It's sufficient to glance at it to be convinced that it has been worked by human hands; the cleanly-cut sections at the ends, and the holes observable at those extremities are in my opinion, irrefutable proof of it. Thus, Messieurs, humans lived in this cavern, In consequence, humans existed in prehistoric epochs, and, to make use of the expression that long scientific discussions have consecrated, that piece of antler was fashioned by an antediluvian human."

All the scientists gathered there yielded to the irrefutable logic of that judgment. Everyone's ardor increased. The Grotto of the Sphinx, which had already furnished such a large contingent of discoveries, still contained many secrets that the expedition would have the honor of extracting from it.

It was therefore resolved to pursue the research insistently, redoubling its zeal and attention.

Meanwhile, William Johnston had not wearied of contemplating that specimen of primitive artistry. "What the devil can it be?" he wondered, in a low voice.

"An insignia of command, some kind of decoration, an ornament?" Monsieur Charmillon speculated.

"Personally, I don't know," the valet Jean-Pierre muttered between his teeth, "but it looks to me like a plate from the handle of a knife."

Monsieur Charmillon, who had heard that reflection on the part of an ignoramus, could not help smiling indulgently and shrugging his shoulders.

Chapter XII

A further meeting of the members of the expedition took place in the large lounge of the *Glorieux*. Arthème Charmillon took the floor in order to acquaint his colleagues with his fortunate discoveries.

"Decidedly, Messieurs," he said, "there is no room for any doubt now that the Grotto of the Sphinx was a dwelling of troglodytes. Far be it from me, Messieurs, to designate by that name the fantastic populations of which Ptolemy, Pliny and Strabo have spoken, and who lived in subterranean dwellings in the vicinity of the Gulf of Arabia and south-western Egypt. No, I merely affirm that the Grotto of the Sphinx has served as a dwelling for savage people who inhabited the Earth for a long period of the Quaternary epoch at the end of the glacial period, traces of whom have been found in the depths of caverns all over the world.

"In these Cretaceous terrains, under the sand that has counted thousands of centuries of existence on this desert island, whose soil has only been trodden at widely-spread intervals and in exceptional circumstances, my friends and I have discovered not merely heaps of shells originating from the meals of these antediluvian humans, but I also have the honor of presenting to you this fragment of antler shaped by human hands, which was found at a depth of about a meter in virgin terrain.

"This fragment, which testifies to the ingenious and artistic intelligence of our ancestors living in the Paleolithic era has been taken, without a doubt, from the antler of a *Cervus elaphus*, a species still extant, or a *Capra primigenia*, a primitive goat of an extinct family.

"These unexpected results, which will cause a veritable revolution in the geology of the austral seas, are of a very encouraging nature. While our savant astronomers are completing their great endeavors of installation, we shall not remain inactive. I have a firm conviction that every day will bring us the recompense of our labor."

The geologist paused, and then added: "Either I'm much mistaken or we shall eventually crown our work by fining more precise traces of the presence in this region of Paleolithic humans. Undoubtedly, the ancient inhabitants of this island must have died in the place where they were born and where they lived. Who can tell whether the discovery of a skull, a humerus or an ulna, or even a complete skeleton, might not grant our wishes and give us further proof of the existence of antediluvian humankind?"

The entire audience applauded. It was agreed that every new discovery would be recorded in a register specially opened for that purpose. Even the two Germans loftily proclaimed their joy at the important and unexpected results obtained thus far by their French colleagues.

Finally, the astronomers declared unanimously that as soon as their installation was complete, they wanted to be allowed to take part in the research of their eminent colleagues.

As can be imagined, Émile Colin was by no means the last to applaud his dear professor. Nevertheless, as soon as the session ended, he left the lounge in haste and ran to carry the news to the dear invalid.

Outside the door of the cabin reserved for Angèle he found Jean-Pierre marching back and forth, with the gravity of a sentinel aware of his duty and responsibility.

"What are you doing?" the young scientist asked.

"Following orders," said Jean-Pierre, in a comically serious fashion.

"What orders, if you please?" asked Émile.

"My master, Monsieur Charmillon," Jean-Pierre replied, without losing any of his gravity, "instructed me to watch over the treasure contained in this cabin and not to let a living soul go into it."

"Very good, very good," said Émile. "I can see that you're fulfilling your duty conscientiously, and I congratulate you. I've come to replace you in that fatiguing function, and I beg you to go ask Mademoiselle Angèle if she's well enough to receive my visit."

The worthy valet did not have a very clear idea of what the obligations of a sentinel comprised, but he yielded to Monsieur Colin's request and went into the cabin, from which he soon emerged.

"Mademoiselle is waiting for you," he said.

"Good, my friend," the young scientist replied. "You can go take care of your own affairs, or your pleasures. I'll be sufficient to guard the invalid from now on."

Jean-Pierre did not make him repeat himself, and hastened to rejoin his comrades in the forward section, the matelots, who had been bemoaning his continual absences in recent days. The ignorant are thirsty for instruction, but by very reason of their lack of knowledge, they are not very selective with regard those who inform them. For them, Jean-Pierre as a scholar, a veritable oracle.

For that reason, all those on deck hastened to form a circle around their instructor as soon as he arrived.

"It's a good job you've come," said Petty Officer Grand-Victor. "We don't understand any of what's happening here, and wouldn't be sorry if you were to explain certain things that seem to us to be stupidities or sorceries."

Jean-Pierre swelled up with pride, and then sat down gravely on a coil of rope.

"Speak," he said. "I'm ready to answer any question you put to me, and even those you don't."

"Tell me, Monsieur Jean-Pierre," Grand-Victor went on, plunged into a kind of contemplative admiration by the valet's aplomb, "what your master and his friends are looking for in the Grotto of the Sphinx, and why they're making us dig holes all over the place."

"That," said Jean-Pierre gravely, "is something I can only tell you proximately. It appears, although our lack of education will doubtless prevent you from understanding completely, that in order to know the age of stones, it's vitally necessary to heap up collections, as they call them, of old oyster-shells, bits of bone and knife-handles."

"It's true, in fact," murmured matelot Le Dall in an admiring tone, "that the filthy devils pick up all kinds of rubbish with great care and take the pieces away with as much compunction as if they were a holy sacrament."

"Yes," my friend, Jean-Pierre continued, his oratorical success inclining him to eloquence, "I've heard it said by Monsieur Émile Colin, who is a clever fellow among the greatest scientists, that everything on earth is worthwhile and nothing is negligible. Can you imagine that he instructed me, while digging the soil, to be careful to collect all the bits of dried excrement I could find, which he calls copperlits,[22] although I don't know exactly why

---

[22] The author inserts a note here indicating that Jean-Pierre means "coproliths."

"With a copperlit, he tells me, one can reconstruct an animal—a funny remedy, all the same. With an animal, one can find the epochs, and with the epochs, one knows the ages, and that's how they determine the age of stones. Does that seem as clear to you as crystal?"

All the matelots nodded their heads affirmatively. Jean-Pierre's scientific reasoning had convinced them. He did not abandon his audience there. "My friends," he added, "it appears that Monsieur Charmillon has done better than that. In the cavern of the Finx he's discovered the foresail[23] man who lived, he said, before the great revolution of eighty-nine."

"Why does he call him the foresail man?" asked Grand-Victor, curiously,

"I didn't ask, but I suppose it's a sort of nickname that was given to him in his youth, unless it's the true name he received from his mother and father."

While Jean-Pierre was holding forth in this manner on the foredeck, the amorous Émile Colin and his intended were not sitting silently either.

The young scientist hastened to tell the invalid about the conversation he had had with her uncle and the old Academician's continued stubbornness.

"Oh, my dear Angèle, I'll never be able to hold to the constraint Monsieur Charmillon is imposing on us. I'll never consent to put off until the Greek kalends the execution of out cherished plans. Truly, I love my benefactor as much as if I were his nephew—what am I say-

---

[23] In order to conserve the intended phonetic resemblance, here as elsewhere, I have Anglicized Jean-Pierre's error, although there might be some significance in the fact that his *faucille* means "sickle."

ing, as if I were his son—but there are times when I can't help cursing his folly. Why, Angèle, aren't you making every effort to change that fatal idea and cure that mania, inexplicable in a man of such great character?"

"My friend," replied the young woman, extended on a chaise-longue with her sprained ankle resting on a soft cushion, "why keep harking back to a subject that is as despairing for me as it is for you, but to which it's impossible for us to apply the slightest remedy?"

"I'd rather die," said Émile, with tears in his eyes, "than live without hope."

"Monsieur Colin," said the young woman, in a severe tone, "you're unjust and you're no longer being amiable. Isn't the chagrin of which you complain mine too? Don't you find any relief from your pain in knowing that I have my large share of it? Believe me, Émile, we shouldn't complain too much, because, in sum, our lot is enviable. We live in close proximity; my uncle, who won't hear any mention of marriage, is glad to see our mutual affection taking flight."

"Yes, yes!" said Émile, in a stifled voice, "all that would be perfect happiness, if only it were combined with a little hope."

"Well, Émile," replied the young woman, impetuously, "I have a heart full of hope! I know, I feel, I'm sure that one day I shall be your wife. It's sufficient to wait and to be patient. Personally, I'm waiting, full of confidence in the future, and full of joy for the present. Calm your impatience, I beg you, and above all, don't destroy the most charming situation because of an impatience that's quite unjustified."

"Truly, Angèle, do you think that we'll be able one day to vanquish the frightful position taken by your uncle?"

"Yes, yes, I hope so! I'm sure of it—but I repeat to you, don't compromise everything by impatience. Look, suppose that Monsieur Charmillon evoked his decision today and accorded you my hand. How would we be any further forward? We can't marry here. We'd be obliged to wait for the expedition to return to Europe. So let's act as if we had my uncle's consent and wait patiently."

"You're right, a thousand time over, my dear Angèle. I'm just a crazy egotist! You've rendered me the pure, limitless joy of faith in the future."

He was interrupted by the sound of footsteps. Monsieur Charmillon opened the door and appeared on the threshold of the cabin. "Well," he said, in a tone of the utmost good humor, "how goes it with our dear invalid?"

"Very well, thank you, my dear Uncle," the young woman replied. "I don't feel the slightest pain as long as I remain still. But how are you, Uncle?"

"I feel twenty years younger, my dear Angèle. Every day brings a new discovery, a new triumph. Hasn't Monsieur Colin told you about the marvelous finds we've made? Why must that accursed sprain confine you to your cabin at the very moment when so much pleasure awaits you in the Cavern of the Sphinx? Anyway, Émile will keep you up to date, and you can imagine my joy at the importance of our discoveries."

From that moment on, far from relenting, the work in the Grotto of the Sphinx took on a further extension, which increased from day to day. Not only did Jean-Pierre expose to the light of day several of the famous coproliths, to which he referred incorrectly as "copperlits," and which are really the petrified excrement of fossil animals, but from one hour to the next, so to speak, new traces of humans were revealed.

The famous deer-anther plate, in which the valet could see nothing but a fragment of the hilt of a knife, was succeeded by all the instruments of the Stone Age. Monsieur Charmillon, whose activity never diminished for an instant, rapidly assembled a rich collection of weapons and tools made of hard stone, in very varied forms, as well as several objects in earthenware and bone.

All of it was generally agglomerated by a ruddy cement with the bones of herbivores, ordinary rats or roof-rats, goats and pigs, terrestrial and marine mollusk-shells, and an enormous quantity of flakes of flint or jasper.

Numerous instruments found in the depths of the cave belonged to the Age of Rough Stone, while excavations carried out closer to the opening revealed tools originating in the Age of Shaped Stone. Among the latter, let us cite four entire axes in diocite and serpentine, a partly-broken ax also in serpentine, two whetstones— "*pietra par affilar*" as the Italian astronomer Enrico della Maria, who was helping with the digging, put it—a sling-stone (*pietra da fronda*), and a ring used in spinning (*fusaurola*) similar to those from the lacustrian habitations of Switzerland.

They also found a disk not pierced by any hole and two weights for a fishing-net; those three items were in terracotta. Let us also mention twenty arrowheads, carved with varying degrees of skill, flint scrapers and an entire bone needle, perfectly conserved, with its eye intact, fabricated—so William Johnston declared—from the tibia of a primitive goat, *Capra primigenia*.

We shall not persist any longer with the procession of precious finds, which soon included everything that the industry of primitive humans was able to create. In additions to the instruments already cited, there were collections of arrows, spears, knives made of agate, flint and diorite, a large anvil-stone that presumably belonged to the Bronze Age, fragments of earthenware jars, triangular blades, and a dagger.

The majority of these instruments, designed to be fitted with handles, had holes hollowed out by human hands into which the wooden handles could be fitted; others, by contrast terminated in a point, in such a way as to be slotted into the body of the handle intended for them, to which they would doubtless be attached by thongs.

Monsieur Charmillon noticed that in the choice of materials destined for the fabrication of weapons and tools, the workman of primitive times had give preference not only to the stones most appropriate to his work by virtue of their tenacity or durability, but also to those that struck his eye by virtue of the disposition and brightness of their colors. It was thus that he observed in his collection carved stones of brightly-colored jasper, in red green or yellow, diaphanous cornelian of the prettiest appearance, and other varieties of flint that were no less remarkable.

That ingenious observation did not escape the attention in France of the savant Monsieur De Cleuziou, who gave just credit to the artistic efforts of our ancestors in his fine book on the origins of our *Art national*.[24]

---

[24] *L'Art national, étude sur l'histoire de l'art en France* (1882-83) by Henri Raison Du Cleuziou (1833-1896). The first volume subtitled *Les Origines*, discusses the carvings and

A discovery no less important than the previous ones was made by the ignorant Jean-Pierre, which confirmed all the others. The valet, cook and maître-d'hôtel had installed his kitchen definitively in a vaulted chamber communicating by means of a lateral tunnel with the principal grotto That chamber had seemed all the better disposed for that installation because of fissures in the vault that gave passage to smoke and permitted the existence of an air current that admirable favored the combustion of the fire.

While searching for the best place to establish his fire, Jean-Pierre noticed that the fine sand forming the floor was mixed with ashes at certain points, as if fires had been lit and maintained there before. On stirring those ashes, the fortunate valet had noticed that they were mixed, not only with the debris of charred bones, but also fragments of incompletely-consumed charcoal. That was further and indisputable proof of the presence of primitive humans in the natural cavern.

That discovery was welcomed with enthusiasm by all the exploratory scientists, especially by Monsieur Charmillon, who, as the head of the scientific expedition, hastened to take new measures in order to ensure ever-increasing order and method in the excavations, so that nothing would henceforth escape the inquisitive eyes of his collaborators.

---

cave-paintings of the Stone Age "Madgalenians." Because Édouard Lartet spent so much time assiduously searching caves he discovered numerous drawings and inscriptions on cave walls, and also numerous carvings in stone, antler and wood representing animals; his research therefore put a heavy emphasis on the artistic penchants and talents of the Magdalenians, inspiring Du Cleuziou's study.

A new order of operations was thus established. The ship's carpenters were charged with constructing a kind of lattice made of closely-positioned pieces of woods solidly attached to one another. That sieve was transported into the grotto of the Sphinx, set up at a slight angle, and the workers were asked to throw each spadeful of soil into it, so that the solid objects contained in the sand would accumulate at the front of the sieve, where it would be easily to collect them. The surface of the grotto was measured out, and the soil removed in layers of thickness approximately equal to the depth of the spade—which is to say, about twenty-five or thirty centimeters.

With the aid of wheelbarrows, the sand removed, after having being searched scrupulously, was carried to the entrance of the grotto and thrown into the sea. They made sure in this fashion that, by proceeding in an orderly manner, no corner of the immense cave would be left unexplored.

The new searches led to the discovery of two objects that excited the highest degree of attention from the scientific missionaries, and provoked hypotheses. They were two bones that had been polished and pointed, doubtless with the intention of fitting them into a wooden sleeve. At first the bones affected a slightly curved conical shape, and natural strata were traced in to direction of their length. A very pronounced depression at the base of the cone left the scientists perplexed, for it seemed to have been made intentionally in order to fit the tool into a piece of wood, which seemed to conflict with the initial hypothesis of an encasement by means of the pointed end.

At any rate, everyone struggled in vain to determine the purpose that such a tool might have served Pierre de

Kolikoff observed that if the bone had a handle fitted crosswise, it might resemble the special hammers used in the modern era by cabinet-makers in order to drive nails with large gilded heads into items of luxury furniture. It was immediately realized, however, that the industry in question must have been too alien to troglodytes for them to have thought of inventing its tools.

Monsieur Charmillon signaled that he wanted to speak. "Messieurs," he said, "notice that these two bones are almost identical, and that their total length does not surpass fifteen centimeters. If they were longer, one could believe that they were used for scraping the soil and serving as a hoe for labor prior to sowing, but the smallness of their dimensions caused me to abandon that hypothesis. If I admit my incompetence to pronounce on the usage of these singular instruments, however, I'm far from renouncing the possibility of determining their nature. My colleagues the erudite naturalists who are surrounding me, when they consider the solid texture of these bones, their polish, their hardness and their yellow color, which is reminiscent at first glance of old ivory, will recognize without a doubt that what we have in our hands are teeth. It is up to them to determine what animal that organ of mastication might have served."

William Johnson approached swiftly, as did Dr. Despierre and the Italian scientist Enrico della Maria.

They examined the curious specimens minutely and then, after a conference in low voices, gave the floor to the English naturalist, who expressed himself in these terms:

"My colleagues and I, after having observed nothing in these two teeth to point us in the right direction, because they do not remind us of any known animal species, believe that we can observe that these precious relics reveal to the world a new race among extinct species. Subsequent studies will doubtless permit us to reconstruct the animal, for which we shall make use of the precious theory developed by the great Cuvier."

As can be imagined, after having made such marvelous discoveries, Monsieur Charmillon was overjoyed. Thus, as soon as he arrived back at his quarters he embraced his niece and Monsieur Colin effusively, the latter not having witnessed the excavations that day because he had gone into the island's interior to enjoy the pleasures of hunting.

Chapter XIII

As we have said, while the naturalists and geologists made their patient investigations in the Grotto of the Sphinx, their colleagues the astronomers did not remain inactive. The construction of the various portions of the observatory was visibly making progress, and they would be able to commence their celestial observations in a few more days.

For his part, Émile Colin, renouncing that day the continuation of the excavations in the grotto with his master, had decided to pursue his own exploration of the isle's interior, and to indulge in the hazards of hunting.

He was, as we know, a skilled marksman. Equipped with his Lepage rifle, he felt strong enough to brave the most ferocious animals, and he did not take long to find an opportunity to demonstrate his sureness of eye and composure.

On the evening of the day when Monsieur Charmillon found traces of ancient hearths and the two remarkable teeth of which neither he nor his colleagues had been able to name the proprietor, he came back from hunting bearing as trophies the remains of a magnificent fur-seal, or sea-lion—which he had felled, not without difficulty or danger.

Fur-seals are, in fact, robust and vigorous animals, which, in spite of their large size and ponderous form, can climb mountains to a height of fifty meters or more. What do those massive animals do in those high places, on ground so little in harmony with their faculties? It is difficult to render an exact explanation, but it is nevertheless an absolute fact.

After having moved silently along the base of the cliff, and having observed the recent passage of a fur-seal by means of the disturbed ground and the vegetation crushed by its weight, he had slipped quietly into the profound furrow that the animal had made as it went upwards. There, most of all, it was necessary to demonstrate a great sagacity.

Those furrows, which he had observed before, were infinitely numerous and ran in all directions. It was a matter, to begin with, of distinguishing the one that had been recently hollowed out, in which he was powerfully aided not only by the condition and appearance of the crushed vegetation but also by the frightfully persistent odor of the creature.

As soon as Émile was sure that the track he had before him was fresh, he started moving along it, crawling, with his finger on the trigger of his double-barreled rifle, which he had been careful to load with two steel-tipped explosive bullets. Ready to fire, he began to creep silently, sometimes veering to the right and sometimes to the left, search for the route in a maze of old and new passages—and then suddenly found himself face to face with one of the stoutest animals in creation.

A less experienced hunter might have hesitated tremulously before that formidable adversary. In that case his death would have been certain, for the fur-seal would have precipitated itself upon him and would infallibly have reduced him to pulp beneath the weight of its body, but the young hunter knew how to impose silence on his nerves. He took aim at the animal's eye, pulled the trigger, and before knowing the result of his shot, leapt with a single bund on to the left-hand edge of the passage.

Émile had understood, in fact, that having attacked the monster from below, it was of vital importance to get out of the path that it was going to follow. The fur-seal, hit in the eye, collapsed in the ditch that it had hollowed out; then the bullet exploded, dispersing the debris of the brain, which blanched the crushed long grass. If the shot had been less fortunate, the young hunter would have been obliged to slip behind the wounded animal and fire a second shot at the weak point of the shoulder as soon as he found himself above the animal and no longer had anything to fear from a fall in the direction of the sea.

One could only take possession of the fur-seal's remains on condition of having killed it cleanly, for if it had not died on the spot it would have precipitated itself into the waves and there would have been no possibility of pursuing it.

The fur-seal, which weighs no less than five hundred kilograms, is interesting in spite of its fearsome appearance. When young, it plays like a puppy, looking at you with an expression of great astonishment, seemingly asking a traveler what he has come to do in the bay that it knows so well, and where it has never seen anything similar. It approaches quietly, swimming, raises its bulging torso half out of the water, and might then give rise to the idea of the sirens of mythology.

The success obtained by Émile Colin in his single combat against the terrible sea-lion was not calculated to cool his zeal, As he have said, he belonged to that race of intrepid hunters who, once departed in pursuit of game, never stop before nightfall, whether St. Hubert has favored them at the outset or they have drawn a blank all day long. Those valiant individual have two axioms that encourage them or console them, in one case or the other As soon as they kill something, they say:

"That's broken the spell." If, on the contrary, everything seems to be in conspiring against them and they have not encountered anything worthwhile, they exclaim: "Courage! It's often at the moment when one despairs that one finds the best game." Anyone who thinks about going home empty-handed, if he conserves his cool head and sharp eye, can make up in an instant for everything that he has failed to encounter during the day. One good shot is consolation for all failures.

So Émile Colin hastened to rejoin the four matelots who had accompanied him, and whom he had obliged to take cover in a fissure in the rock during his perilous pursuit.

"Come and see, my friends," he said to them, "Hazard has favored us and I've just killed a beast that all five of us would have difficulty shifting."

They carefully marked the place where they left the dead animal and set out again, not without having made a resolution to come back that evening on the way back, in order to take a few trophies of a nature to honor the valiant hunter.

The goal the Émile had chosen was the ascension of Mount Reclus, a beautiful mountain, majestic in appearance, and the highest on the island. The route could be followed without too many difficulties.

As he rose in altitude the ground became form, and if game seemed to be completely absent from the slopes, at least the attention of the naturalist, replacing that of the hunter, was able to wander over specimens of magnificent mosses. There were some as fine as human hair, greenish-yellow in hue, similar to linen or silk; others bore peduncles reminiscent of little mallets; yet others extended in long plaques, contorted like huge ears and offering lace-like delicacies in their center.

On that desert island, so far from the shipping routes, nature seemed to delight in giving those mosses all kinds of forms and endowing each variety with tender and slightly faded colors in harmony with the sky, whose tint rarely achieved the profound blue of the topics in these latitudes.

Struck by that observation, Émile could not help admiring that harmony and attempting to explain it.

"Is not light the great generator of colors," he murmured, "and is it not lavish with red, bright yellow and intense green where its rays attain their maximum strength?"

While philosophizing in that manner, the young man continued climbing, accompanied by his matelots. After two hours of strenuous marching they arrived at the pass that separated the Bay of Deliverance from the Western Valley. Émile had not yet seen that part of the island. Before his eyes, to the right of a valley, an escarpment rose, beyond which the sea extended. To the south, the tranquil blue-tinted waters of a lovely lake were sparkling.

The view was so beautiful that, in order better to enjoy it, the young scientist climbed up a stone ladder to the top of a little pointed hill, from which the spectacle was even more grandiose. For one thing the weather was favorable: little sun, little wind; in the distance, to the west, an appearance of mist and—an ominous sign—cirrus clouds overhead.

Émile admired the magnificent panorama. In front of him was crumbling mountain, half of which had already disappeared into the waves, and the fracture was imposing in its aspect. The young scientist's mind, reaching out through ages to come, wondered when a second fracture would occur, and which part of the island would then be swallowed up by the waves.

On the far side of the lake, another summit, half rounded and half flat, was linked to Mount Levasseur by another pass, which separated the lake from a bay situated to the south. The waves to the west and south seemed scarcely elevated, the edge of the water was white with foam; at sea, there was nothing but the aqueous horizon mingling with the gray of the sky, without it even being possible to trace a line of demarcation.

The four matelots, the hunter's traveling companions, felt ill at ease as they plunged their gaze into the immensity. A sea without ships and sails seemed singular to them. Since the arrival of the expedition, no ship, great or small, had been sighted close by or far away.

When the young hunter turned his gaze away from the sea he saw the whole of Mercury Bay extending to the east. The launch appeared as a dot, very close to shore, and three small white patches could be seen, which represented the roofs of the camp.

He decided to attempt the ascent of the western mountain. Between him and the peak he could see a few white dots standing out against the gray-green background of the vegetation.

"Good!" he exclaimed, loudly. "I'll be luckier today than we were the other day, for that's certainly a whole series of young albatrosses on their nests.

The route they followed did not take long to lead the little caravan to one of the young birds, already almost ready to launch itself into the air. The unfortunate was massacred pitilessly, and several more besides, by the mariners of the escort.

What drove the matelots to shoot those birds was not the pleasure of putting a large animal to death. What they desired above all was to possess the foot of an albatross, which could then be converted into a tobacco pouch, and a leg-bone, which could be transformed into a long and elegant pipe-stem. Such were naval traditions, at least of those matelots who sailed the Southern Seas. It is necessary to know much how those objects are coveted aboard ships that double Cape Horn to understand the desire of the matelots of the *Glorieux* to make a collection of them in memory of the land to which, undoubtedly, none of them would ever return.

At that moment it was about eleven o'clock; the wind was beginning to blow more forcefully; wisps of vapor were beginning to accumulate at the summit of the mountain. The hunter and his companions increased their pace, and, climbing straight ahead, soon arrived at the first of the three steps that formed that side of the western mountainous massif.

To the left, the rock, forming a steep wall forty meters high, was insurmountable; to the right, heaps of boulders offered an analogous difficulty. There remained the center, where mosses and saxifrage formed occasional patches of verdure here and there. It was there that the ascent was attempted, and after a quarter of an hour all five of the travelers had embarked on a series of escarpments where retreat became impossible. It was necessary to advance no matter what the cost—and to put a cap on the misfortune, fog began to envelop them.

The first matelot, who was preceding the caravan was, in any case, not thinking about the means of descending again, nor about the mist that was thickening incessantly.

"We'll get through it!" he kept repeating. That was his only response to the various question that were addressed to him, and the hunter soon perceived that he objective of the intrepid ascent had ceased to be climbing the mountain but was, instead, the pursuit of a big black bird that was reminiscent of both an eagle and a seagull.

That rare bird, whose capture excited the greatest desire in Émile Colin, was recognized by him as the great Cordonnier.[25] The guide supposed, with some justification, that the nest of the bird could not be far away and, in order to pursue it, he made all kinds of zigzags, while gradually veering eastwards. Wherever he went, his comrades and the young hunter followed on his heels, sometimes scarcely having room to place a foot on a ledge, or being forced to hang on with both hands.

The enthusiastic nest-hunter continued marching until the moment that he uttered a cry of triumph: "There she is!"

The travelers stopped, and peered, as if wondering what the use of the feminine signified.

It was the female, on her nest with two young ones, while the vigilant male soared overhead.

While the matelot hung by his arms from the edge of the nest, one of his companions, his legs braced by a third, climbed over him. That double appearance surprised the winged family so much that they did not even

---

[25] The literal meaning of *cordonnier* is "shoemaker," but the term was attached to a large bird, allegedly on the authority of previous French navigators, by Étienne Marchand, who published an account in 1809 of a circumnavigation of the world made in 1790-92. The successors of the Comte de Buffon quoted Marchand's reference when updating new editions of his *Histoire naturelle* in the 19th century, but were unable to identify the bird in question, and it appears to have disappeared from the record thereafter, save for the occasional literary reference.

try to avoid the entrance to the sack, in which all three of them were engulfed.

"Bravo, my friends!" cried Émile, and then said to himself: *How glad Angèle will be when I bring her the entire family to rear!*

For one thing, they were superb creatures. The mother had a wingspan of about four feet. The body color was black with a hint of red; the beak was strong, the sharpened talons indicating at first glance the category in which the bird as to be classified. Their cry was a kind of bark, resembling quite closely that of a dog.

The nest, which the your scientist examined with extreme care, consisted of a cavity hollowed out naturally in the rock and indicated by its rudimentary form that the inhabitants of the locale had not yet contracted any habit of softness. Finally, the debris of fish, cuttlefish and sea-spiders that strewed the ground around the nest proved that the nourishment of the birds did not borrow anything from the dry land.

"Come on, my friends, courage!" cried the hunter, cheerfully. "We're a long way from the goal we set out to attain, and I confess that I'd regret not having been able to gaze at the horizon from the height of that summit."

The little caravan set off once again. A little higher up than the nest of the cordonnier there was a terrace covered in vegetation even thinner than that down below. There were no more mosses, but Alpine plants and wild fennel to carpet the ground. Further on, a second buttress was scaled, no less easily than the first. The path they followed slanted westwards and served as the bed of a little stream.

A few minutes later, Émile and his companions arrived on an elevated plateau not far from the true summit, the goal of their ascent—but the mist was so dense that they could not see two paces in front of them. What were they to do?

The young hunter reflected for a few minutes. "No point in trying to march on," he muttered, between his teeth. "On the other hand, it's impossible to go back by the break-neck route by which we came up." In a louder voice, without forsaking his good humor, he said: "In truth, my friends, my opinion is that we've forgotten to eat, and that there's nothing better we can do for the next quarter of an hour than to surrender to he joys of gluttony."

The matelots sat down on the grassiest spot they could find, and hastened to unpack the provisions they had brought with them. They ate with a good appetite and drank with enthusiasm.

From time to time, the young hunter stood up to consult the horizon, but each time he sat down again after having observed that the same opaque gray circle enveloped them.

Suddenly, there was a slight increase in brightness. Émile looked at his watch. It was two o'clock.

"Bravo!" he exclaimed. "Look, my friends, only a few meters separate us from the summit. Let's hasten to climb up and plant the French flag there.

A few minutes later, in fact, the folds of the tricolor flag were deployed in the air.

"The Germans will be annoyed if they see this from down below!" said the Breton matelot Le Dall, with a hearty burst of laughter.

"They can say and do as they like," the hunter replied, with a smile. Thinking about the difficulties of the ascent, he added, not without malice: "I don't think, at any rate, that they'll be tempted to come and take it down."

Taking advantage from the bright spell, which was increasing, Émile paraded his marine telescope in all directions, uncovering various features as the thick mist retreated. Suddenly, he felt something akin to an electric shock.

"What's the matter?" asked Le Dall, seeing him shiver as if he had been struck by a bullet.

"Nothing—it's nothing," replied the hunter, directing his telescope once again at the north-western tip of the island, which no one had yet thought of trying to reach, and which, in all probability, never would have been visited, because of its distance from the camp and the difficulties to be overcome in reaching it.

"My friends," the young scientist went on, "I've just seen down there, thanks to my telescope, a prey worthy of me, and I've made a firm resolution to get to it. To take you with me would render the task impossible, because, in spite of the agility of which you've just given me so much proof, one or other of you would slow me down. You have mariners' feet, whereas I'm a mountain man. You scale masts; I scale rocks."

After a moment's reflection, he added: "In any case, each of you is carrying a burden, while I only have my rifle. You're going to descend from here along the slope that runs eastwards, and which we were wrong not to have seen from below. The course will be short and relatively easy. Go and wait for me where I left you this morning when I went to shoot that huge mass of oily meat. You can take it for certain that I'll join you there before nightfall."

The matelots knew that they had been placed under the young man's direct orders for as long as the exploration lasted. None of them had the slightest idea of raising any objection to the leader's plan. Each of them picked up his pack, lightened by the weight of the meal, and the four sailors headed eastwards, while the intrepid hunter disappeared on his own through the escarpments of the opposite slope.

The mariners did not take long to recognize the wisdom of the advice that the young scientist had given them. The slopes on to which they ventured did, indeed, constitute the best route. A landslide had taken place on he first terrace and the sliding rock had carried away part of the second. The slope was steep, but not vertical. If he ground had not been miry they might have had the pleasure of letting themselves slide down astride an Alpenstock.

When they had arrived at the place fixed for the rendezvous they lay down idly on the thick grass that garnished the soil and then, warmed by the sun's rays, smoked their pipes philosophically, drinking a mouthful of cider-brandy from time to time. The hours went by without the admirably-disciplined individuals showing the slightest sign of impatience or anxiety.

However, when the sunlight had given way to dusk, Le Dall, without saying a word, rose to his feet and went to take a walk, straight ahead and then to the left of the designated point, looking into the distance in all directions to see whether he could see the hunter approaching.

As time went by the light grew weaker. All four companions came to their feet and gathered in a group to deliberate.

"I'm beginning to fear for the bourgeois," said one of them, in a low voice.

"If he isn't back before the night turns black, I wouldn't give a nail for his life," said another."

"Damn!" said Le Dall. "He'll be frozen in a corner if he stops, or fall into a hole if he keeps going."

"I'm not worried, myself," said the fourth sailor. "Monsieur Colin's a rude walker, and it's sufficient to have gone into the fields once with him to be sure that he's not scared of anything."

"All the same," said the Breton, "I wouldn't be sorry to know what the fine prey was that he saw through his telescope."

"Who can tell?" replied another. "These scientists have such odd ideas! Perhaps he's still running after some stinking beast, good for nothing—not even nailing on a door."

"If Jean-Pierre were here," affirmed Le Dall, "he wouldn't fail to tell us what was at the bottom of it—for it goes without saying that there's a fellow who has an education."

At that point in their conversation the four matelots pricked up their ears. Distant sounds were audible.

"Bravo! Here he comes!" exclaimed the four, with one voice.

And indeed, from the shadows of the dusk, they saw the silhouette of the hunter emerge.

"Yes, my friends, it's me," he said, approaching and dropping a dead body in front of them, which they recognized as a goat. "And here's what I was hunting," he added.

Chapter XIV

When he went back aboard, Émile Colin had a pre-occupied expression. He went directly to Angèle's cabin, and the two of them had a long conversation. As they had been careful to close the cabin door securely, nothing of their conversation leaked out, and we shall remain silent on the subject.

Let us say, however, that an observer who had looked attentively at the young man when he emerged from his fiancée's room would easily have recognized an unaccustomed phenomenon: his anxious expression had given way to an air of gaiety and good humor that people were scarcely in the habit of encountering in him.

From that day on, the young scientist was gripped by a kind of recrudescence of his love of hunting and solitary excursions. He renounced the accompaniment of one or several of the ship's matelots. Doubtless he judged that his acquaintance with Seal Island had become sufficient for him to travel around it alone and without danger. As he frequently brought back a kind of wild pig, reminiscent of a wild boar, that he had discovered in the mountains, the explorers' table was enriched by that precious meat, and no one—not even Monsieur Charmillon—thought of reproaching him for his vagabond humor and his frequent absences.

While he was devoting himself to his cynegenetic passion, we shall leave him to stride over the mountains and the valleys, and return to follow the savant and fruitful investigations of the members of the expedition in the Grotto of the Sphinx.

The astronomers had finally put the finishing touches to the installation of their instruments in little cabins built from wooden boards brought from Europe, carefully divided into labeled sections, ready to be connected up hermetically. Freed from that enormous care and ready to commence their celestial observations, the amiable scientists were glad to associate themselves with their colleagues' research and labor.

Every day brought new discoveries more previous than the last.

To the traces of human presence already found in the marvelous cavern others were soon added, no less important, which left no one in any doubt at all regarding the presence in that location of Paleolithic humans.

The two Germans, finally understanding that no one would associate themselves with their indelicate enterprises, any more than their isolation, had stopped sulking and had come to lend assiduous assistance to the excavations carried out in the first grotto, and then in all the tunnels opening to the right and the left of the principal cavern.

In one of these excavations they found a fairly considerable number of tools and weapons of the primitive age. Some were made of bone or the antlers of red deer, others of stone.

The former were not very numerous, unless all the bones broken by human hands that hand one ends sharpened to a point are considered as tools. We shall only count the objects whose usage could be clearly determined.

Monsieur Charmillon pointed out that on none of the debris was there the slightest race of drawing or engraving. Only one body fragment, whose employment was difficult to determine, split longitudinally, about six

centimeters long and broken at both extremities presented two series of three parallel transversal grooves, separated from one another by an interval of slightly less
than two centimeters.

"Look, my friend," said the French geologist, addressing the English naturalist William Johnston, toward
whom an ever-increasing increasing sympathy drew
him, without him being consciously aware of it, "examine these grooves carefully. It seems impossible to me,
given their depth, their small number and their regulari-
ty, that they served as some kind of sign of numeration. I
could believe more easily that they were simply a particular mark of the object, weapon or instrument, or even a
distinctive sign of the man to whom it belonged individ-
ually, and was perhaps an important chief. I confess,
though, that I haven't yet seen staffs of command anywhere else affecting such a form and bearing such ornaments."

As this scholarly conversation was taking place, the
matelot Le Dall brought another instrument found in a
lateral cavern at a depth of 2.10 meters. That object
seemed even more curious than the preceding one, and
the scientists racked their brains in vain to explain the
purpose for which it might have been employed.

The item, which was recognizable as a fragment of
the horn of an ox, was fifteen and a half centimeters
long, narrow, thin and semicircular, about five centimeters broad. A little hole had been bored through the
rounded extremity, which suggested that the end of the
instrument might have been embedded in a wooden handle and retained by a thong passed through that opening.

The object was slightly curved lengthwise; it bore
superficial transversal grooves on both faces, numbering
thirty on the concave surface and twelve on the convex

surface. The grooves, regularly spaced, were separated from one another on each face by an interval of slightly less than a millimeter; there were contained within two almost-parallel lines traced longitudinally.

"This time," said Monsieur Charmillon, after a long examination and a meditation that everyone took care not to trouble, "I'm almost certain that these marks really must have served as marks of numeration. I'm not far from thinking that this object must have served as a staff of command; in that case, the interior marks would doubtless indicate them number of men forming a company, and those placed outside might have marked the number of companies that the chief had to direct."

Everyone, including the jealous Germans, agreed in recognizing the ingenuity of this explanation.

William Johnston, glad to show the French scientist the extent of the reciprocal amity he professed for him, added: "The lucidity of the explanation given by Monsieur Charmillon is such that I propose that it be admitted as sufficiently demonstrated, by virtue of the scientific axiom that a hypothesis ought to be admitted as a certain fact when no plausible alternative can be found."

That motion, so honorable for our compatriot, was passed unanimously by all the scientists present in the grotto.

The bone instruments found in the excavations carried out in the cavern of the Sphinx could be divided into several groups:

Firstly, arrow-heads, generally crudely carved and various in form. Their number remained very limited.

Secondly, awls, mostly quite beautiful, which were also the most numerous. A few were cylindrical throughout their length, others had one extremity flattened, while the other was cylindrical and pointed. One of them, about four centimeters long, formed a double awl—which is to say that, broad in the mid-section, it terminated on both sides with a tapering and pointed extremity. Others were only fragments of long bones, split as if someone had wanted to such the marrow from them, and whose tip had been sharpened and polished by friction. All of them had been used to pierce holes in wood or in hides destined to make garments.

Thirdly, needles, none of which was entire, possessed of a complete eye, the broader extremity being broken in every case, only the point being intact and well-sharpened. Almost all of them were made from fish-bones.

Fourthly, a chisel, whose form sufficiently indicated its usage, made of a bone perfectly cylindrical along its length—the tibia of a deer or primitive goat—but more voluminous than those of the awls. It terminated by narrowing slightly and flattening out in the form of a thick, rounded blade.

Fifthly, a smoother. It was Monsieur Charmillon, again, who had the honor of recognizing the primitive usage of that instrument.

"I have the conviction," he said, "that this object can be considered as having served the purpose of flattening the stitches made in animal skins, and had been constructed from the horn of an adult male *Capra primagenita*. Only the point has been worked in order to offer a flat surface on one side about a centimeter broad; the smoother had a rounded surface on the other side and the rest of the horn conserves its natural form."

The stone weapons and instruments, much more numerous, were no longer counted in hundreds but in thousands, including the nuclei and the flakes chosen from among the most interesting. They were generally well-preserved and often entire. The predominant form was that of the scraper. Their hues were also more varied; as we have already had occasion to say, the various colors indicated differences of origin, which did not escape the knowledgeable French geologist. He identified the presence of pudding stone, flint, limestone flint, agate flint, etc.

"Look, Messieurs," he repeated one day, in a fit of enthusiasm justified by a sudden rush of discoveries. "In the choice of materials destined for the fabrication of weapons and tools, the workman of primitive times has given preference not merely to the stones most appropriate to his work by virtue of their tenacity and hardness, but also to those which charmed his gaze most by the disposition and brightness of coloration. As soon as humans appeared on earth thy revealed themselves to be artists! Glory, therefore, to our ancestors in the remotest epochs."

The flint weapons and instruments collected in the various caves of the Sphinx could be divided into scrapers, awls and blades or arrowheads, the last-cited category presenting objects of two different types, one characterized by a shape like an almond or a "cat's tongue," the other consisting of stones carved on both sides. There were also sharpened punches, quite well-finished, shaped along the edges and both extremities.

"Behold, Messieurs," said the indefatigable Monsieur Charmillon, "the primitive hammer, the instrument with which our ancestors attacked the hard masses from which they constituted their first tools. Today, miners and quarrymen still make use of punches, but they're made of steel, almost as hard and diamond and a thousand times more resistant."

Let us also cite among the instruments found, disks and knife-blades, fairly rare and crudely carved, as well as hammers of a less primitive form than the plungers. We should also mention whetstones, sling-stones, weights for nets, triangular blades in flint, agate, diorite or serpentine, and even jade, daggers, and other tools whose imperfect forms did not allow their usage to be divined, and which might only have been fragments of stones.

No richer collection of prehistoric objects had ever been assembled so rapidly, and unalloyed joy already reigned among all the members of the expedition when a further discovery, leaving far behind all those that had preceded it, brought the pleasure of all the erudite individuals to the point of enthusiasm.

In order to illuminate the work in the profound darkness of the grottos they were exploring, Monsieur Charmillon and his colleagues—especially the chemist Guébard—had set up an ingenious apparatus with which a mixture of hydrogen and oxygen was manufactured. That mixture, when ignited, inundated the most distant walls of those profound retreats with bright light.

The work, carried out with zeal, was progressing with an ever-increasing activity when the workers, involuntarily interested in the research that they did not understand, brought to the scientists assembled around a table installed in the grotto bones that drew simultaneous cries of joy from Johnston, Pierre de Kolikoff, Enrico della Maria and Monsieur Charmillon, who were unanimous in recognizing their origin.

"Here, finally," exclaimed the French geologist, "is the recompense for our fatigues, for I defy anyone to deny that this debris, extracted from an excavation no less than two meters deep, belonged to the human species."

It was a metatarsal and a big toe, which, without a doubt, had been part of the skeleton of a human of the paleolithic era. Indeed, the remainder of the skeleton was soon found.

They resolved to extract the human remains without displacing them and to remove them along with the sand that surrounded them and in which they were, so to speak, molded.

That was not an easy task, if one takes into account the difficulty of touching the fragile and delicate remains without reducing them to powder. The disengagement of the entire skeleton and its transportation in a box constructed expressly for that purpose and covered with window-glass, the obligation to leave it half-buried in the sand, detritus, ashes and various objects surrounding it, necessitated ten days of uninterrupted and extremely scrupulous labor.

The fossil man was lying on the left side, the left ulna being parallel to the longitudinal axis of the cavern, ten meters from the entrance, near the left side-wall. The body was lying on a line from south to north. His attitude was that of repose—that, for instance, of man surprised in his sleep by sudden death without any violent death-throes.

In front of the mouth and the nasal fossas, about six centimeters from those openings, a perfectly regular furrow was intentionally hollowed out, eighteen centimeters long, four centimeters wide than thirty-five millimeters deep. That furrow was filled with a pulverized reddish yellow substance, which the Swedish geologist Otto Eliaison recognized as the iron oxide commonly known as rust.

"Take note, Messieurs," said Monsieur Charmillon, "that this observation is immensely important. In fact, these residues can only originate from the oxidation of a tool or an iron instrument belonging to the man whose skeleton is before us. Thus, in the epoch when he lived, the uses of metallic iron were known, and yet, in spite of the seeming contradiction, no one here, I'm sure, would dare to emit the opinion that this man lived in an epoch more recent than the Stone Age. Anyone who did would quickly see his paradox crushed by the mass of irrefutable proofs that demonstrate the contrary.

"Do not let that result astonish you too much, because it is not without precedent. When Émile Rivière, our illustrious colleague, discovered a human skeleton of the paleolithic era in the caves of Balzi-Rossi in Italy, known as the grottos of Menton, a furrow of the same kind as the one we have before our eyes was observed in an almost analogous situation.[26] However, the substance

---

[26] Émile Rivière (1835-1922) first visited the caves of Balzi-Rossi on the Italian Riviera in 1869, in company with Stanislas Bonfils, who had assembled a large collection of natural history specimens in the nearby town of Menton, just over the French border, to which the Balzi-Rossi finds were added. Rivière discovered the skeleton that became known as "l'Homme de Menton" in 1872; he discovered another three the following year and two more in 1874. He published a book on his discoveries, but not until 1887, some years after the present text, having submitted a preliminary text to the Académie in 1884. Numerous popular articles about the discovery of the Menton skeleton were published in 1874, however, some including a photograph showing the reassembled and posed skeleton lying on its left side, surrounded by various objects found in close proximity, which appears to have

that filled it was a shiny gray, and was nothing other than hematite, an iron oxide in powdered form. That singular material was not only observed there, but numerous particles of it were found on the surface of the teeth and bones of the skeleton, as well as on the surface of the weapons buried close to him and various objects of adornment covering the skull and ornamenting the left leg. The human bones had taken on a rather pronounced brick-red coloration with a certain metallic gleam."

"Do you conclude from that, Monsieur Charmillon," Kolikoff put in, "the absolute certainty that primitive humans had knowledge of iron and its uses, and that if their weapons, ornaments and tools were fabricated in stone, it was merely by virtue of an as-yet-inexplicable preference?"

"Certainly not," replied the Frenchman, "but I conclude, or at least suppose, that the iron employed by the first humans only came from a few parcels of native iron, which, for them, represented a luxury metal of which they fabricated jewels and ornaments. It nevertheless remains established that they did not know how to extract iron from the mineral that contains it, and that, in consequence, they were obliged to be content with their primitive weapons for a long time."

Everyone recognized the justice of this remark and adopted the formulated hypothesis without contest; everyone's attention redoubled and was directed to the various constitutive parts of the discovered skeleton. Apart from the traces of rust contained in the furrow, however, they were unable to discover any coloration similar to that so remarkably observed on the Menton skeleton.

---

been used as the basis of Gros' description of the attitude of his fictitious skeleton.

The head, slightly more elevated than the rest of the body and slightly tilted forward, was gazing into the depths of the cavern. It was resting on the ground by the left side of the skull and the face. The lower jaw, in natural and immediate contact with the upper jaw, was supported on the ultimate phalanges of the left hand. The base of the skull, as well as the posterior region of the trunk as far as the pelvic girdle, were supported by a number of stones of varying volume, not shaped and irregular in form, which appeared to have served as a support for the body during sleep.

That skeleton, the first of the Paleolithic epoch to be found in the austral regions, was well-preserved and almost complete. In spite of the minute care taken by the laborers working under the anxious eyes of the entire commission of illustrious men, a few bony parts had been damaged by spades and other tools. Thus, one of the ungular phalanges had been broken off one hand and had disappeared. It was the same with the short stout bone forming part of the tarsus forming the bony part of the heel, known as the calcaneus. The astragalus, the scaphoid, the cuboid, one of the cuneiform bones and the first metatarsal having disappeared, the left foot could only be partially extracted, but the right foot, of unusual dimensions was composed of the calcaneus, the astragalus, the three cuneiform bones, the first three metatarsals and the first phalange of the big toe.

Monsieur Charmillon, who had the honor of putting in evidence, every time the occasion arose, the discoveries of the French scientists, hastened to make use of the method developed by Dr. Broca and described in his paper on "The Relative Proportions of the Arm, Forearm and Clavicle Among Negroes and Europeans."[27] Comparing various pieces of the skeleton, he was soon able to make a statement of the following observations, whose importance will not escape our readers:

"Messieurs, if the humerus is represented by the fugure 100, the length of our subject's radius gives the enormous figure of 82.90, while the mean of negroes is only 79.43 and of Europeans 73.82.

"Let us now pass on to the clavicle, which, as you all know, also exhibits differences in length in various races. Still using the humerus as 100, we obtain the formidable figure of 54.17. Among negroes the mean found by Dr. Broca is 45.89, while among Europeans it is only 44.32."

These observations having been made with the minute attention they merited, he passed on to the skull of the antediluvian human. The cranium was elongated, very dolichocephalic. Skulls are thus designated whose cranial cavity is oval in form and whose maximum longitudinal diameter is longer by more than a quarter than the transversal diameter.

William Johnston, who is well known for his admirable anthropological endeavors, hastened to remark that the numerous savages of Oceania, among whom he cited

---

[27] Paul Broca (1824-1880), one of the pioneers of physical anthropology, published numerous papers detailing the comparative measurements he made of the physical structure of humans and other primates. He founded the Societé d'Anthropologie de Paris in 1859; the paper cited was published in the Society's Bulletin in 1862, and is nowadays widely cited in fashionable academic exercises in the history of racism, by virtue of the unfortunate conclusions that are echoed in the present text, as well as many other works of fiction published in the *Journal des Voyages*.

the Kanaks of New Caledonia, are dolichocephalic. That little dissertation was greeted with the favor it merited.

The rather narrow skull, scantly developed in the anterior frontal part, presented, by reason of that frontal depression, a rather bestial aspect. The sutures, all sealed, where not very apparent, by reason of the thick patina that covered the surface of the skull. The parietal foramen was very apparent. The orbit was extremely remarkable in terms of its dimension and its round form; the transversal diameter was only a little more extensive than the vertical diameter; the upper orbital rim was as hard and thick as the lower orbital rim. The facial angle, very acute, like the frontal depression, denoted a mediocre intelligence in the primitive race.

The naturalists exhibited surprise on examining the jaws; the nasal bones had almost disappeared and, in terms of their origin, seemed never to have had a very considerable development. Monsieur Charmillon called attention to this fact, reminding his listeners that there was nothing strange about the fact that early humans had had snub noses like negroes, who are themselves new or inferior races. The double maxillary prognathism was also very apparent—which is to say that the jaws were noticeably pre-eminent, constituting a further point of similarity with black nations.

The teeth, perfectly white and well-conserved, were almost entirely devoid of caries, but the four canine teeth were absent and left wide gaps in the dental array. Nevertheless, the maxillary arcade formed a continuous curve, the teeth in the upper range being more voluminous than those in the lower, as in the majority of human races.

The absence of the canine teeth from jaws so admirably conserved gave much cause for reflection on the part of the scholars present; there was a mystery therein that might perhaps be difficult to solve. Monsieur Charmillon hastened to point out it was another subject of astonishment, as yet unexplained, that was also manifest in the prehistoric human skeleton of Balzi-Rossi.

The observation of the scientists did not stop there, however.

Mr. Johnston pointed out that the grinding surface of the teeth in the lower jaw did not present any protrusion or depression; it was completely flat and smooth, with no curvature forwards or backwards, neither in the incisors nor the molars, and that the upper set were similar.

Was the age of the subject, which did not appear to be very advanced, considering the conservation of the bones, sufficient to explain that wearing away of the teeth? Was it a characteristic of the race, or was it the result of a mostly vegetarian and frugal diet?

Monsieur Charmillon immediately came down firmly in favor of the latter hypothesis, which was rejected no less ardently by the two German scientists, who had remained attentive but silent spectators until then. Our compatriot thought it a matter of good taste not to insist further, for fear of seeing a renewal of the unfortunate scenes that had occurred before.

Furthermore, the English naturalist William Johnston took the floor, and Monsieur Charmillon, yielding to the evidence, hastened to rally to the opinion of his adversaries as soon as a decisive argument caused him to change his initial opinion.

"Messieurs," the Englishman said, "in spite of the high esteem that I profess for the expertise of Monsieur Charmillon, I have the regret, for this time only, of not sharing his view. I believe that the wearing away of our skeleton's teeth cannot be attributed to the exclusion of meat from the diet, for which I require no more proof than the enormous quantity of animal bones found in these caves and broken by humans, their contemporaries.

"These bones, without a doubt, are mostly culinary debris; that is why I agree with Messieurs Müller and Henrich, even though I renounce explaining the phenomenon with which we are confronted. One observation, however, which justifies the error of our dear French colleague is the brevity in the lower jaw of the coronoid apophysis, which ought to permit very extensive movement of that jaw relative to the upper one—movements similar to those of a millstone, which must have singularly favored the crushing of vegetable nourishment."

Note was taken of these phenomena, and the scientists, renouncing their explanation because of their diversity, decided to wait until further discoveries supplied the key to the enigma.

The thought that predominated, however, was that the suppression of the canines and the wearing away of the teeth observed in the Grotto of the Sphinx as well as the cavern of Menton, could not have any other cause than a superstitious practice of the humans living in such a distant epoch.

All the parts of the skeleton were studied successively and analyzed. The unusual length and breadth of the radius and ulna, which formed the forearm, denoted a colossal strength in primitive humans. The ensemble of bones composing the hands had an enormous surface area. The long and stout tibias were slightly curved inwardly. What seemed to be the most remarkable characteristic of primitive humankind, however, was the enormous amplitude of the chest, the bony cage of which was no less than 1.35 meters around.

On taking account of the development of the humerus, forearm and hands, and the breadth of the shoulders, Monsieur Charmillon pointed out to his astonished colleagues that the horizontal reach of the skeleton attained 2.20 meters. Let us add to these details that the skeleton itself occupied a length of 2.05 or 2.06 meters, which indicated gigantic proportions and a Herculean strength on the part of the man to whom the bone-structure in question had belonged.

After having concluded these studies, measurements and a considerable number of anthropological observations for which there is no room within the narrow frame of this story, the savant voyagers directed all their attention to the minute observation of the external objects that had been found in close proximity to the skeleton.

The skull was still ornamented with a decoration of shells of various kinds, which must have been linked together as a necklace by a thread that had subsequently disappeared, for all of the shells had been perforated by a human hand. Several of them belonged to the *Massa* genus,[28] which is only found today in the Mediterranean, and is absolutely foreign to the polar region. Other shells of a more elegant form belonged to the immense family of the *Helicidae*, which are found all over the world. In that crown of sorts, it was observable that the shells were

---

[28] There is no such molluskan genus, and the information given is too slight to enable the deduction of the genus to which the author is referring, although it does rule out the species *Lyrodus massa*.

separated in pairs by the canine teeth of red deer, similarly perforated by a human hand.

A bone instrument or weapon, undoubtedly derived from the tibia of a hippopotamus, shaped and polished by a human hand, about eighteen centimeters long, was applied to the skull at the front, and must have been part of the crown or lattice that served to ornament the head. An articulatory facet of the primitive bone was still visible at the broader extremity of the ornament, which presented the form of a flat dagger in the upper part and was terminated cylindrically by a well-conserved point. Two holes had been bored in one end of the instrument.

That head-ornament could be compared with the long spikes in ivory, coral or bone that were popular only a few years ago and with which elegant women transpierced their hair. Several savage tribes, at various points of the globe, also use ornaments of that kind frequently.

The precious box containing the remains of the Paleolithic human was eventually sealed and transported with pious care to the *Glorieux*, where a specially-prepared cabin received it. The door was carefully closed and the key confided to Monsieur Charmillon in person.

All the members of the expedition agreed that a common report would be drawn up, including the slightest details of the admirable discovery, in order to reveal to the scientific world, when the expedition returned to Europe, all the new information that the unexpected find had provided.

Unanimously, save for two votes—doubtless those of the Prussians—Monsieur Émile Colin was designated to draft that report under the supervision and direction of his illustrious master.

Chapter XV

We shall leave the members of the international scientific expedition to celebrate the admirable discoveries made in the Grotto of the Sphinx and to prepare the drafting of the report destined for the various scientific societies of Europe, and momentarily follow our friend Jean-Pierre, exercising his pedagogical sacerdocy on the foredeck.

The enthusiasm of the scientists had been so noisy and so expansive that it could not have escaped the crew of the *Glorieux*. In any case, had the manual labor that had led to such fine results not been carried out by the zealous matelots? The latter, however, remained utterly perplexed, for they had not understood any of the searching for pieces of stone, bone or seashells, and had even less understanding of the purpose of the exhumations of the Paleolithic human skeleton and the precautions taken to avoid disturbing anything, either of the disposition of the bones or the economy of the terrain containing them.

That series of astonishments was loudly manifest in shipboard conversations, and outstanding in the first rank of the orators were the fine petty officer from St. Malo, Grand-Victor, and his Breton accomplice Le Dall.

"Can you imagine what's happening?" said the latter. "What the devil do those men want with the human remains they collected with so much care?"

"Personally," replied the petty officer, "I'm completely at a loss. I've seen a great many strange things while sailing, but word of honor, nothing has ever seemed as strange to me as the work to which everyone here, including our Commandant, is devoting so much ardor."

Hearing talk of extraordinary things, the matelots scented the possibility of getting Grand-Victor to recount some of his adventures. It was Le Dall who attempted to provoke that disclosure. In a detached tone, as if he wanted to show that he out no great store in the stories he was about to hear, he said: "Really, countryman, you've seen marvelous things? May we at least know where that happened?"

Grand-Victor, as his compatriot had anticipated, felt his tongue loosen, and had no need to be begged to enter into the matter.

"Where?" he replied. "In all four corners of the globe! I've seen Greenlanders, Eskimos and Tschoutsches drink stinking fish-oil out of full bowls and fall down drunk, as if they'd absorbed apple- or grape-brandy."

"Pooh!" Le Dall contented himself with saying.

"In India," the petty officer continued, "I've seen widows throw themselves voluntarily under the wheels of the carriages that were taking their husbands to be buried. In New Caledonia, those same widows, to testify their grief, hang themselves in clusters from the braches of nearby trees."

"That's a bit much!" exclaimed those around him.

"You think that's a bit much?" said Grand-Victor, becoming animated. "Well, that's just small beer. In Africa, I've seen Moorish kings who take a kicking without complaining in order to get hold of a drop of eau-de-vie. I've seen fathers sell their children for a handful of salt, which they swallowed like sweets. I've seen black princes who, in order to amuse themselves, had the throats of a hundred or two hundred people cut, including their relatives and ministers."

"All that's true!" Le Dall put in, visibly interested. "I can guarantee it, because I've seen it myself, in person."

The audience was enjoying the stories, and Grand-Victor was about to continue his list of extraordinary things when Monsieur Charmillon's valet appeared.

"My friends!" cried the petty officer. "Enough of this foolery and shut up. Here's Monsieur Jean-Pierre, who's going to explain to us why those Messieurs the scientists so carefully removed the bones of a fellow buried I don't know when on an island where no vessel ever calls, and where, in order to drop anchor, it would have to be carrying an entire band of men bitten by a tarantella."

"You mean a tarantula," Jean-Pierre observed, modestly. "Well, since you desire it, I'll let you know at least proximately, and taking account, as Monsieur Charmillon says, of the modicity of your interrigence, what the great scientists have found in discovering the foresail man, or the enterdiruvian man.

"First of all, know that that skeleton belonged to a great man; I heard that said textually by Monsieur William Johnston, who knows, and who certainly hasn't got blinkers on when it comes to the history of naturals. Probably, the fellow named Foresail was the victim of the ingratitude of his concitizens, who must have deported him to this island as if he were a mere Communard,[29]

---

[29] Just as memories of the Prussian invasion would still have been fresh in French minds in 1876, so would memories of the fate of the ill-fated supporters of the Paris Commune; those who were not summarily executed had been deported to New

and where, for lack of sufficient sustenance, he went and died."

Jean-Pierre, whose audience always listened to him meekly, was about to continue his bizarre narrative when the severe face of Monsieur Charmillon suddenly appeared before him, like the head of Medusa.

"Monsieur Jean-Pierre," said his master, in a tone of voice that did not permit any reply, "do me the pleasure of going to my cabin, to which I shall follow you."

The valet bowed and withdrew, not without muttering between his teeth: "These scientists always want to protect themselves against the envy to which the talent and success of others give birth in them!"

Monsieur Charmillon approached Jean-Pierre's audience and said, in his soft and sympathetic voice: "My friends, forget what that imbecile has just told you. Everything that comes out of his mouth is a tissue of gross stupidities. One of these days, if it would be agreeable to you, I'll gladly say a few words to you about our discoveries and will try to enable to you understand the goal of our research." He smiled and added, "In he meantime, know that it's not a matter of a fellow named Foresail, but of a *fossil* man, which simply means a man who had just been taken from the earth where he's been buried since very ancient times. That man wasn't a great man, but a very big man, tall and very strong, who was a frightful savage a long time ago.

"The objects in bone and stone, and the shells that we've taken out of the ground in the Grotto of the Sphinx are the weapons, instruments and tools that were

---

Caledonia, where they were still imprisoned in that year, although by the time Gros wrote the story they had been pardoned and allowed to return to France.

used at the time of his existence, or the remains of his meals. My companions and I are glad to have discovered those remains, which prove that the earth is much more ancient than ignorant people think, and that the human species even lived in these cold regions in a period when it had no weapons and tools except those made of stone; that's why we call that epoch the Stone Age—not the age of stones, as that donkey Jean-Pierre has told you."

When he had concluded that benevolent little lesson, Monsieur Charmillon bowed to his naïve audience and returned to his cabin,

As soon as he had disappeared, Petty Officer Grand-Victor could not hold back the expression of his indignation. "That dirty dog of a domestic will pay me back!" he said. "He's made fools of us! Well, I'll reserve a few good punches for him that he'll remember for a long time!"

"Bah" said the matelot Le Dall, ever skeptical. "Who knows, after all, whether it's the master or the domestic who's right? For my part, I'd as readily believe both of them or consider them both as jokers. A good plug of tobacco's always worth more than these clever speeches, and so far as I'm concerned, it's better to go take a look than believe what anybody says."

From the day when the great discovery of the paleolithic man had been made, everything changed aboard the *Glorieux* among the colony formed by the members of the scientific expedition. If, on the one hand, they considered it unnecessary to continue digging in the Grotto of the Sphinx, on the other hand, they multiplied the scientific conferences in the large common lounge.

Each of the erudite individuals was charged with recording his own impressions of the objects found and their classification. Those personal and combined works soon filled an enormous file, which was discussed in general meetings and from which the quintessence was extracted in order to make a major scientific report. William Johnston and his compatriot Wilson, Pierre de Kolikoff, Otto Eliaison, Enrico della Maria, Dr. Despierre and several others, including the Germans Walter Müller and Franz Henrich, who seemed to have definitively abandoned their hostile projects, lent the collaboration of their enlightenment and knowledge to Arthème Charmillon.

Émile Colin, appointed as secretary/reporter was obliged to renounce his cynegetic excursions completely, at least for a while, for the employment incumbent upon him was far from being a sinecure. Every day there was a heap of memoirs, notes and classifications to go through, and often to copy out neatly. Thanks to all the combined efforts, however, the work made progress every day, and within a fortnight, the great report destined to be communicated to the scientific societies of Europe was complete.

Émile Colin was charged with compiling the final draft and copying it in his finest handwriting.

When the beautiful document was finished and the secretary was able to read it to a gathering of al the members of the expedition, everyone wanted to shake young Émile's hand and thank him for the care with which the precious report had been transcribed on fine ministerial paper. That document, the result of the collaboration of so many illustrious men, contained no less than sixty pages of compact and magisterial handwriting. A large blank sheet was appended to it to receive the signatures of all the members of the expedition; when everyone had added his name to it and Monsieur Colin had added the titles and qualifications to each one, the manuscript was reread in public and the young secretary was solemnly requested to put it in a large envelope and put a seal on it that would make and subsequent amendment impossible.

"That measure," said Monsieur Charmillon, "seems all the more necessary to me because the sealing of the envelope will be equivalent to a certification of the date of our discovery and will ensure us of priority over any other find of the same sort in the old or new continent."

In consequence, Émile Colin, after having furnished himself with all the instruments necessary to the grave task that had been confided to him, shut himself away in his cabin and set to work to complete his mission. The young scientist, as we know, was far from being a dunderhead. He knew that it is not as easy as it is commonly believed to place one or several wax seals on an envelope in an appropriate fashion. The substance to be employed needs to be neither too hot nor too fluid; it must be spread out broadly and amply, without economy but without prodigality, over the folds of the envelope to be sealed, in such a fashion that the seal that the wax is called upon to reproduce is molded there in a correct and irreproachable fashion.

He was also aware of the deadly effects caused by a smoky flame to which one brings the wax to warm it. The bright red of the seal is marked with black patches and instead of an artistic sea you no longer have anything but a common and dirty one. Émile therefore placed the seal to be reproduced close at hand, moistened it slightly to avoid an inconvenient adherence, and then picked up the stick of sealing-wax, rotated it above an alcohol lamp until the moment when the odorous material began to melt, and was able to extend a beautiful horizontal plaque on the united folds of the envelope to be sealed.

The seal entered profoundly into the liquid paste, and, when the young secretary withdrew it, after a sufficiently long pause to cool the molten material, he was able to observe, joyfully, that it had been molded completely and had left an irreproachable imprint.

Meanwhile, enthusiasm was increasingly taking hold of the happy scientists. Monsieur Charmillon's words relative to the necessity of ensuring the priority of the discovery of the prehistoric skeleton had moved his audience profoundly. Everyone was wondering, in fact, whether, during the prolonged sojourn that they were required to make on Seal Island, someone no less fortunate than them, in Europe, Asia, America or Oceania, might discover a fossil human. Their glory would be significantly diminished, if not totally extinguished.

It was the English naturalist, William Johnston, who was the first to voice his fears on that subject.

"Messieurs," he said to his friends gathered in the saloon, "it's a fact that I won't attempt to explain to you, but which nevertheless procures me considerable and serious concern. Great discoveries allow themselves to wait for thousands of years, and then one suddenly sees them springing forth simultaneously at several points on the planet. Isn't it for that reason that three men in Europe dispute the glory of having discovered gunpowder: Roger Bacon, Berthold Schwartz and Albertus Magnus? Similarly, without being given the word, the American Fulton and the French Marquis de Jouffroy each constructed a steamboat. I could multiply examples, but you know those stories as well as I do. The thought that we might not be the first signal to the presence of antediluvian humans in the polar seas haunts me in spite of myself, and I believe that it's important to our glory to ensure ourselves of the priority of the discovery."

A murmur of approval greeted those words.

The English scientist continued: "The transit of Mercury won't take place for another month. It will only take a fortnight for the *Glorieux* to accomplish the voyage from here to Melbourne and back. On the other hand, the work of installing the astronomical instruments is complete, and those whose objective is to procure us comfortable lodgings on shore are nearly complete. In two days, our fine ship and its amiable Commandant Beaudin could take to the sea and head for Australia, bearing the precious document that will make our work and discoveries known to the scientific world of Europe. I propose, in consequence, that we take a vote here and now on the prompt departure of the vessel, so that our report can be put aboard one of the big liners that maintain a regular postal service between Australia and Europe, and that it be addressed without delay to the Académie des Sciences in Paris, which will send copies of it as soon as possible to all the scientific bodies represented here."

That motion, which responded to the secret desires of all of the members of the expedition, was greeted with an indescribable enthusiasm. It was voted by a show of hands of complete unanimity.

Monsieur Charmillon asked to speak.

"I believe," he said, "that it would be a good idea, in order that none of us appears to have wanted to separate himself from his colleagues, to make a solemn engagement of honor not to send any private note to Europe, so that our report, so conscientiously drawn up, will remain the only official document testifying to the nature and importance of our endeavors."

Like its predecessor, this proposal did not give rise to any opposition, and was adopted by a unanimous vote. Everyone, including the Germans, agreed in recognizing that it constituted an important measure of order.

Only Commandant Beaudin might have been able to find a more-or-less reasonable objection to the departure of his ship, but he did not do so, and put himself entirely at the disposal of the scientists when they expressed the desire that they had just formulated.

This, on the twenty-first of November, a little more than a month after the arrival of the voyagers of Seal Island, the *Glorieux* set out to sea again, under the guidance of its worthy Commandant, and soon disappeared into the distant mists of the horizon.

All the scientists gathered on the beach sent their good wishes to accompany the ship that was about to revolutionize scholarly Europe.

That same day, Émile Colin had a long conversation with Monsieur Charmillon's niece, which remained secret but terminated with a loud burst of laughter on the part of the young couple and a handshake testifying to the fact that their mutual affection, far from weakening, was increasing every day. Angèle, in particular, had a triumphant expression. As she watched her fiancé disappear around a bend in the corridor, she gave him one last wave of the hand and placed her index finger over her lips, as if to recommend him to discretion.

Émile contented himself with smiling.

Chapter XVI

The day after the day when the *Glorieux* had quit Seal Island—which is to say, the twenty-second of November—all the sailors left at the service of the members of the expedition set to work ardently to complete the embellishment of the improvised colony on the shore.

The European scientists were installed in wooden houses affecting the form of cheerful chalets, which gave the landscape an Alpine character unmistakable reminiscent of the mountains of Switzerland.

Before his departure, Monsieur Charmillon had bought a delightful little chalet from Walker's in Paris, doubtless constructed to form a nest for a young married couple in the vicinity of the capital. That light and pretty wooden house had been divided into labeled sections and constructed in such a fashion that it could be dismantled and reassembled without difficulty. It had been possible to reassemble it on the coast, at a point fairly high on the cliff; it was reached via a rustic stairway hollowed out in the ground, and made an admirable effect there.

The matelots charged with the installation had taken care, with a taste that did them the greatest honor, to surround it with arborescent ferns. The plants with broad green delicately serrated leaves framed the rural house, forming a veritable nest of verdure all around it.

As small as Socrates' house, the ground floor of the chalet contained a kitchen, a dining room, a drawing room and a closet, which became Jean-Pierre's bedroom. The first floor, divided into four rooms, offered a bedroom for the uncle, one for the niece, a study for the

Academician and, finally, a bedroom for the amorous secretary.

Thanks to the activity of Angèle, completely recovered from her sprain, and that of the valet Jean-Pierre, Monsieur Charmillon's new dwelling soon left nothing more to be desired in terms of its internal fitments and comfort.

The scientist's collection and library were installed in his study by Émile Colin, under he gaze and in accordance with the advice of his master. Two sculpted oak tables with twisted feet were set up to serve the two workers as desks. Angèle took charge of the rest of the furnishing.

On the evening of the day when they entered into possession of it, the new tenants of the elegant chalet declared themselves to be as comfortably installed as they would have been in Paris, in their old domicile in the Rue de Fleurus.

It seems that a baleful law regulates humankind, no matter where on the globe they live, and that no happiness can last for long.

Scarcely were the erudite astronomers, geologists, naturalists, geographers, chemist, botanists, etc. definitively installed in their new habitations, and the table service had been conveniently established, when everything seemed to be smiling on them, and they were no longer thinking about anything but the glory that awaited them on their return to their fatherlands, than something happened that reduced all their legitimate hopes to nothing at a single stroke.

The temperature was becoming more clement every day; only the members of the expedition who had devoted their anterior studies to the history of our planet and its first inhabitants ordinary remained indoors, in the silence of their studies, classifying and labeling the treasures amassed in the Cavern of the Sphinx. As for the others, they loved to stroll, sometimes on the shore, sometimes on the summits and sometimes in the profound valley.

One day, shortly after sunrise, before the first meal to the day, which even the most indefatigable excursionists had the custom of taking together, a considerable number of the scientist were sitting on the jetty gazing out to sea and perhaps thinking of their distant homelands, when they saw a little company emerge from the interior, the sight of which did not worry them unduly at first.

"Look," said Batschkoff, pointing out the arriving group to his Russian colleague Kolikoff. "It appears that our matelots have acquired, like some of us, a love of adventure and excursions. There are some of them coming back in the early morning, who must, I'll wager, have gone out by night along the coast, fishing by torchlight or hunting seals."

Kolikoff took a marine telescope from his pocket and aimed it in the direction indicated by his colleague.

"Damn!" he murmured, between his teeth. "Damn!"

"What's the matter, my dear friend?" Batschkoff asked him.

"It's…it's…well, if they're matelots they're putting on a singular masquerade." As he pronounced those words he passed his telescope to his companion, who set about inspecting the new arrivals in his turn.

"No! No, they're not our men!" exclaimed the Russian ethnologist, more disturbed than he wanted to appear.

At the same moment, several other scientists dispersed along the beach came back toward the two observers and asked them for information regarding the visit that they seemed to be about to receive.

No one finding any way to provide information regarding that problem, they resigned themselves to waiting patiently.

As the little troop drew nearer, the silhouettes of those making it up stood out more clearly on the horizon.

They could even count them: there were five.

"But they're savages!" cried the Swede, Otto Eliaison. "Eskimos!"

The astronomer Chauvin, who was present, permitted himself a smile. "It would be surprising to find Eskimos in the austral seas," he said.

"You're surely right, a hundred times over," replied the geologist from Stockholm, "but the devil may take me if I can work out who we're going to be dealing with."

Indeed, the strangers were still drawing closer, and it was soon easy to distinguish not merely their costumes, which were more than singular, but their faces. They were white men, but how strangely dressed! Animal skins, fur outwards, covered them from head to toe, which made them resemble rather closely, as Otto Eliaison had said, the Eskimos, Samoyeds or Tchoutsches who live on the shores of the northern polar seas. A broad sealskin belt retained those primitive garments around the hips. A weapon of singular form, part dagger and part saber, was suspended from the belt in question by means of a sleeve curved like the handle of a walking-stick and a sealskin strap. Behind the back each of the savage men carried, instead of a quiver, two toothed harpoons doubtless designed for hunting walrus, sea-lions or large cetaceans. In the hand they held a curved bow fabricated from whalebone. The string of the bow had doubtless been furnished by the intestines of seals of some other marine animal.

Unkempt hair whiter than snow undulated over the shoulders and surrounded the face at the whim of the wind; long white beards, no less white, falling in compact waves over the breasts of the new arrivals completed a patriarchal appearance that imposed simultaneous sentiments of compassion and respect.

When they arrived within range of the voices of the members of the expedition, one of them, who was marching at the head and appeared to be the leader, approached the scientists, bowed politely and, in a firm voice, said in excellent French: "Whoever you might be, white men, our European compatriots, whatever language is spoken in the place that gave you birth, we beg you to help unfortunates for whom you have arrived here like a providence for which we have no longer dared to hope for a long time."

He fell silent and tilted his head, like a man determined to wait for a response before continuing his discourse.

Monsieur Charmillon approached the newcomer and offered him his hand.

"As you have said, my friend, we are compatriots. Personally, I am honored to belong to France, the language of which you speak. Hasten to tell us who you are, and as a result of what misfortunes you find ourselves in this cold and desolate land."

"Monsieur," replied the leader of the newcomers, "you see in us unfortunates condemned to live here for thirty years, without resources and without hope. My four companions and I are French, honest mariners whom the tempest once cast away here on this sterile shore, without shelter, without weapons, without bread and without resources."

"But then, my poor friends," said Monsieur Charmillon, with tears in his eyes, "how have you triumphed over so many obstacles. How do you come to be still alive at the present moment?"

The man who seemed to be the chief of the castaways was about to reply to that perfectly natural question and begin the recitation of the terrible epoch that had reduced the men to the savage state in which they were seen, when the English naturalist William Johnston approached in his turn.

"Monsieur Charmillon," he said, "it seems to me that, in the present circumstances, the wisest and most urgent thing is to restore these unfortunates with a substantial meal, and then procure them more comfortable clothing. We'll still have time to listen to the account of their misfortunes."

In spite of the legitimate curiosity that had invaded the hearts of all the members of the expedition assembled at that moment, they all recognized the justice of the English scientist's observation, and they all hastened to guide the castaways to the camp where a good meal awaited them.

The unfortunates did not have to be begged to sit down at the table and do honor to a meal such as they had not encountered for a very long time.

The use of spoons and forks seemed to have become foreign to them, and they only made use of such utensils with an awkwardness that amused the spectators greatly. Red wine caused them to make ugly grimaces, and only the one who had served as spokesman and was easily recognizable as their chief declared that, to his great astonishment, although born in Burgundy on the fertile hills of Nuits, he found the vermilion liquid intolerably acidic.

"Sapristi! You're difficult to please, my lads," said the astronomer Chauvin, laughing. "What you're drinking there, and seem to be disdaining, is nothing lees than authentic Clos-Vougeot."

"You see me confused," said the leader of the castaways. "Our palates have lost the habit of savoring that divine nectar."

"What do you drink here, then?" asked Kolikoff, interested to the highest degree by this unexpected visit.

"Sometimes a little water, always foul, saturated with vegetable detritus, sometimes brackish and sometimes containing salts in solution that give it an insupportable odor of rotten eggs; otherwise, and more frequently, seal oil, which protects the body against the intense cold of winter, makes the limbs supple by penetrating into the pores of the skin, and procures, by satiation, a kind of wellbeing that is somewhat reminiscent of the drunkenness produced by alcoholic beverages."

Monsieur Charmillon left the dining room and went back to his chalet. He soon came back clutching two bottles whose necks ere garnished with silver paper.

"My friends," he said, cheerfully, to the castaways, "Here's a kind of champagne that will reconcile you with the wines of France."

Jean-Pierre came running at that moment, carrying crystal glasses.

The unfortunates drank the sparkling liquid, and proclaimed that since the day of their shipwreck, nothing had seemed as succulent to them.

"I was sure of that result," said Monsieur Charmillon, turning to his savant colleagues, "for all the peoples of the Far East—the Japanese, the Chinese and the Annamites—who cannot accustom themselves to the acidity of our red wines, drink our great wines of Champagne with pleasure, and willingly push their enthusiasm for that liquor to the extent of drunkenness."

When the castaways had had their fill they were brought a trunk full of the warm garments in use in the navy, but after they had thanked their generous hosts effusively they asked to be permitted, at least temporarily, to retain the primitive costumes to which they had been accustomed for so many years, promising to try on the European garments in more discreet circumstances, and to familiarize themselves once again with their employment before showing themselves in public thus clad.

Monsieur de Kolikoff asked them to tell the story of their adventures.

After raising a cup of hot tea that had been set before him to his lips, the troop's spokesman stood up and spoke in a firm voice, which emotion sometimes caused to vibrate in a patriotic fashion.

"It will soon be thirty years since we quit the southeastern coast of equatorial Africa; we were bound for Melbourne, to which we were taking a rich cargo of ivory and ostrich feathers. Our ship, of which I had the honor of being second in command, was caught by a cyclone a little beyond the islands of St. Paul and Amsterdam, in the middle of that immense sea on which there is not a single islet or spur of land—not even a rock to serve as a shelter for navigators in danger.

"From the very first blasts of the wind, Captain Joly and I understood that all hope of salvation was lost for the ship and crew; our masts had snapped like wisps of straw and our schooner, the *Françoise*, was carried at the whim of the waves across the immensity, like a pontoon or a mere nutshell, tormented by the swell, besieged, lifted up toward the skies or precipitated into the depths of liquid abysms in accordance with its caprice.

"You will find, Messieurs, the account of our ship-wreck—or rather, its long agony—in the ship's log, which I had the good fortune to save. Captain Joly kept it conscientiously every day until the moment of his death; after that, when I took command, I understood that duty bound me to continue that account, and I wrote every day, until the moment when the last piece of paper saved from the wreck was so soiled, so full of writing, intersecting in all directions, that it became impossible to add anything more without destroying what it already contained."

The orator paused, as if to draw breath. Monsieur Charmillon darted an investigative glance around him, as if searching for someone in the crowd of spectators.

"Where can Monsieur Colin be?" he murmured, in a low voice.

Kolikoff heard him. "Undoubtedly," he said, "in accordance with his habit, our intrepid hunter departed at dawn to set out in pursuit of some wild goat, which will bring a little fresh meat to our meals."

"Monsieur," said the amiable French scientist, addressing the castaways' spokesman, "I would like to introduce you to my secretary. I'll put him at your disposal from today, to copy and clarify your precious manuscript. But please continue, we beg you, the interesting account of your misfortunes."

The castaways' spokesman resumed his story.

"Our unfortunate ship remained prey to the chaotic caprices of the tempest for three days and three nights; we no longer knew where we were, for the sky had remained as gray as dusk throughout that time and we had not had a single moment when we might have taken a point. Furthermore, under the influence of inexplicable electric phenomena, the needle of the compass ran madly through all the divisions of its frame.

"When it becomes absolutely certain that all effort is futile, one easily yields to discouragement. As for us, we had long renounced the struggle, and were watching impassively the terrible spectacle of our own agony. The sole precaution that we demanded of our companions was that each of them, like the captain and me, should put a lifebelt round his waist. The duty of a man, even in the most desperate circumstances, is to resist until death. We waited for our unfortunate *Françoise* to be swallowed up under the weight of one of the thousand waterspouts that were swirling around us like liquid colossi serving as bonds of union between the sky and the vast sea.

"To speak more precisely, we knew that we were going to perish, that it was only a matter of hours, perhaps of minutes, but we would have found it very difficult to say what kind of death was reserved for us. Lightning was furrowing the sky with sinister steaks and the thunder was ripping our ears. Was it about to blast our frail ship apart? Would the heavy packets of sea-eater that fell upon her incessantly, as if hurled by a catapult, succeed in splintering her frame and smashing her to smithereens? Or would the force of the waves, as unconscious as it as indomitable, drag us on to some rock at surface level, on which we would shatter like glass? Those various possibilities seemed no less probable than seeing the *Françoise* dragged down by some whirlpool and crushed by the immense pressure of the column of water in the depths of the Ocean.

"Whatever our fate was to be, the order was given to throw ourselves into the water at the supreme moment and to try to swim until the last second.

"We no longer had a watchman, but we were solidly lashed to the masts in order not to be carried away by the surges of the sea. Doubtless we would have suffered less enclosed in the hull of the ship, still watertight, but none of us had consented to go down there; we preferred to look death in the face rather than waiting for it cowering in a cabin. There is, besides, an involuntary providential sentiment that humans cannot dispel, which is resistant to everything: that is hope.

"'Who can tell,' said that secret voice, 'perhaps the caprice of the tempest is bringing us closer to inhabited land without our being aware of it; perhaps the visage of some savior will appear before out eyes at any moment; perhaps we shall find on our route some ship, prey like us to the tempest but better able than we are to resist it; perhaps, finally, good weather will suddenly succeed the storm and, even though the *Françoise* is entirely disabled, who knows whether she might not be able to stay afloat long enough to reach some land, or perhaps obtain assistance from another ship passing within view?'

"That last hypothesis seemed for a moment to have been realized; in the afternoon of the third day, the tempest calmed down for a while. We took advantage of it to have a copious meal, which rendered us strength and the hope of salvation. Unfortunately, the calm only lasted two hours, and the wind returned, redoubling its fury, laden with hailstones and thunder.

"We continued that mad course all night; the next day, at dawn, I paraded my marine telescope over the mists of the horizon. Suddenly—O joy!—I seemed o see a small black dot appear in the distance.

"'Land! Land!'" I cried.

"All my companions directed their gazes in the direction in which I was pointing. It really was land; it appeared, blackly, against the sky. We threw ourselves into one another's arms, for salvation appeared to us if not certain, or even probable, at least possible.

"The wind to which we were delivered without defense, for it was so violent that a sail as big as a pocket handkerchief would have been ripped apart, no matter how strong its canvas might be, seemed to have taken pity on us, for the land was visibly growing, and we were evidently approaching it with a frightful rapidity.

"'Lieutenant Lefort,' the captain said to me, chopping his words like a man who understands the importance of time, 'pick up a compass and a sextant. I have my chronometer.' Then, turning toward the fifteen men who formed the crew, he said: 'Hurry up and grab food and clothing, everything that you want to save.'

"Without saying a word, I did as the Commandant ordered, and put a compass in my pocket, while I slipped a strap around my neck attached to a sextant carefully enclosed in its case. I had understood that the *Françoise* would never be able, without a rudder or any way to maneuver, to reach an inlet in the land-mass that was surging toward us. She would inevitably be broken, whether she was hurled against the sheer coast that we were beginning to discern, or rent apart by submarine rocks.

"That as the last misfortune that struck us; although disabled, we were flying with a rapidity for which I can find no other point of comparison than descending one of the roller-coasters that had become fashionable in the great cities of France before our departure.

"'Yvon,' said Captain Joly, addressing a Breton matelot, 'untie Pongo and do everything possible to save him.'

"'Yes, Commandant,' the brave mariner replied.

"Pongo was the captain's pet monkey—but I confess that for my part, I had other things to think about at such a moment.[30]

"Suddenly, we felt a frightful shock, accompanied by a terrible cracking sound. An immense, immeasurable force seized every one of us and, before we could even take account of the situation, it hurled us into the icy water, carrying us so far from the *Françoise* that I turned

---

[30] Although the term *singe* [monkey] has a very wide range of meaning, the fact that the captain's pet is called Pongo caries a certain implication, by virtue of the fact that that term had been used by the Comte de Buffon in his *Histoire naturelle* (1749-1788) to denote the larger variety of the single great ape species that he initially attempted to describe therein on the basis of vague second-hand accounts, without any specimens on which to base his assessment but a few of the "Jocko," or chimpanzee. He was subsequently obliged to acknowledge that the larger "Pongo or Ourang-Outang" must be a different species, but still declined to distinguish between reports of larger apes originating from Africa and Indonesia, although his contemporary Carl von Linné (Linnaeus) did identify the orangutan and the gorilla as distinctive species in the 1760s, on the basis of hearsay. Both species had a fugitive presence in Vernian literature in consequence, where the close analogy between the largest great apes and humans inevitably gave rise to various speculations, which continued to echo and proliferate in speculative fiction until well into the twentieth century. Even in 1876, however, no European scientist would have seen a live orangutan or gorilla, or even a skeleton, only a few much-traveled seamen having had the chance to encounter either species.

round in vain; nothing indicated her presence to me, in front or rear, to the left or the right. Doubtless, split in two by the impact she had suffered, she had gone straight down.

"It seemed to me, from the first moment, that I could hear sounds in the midst of the din of the tempest that must be coming from a human mouth, and, desiring myself to let me comrades know where I was, I shouted as loudly as I could: 'Friends! Friends! Lieutenant Lefort is here!'

"The furious waves had probably scattered us so widely that my words couldn't be heard, for no voice replied to mine. The lifebelt that I had been careful to put on was immensely useful to me. Half my body remained out of the water without any effort, and while the waves tossed me around like a cork, I was able to reflect on my situation.

"The essential thing was to take account of the position of the land toward which an indomitable current had driven us until then, and to find out whether I was still getting closer to it or whether the inconstant waves were dragging me out to sea. I took advantage of a moment when an immense wave griped me to lie down upon it as a rider lies down on a horse when he wants to resist a shock produced by a hectic gallop, and I allowed myself to be carried by the ascending movement of the swell. When I reached the summit of that liquid mountain I did my best to raise myself up and look in front of me.

"A high black wall loomed up a short distance away-an abrupt and vertical wall. I felt that all hope was lost and that the ballistic force that was dragging me was about to crash me into the obstacle.

"The instinct of self-preservation is so profoundly anchored in the human heart that it did not even occur to me to give up the struggle. I took off the lifebelt and dived down into the wave, steering in the direction of the obstacle.

"Against my attempt, instead of being drawn up again, along the smooth wall of rock and thus rising up to a point where I could cling on to some ledge or fissure, I felt myself gripped by an inexplicable force, which, seizing me like a vice, dragged me down into the aquatic depths.

"This time, I thought that I was definitively doomed, for I could not hold my breath any longer, and a terrible buzzing in my ears made me understand that asphyxia was commencing. On the other hand, a mortal cold had invaded my entire being and paralyzed my limbs. I stopped struggling, closed my eyes and lost consciousness."

When he arrived at that point of his interesting narrative, Lieutenant Lefort stopped and raised the cup of tea to his lips.

His listeners perceived that it was empty.

"In truth, my friends," said Monsieur Charmillon, "at the risk of depriving you momentarily of the satisfaction of your legitimate curiosity, I observe that the orator is thirsty, and I beg him to suspend his story until I come back, to offer him and his companions a few bottles of the champagne that so justly appreciated, and which I consider to be one of the best of our French wines."

"Personally, Messieurs," said the savant author of the book on the origin of the Slav nations, the Russian Batschkoff, "I applaud the generous thought of our friend Monsieur Charmillon, but I request to complete it be offering my colleagues a few bottles of Madame Veuve Cliquot's wine. By clinking glasses with our unfortunate guests, we can devote ourselves to a comparative study of the brand adopted by our colleague and the one that enjoys the favor of the entire Russian nation."

Chapter XVII

When the two generous scientists came back, followed by their valets carrying two bottles of the sparkling liquid, it was announced that the morning meal
was ready, and that the meal awaited the guests in the
dining room. The members of the expedition invited the
castaways to follow them and sit down at the table. The
latter protested at first, and declared that the snack that
had just been given to them had reduced them to impo-
tence.

"Bah!" exclaimed Dr. Despierre. "The merit of
good cuisine consists precisely in giving birth to desire
in the individuals seated, and it's high time that the
proverb 'appetite comes while eating' traveled the
world."

"I propose," said Monsieur Charmillon, "that since
the champagne is here, it becomes the only beverage
employed this morning during the meal. I've put that
method into practice more than once, recommended by a
gourmand as witty as he is distinguished, Dr. Véron.[31]
Another litterateur, as well-known for his refined gluttony as the delicacy of his wit, Monsieur Monselet,[32] has

---

[31] Louis Véron (1798-1867), the one-time director of the Paris
Opéra, who had earlier made a fortune selling patent medicines, famously wrote in his *Mémoires d'un bourgeois* (1853-
55) that he had been drinking champagne for thirty years and
never found fault with it; the quote is still used in promotional
material today.

[32] Charles Monselet (1825-1888) was one of the pioneers of
gastronomic journalism, nicknamed "the king of the gastro-

kept me company many a time during such meals, with an iced champagne that he declared exquisite.

Everyone agreed, and the table was covered with silver-necked bottles; the corks were soon leaping up to the ceiling, producing a series of joyful detonations in the dining room. The two kinds of champagne poured into iced flutes were appreciated equally, in such a way that the trial continued, and no one dared pronounce a definitive judgment.

As always, the meal was composed of delicate dishes, a large number of which came from tins furnished by Maison Chevet[33] of Paris: edible mushrooms, including morels and truffles; pâtés of game or *foie gras*; and vegetables that emerged from the tins as green and tasty as the moment when they had been picked. All those good things, as Dr. Despierre had prognosticated, reanimated the expiring courage of the castaways, who did honor to them as if they had not already left the table.

The meal was, therefore, cheerful and animated, the glasses overflowing with foamy wine being filled up and emptied rapidly. Good humor rendered everyone more communicative.

When they reached dessert, in which tinned Europeans fruits took pride of place, Lieutenant Lefort announced that he was ready to continue his story. A great

---

nomes," although he also wrote prolifically on other subjects, especially literature, and wrote satirical comic novels.

[33] Direction of Maison Chevet, which catered formal dinners in Paris and elsewhere as well as selling its produce as preserves, was assumed in 1876 by the "*roi des cusininiers et cuisinier des rois*" [the king of cooks and the cook of kings] Auguste Escoffier.

silence succeeded the general hubbub, and the castaway resumed speaking in the midst of a religious attention.

"Generous compatriots," he said, "I wouldn't want to abuse your kindness, so I shall try to conclude the tale of our misfortunes as briefly as possible.

"As I had told you, I had completely lost consciousness after having passed through all the agonies of death by asphyxia. How long did my unconsciousness last? I can't say. At any rate, when I came to, I opened my eyes and fund myself plunged in the most profound obscurity. The idea that I had suddenly gone blind took possession of my entire being.

"*I'm not dead*, I said to myself, *but what good is salvation to me if the celestial light has been taken away?*

"I stretched out my hands and felt the objects that surrounded me. I found that I was lying on a bed of fine sand; in the distance I could hear the sound of waves striking rocks; enlightenment gradually dawned in my mind as my memory returned. I realized that when I had plunged into the wave that was carrying me I had been gripped by a submarine current and deposited on a beach.

"I thought about my traveling companions and, gathering all my strength I uttered a cry of distress: 'Help, help me, my friends!'

"A kind of funereal croak responded, coming from some distance to my right. I tried to get up in order to grope my way to where the voice had come from, but my entire body was aching so much that it was impossible for me to stand. I dragged myself over the soft ground, crawling in the direction in which I hoped to encounter a human being, and then made a new effort.

"'Is there anyone there?' I shouted, again.

"A second groan replied to me, more distinctly, closer at hand, and, so to speak, more human. I continued on my way, on my hands and knees, and did not take long to bump into a mass that uttered a croak in which I thought I could distinguish the question: 'Who's that?'

"'It's me, Lieutenant Lefort—but who are you, my friend? I can't see you because I'm blind.'

"My voice seemed to galvanize the man lying beside me; I felt him shiver, and make every effort to sit up. Doubtless he had been no less maltreated than me, for he collapsed, and it was only after a few moments of silence that his voice made itself heard more firmly. 'Lieutenant,' he said, 'I'm matelot Jean-Marie of Le Havre. My eyes, like yours, are closed to the light. I've opened them in vain; I'm plunged in the most absolute darkness.'

"Those words rendered me a little hope. 'Perhaps we're in a dark cavern,' I said.

"I did not take long to assure myself that I was not taking refuge in a vain delusion. I remembered that I had a flint lighter in my pocket. I had no doubt that the tinder would be unusable, the water having certainly penetrated the case, but by striking the flint against the stone I would certainly obtain sparks, and would be able to check my eyesight and get a glimpse of where I was.

"I therefore took the instrument out and struck it feverishly, with an ill-assured hand. At the first stroke, not the slightest spark appeared. 'Did you see anything, Jen-Marie?' I asked.

"'Nothing, nothing,' my unfortunate companion replied, despairingly.

"I repeated the experiment. This time—O joy!—I saw a shower of bright sparks, which traversed the obscurity, like the little sparks that fly away from a

Christmas log and light up the dark hearth. I wasn't blind!

"A cry of joy from Jean-Marie mingled with my delight. 'Lieutenant, Lieutenant, I can see! I saw the sparks springing from your lighter.'

"I felt reborn, and strength returned to me with an incredible rapidity. I was immediately able to sit up. I felt intolerable pains in all my limbs, but with the certainty of not having lost the use of the most precious of my senses, I felt my courage and my energy reviving.

"After having remained in a sitting position for a few moments I made a further effort and succeeded in standing up. I leaned over my companion in misfortune and held out my hand to him. 'Courage, Jean-Marie,' I said to him. 'It's important now to find a way out of here, for hunger won't take long to make itself felt, and it's necessary that it doesn't complete the work of the tempest.'

"The brave matelot revived in his turn; with my help he stood up, and both of us, each holding on to the other's arm in order to steady ourselves, advanced at random, groping ahead of us with our free hands.

"We arrived thus at an obstacle that presented itself in front of us, vertically. 'Lieutenant,' said Jean-Marie, 'we might not be alone here. We'd do well to unite our voices in order to make ourselves heard by our companions, if, by chance, they've been dragged into this cavern like us.'

"The suggestion was good, and I agreed wholeheartedly. For a few minutes we applied all our strength to our lungs to make the grotto resound with shrill sounds, but although we strained our ears, there was no response to our appeals.

"'It's a matter of following the wall we're leaning on,' said Jean-Marie, 'but which way shall we go? Perhaps, instead of going toward the light, we'll be going deeper and deeper into the entrails of the earth?'

"Jean-Marie fell silent for a moment or two, like a man reflecting, and then he suddenly said: 'Can you hear the sea?'

"'Undoubtedly,' I said, 'and I think we ought to go in the opposite direction, in order to avoid being gripped by it again,'

"'I don't agree,' he said. 'The tempest must have ceased, or diminished considerably in intensity, since the waves are a long way from the place where they left us. If we go toward the sea we'll find ourselves at its edge. Even supposing that no light arriving from outside comes to our aid, we'll find shellfish by groping, and thus be able to combat hunger, the most terrible of our enemies, for the moment.'

"I understood the justice of that reasoning, and yielded immediately. We therefore went in the direction of the sound that had struck my ears as soon as I recovered my senses. We only went slowly, one step at a time, not daring to put our feet to far forward for fear of colliding with an unexpected obstacle or falling into some hole.

"'Jean-Marie,' I said, suddenly, 'have you noticed, as I have, that as we go further forward, the sound of the waves, instead of getting louder, is diminishing?'

"'Of course, Lieutenant!' he replied, without concealing his joy. 'It's because the tempest has died away completely and the sea has resumed its level. Who can tell whether we might not find an issue shortly that will permit us to swim to a point on the cost more habitable than this dark hole?'

"Scarcely had he finished speaking than hazard seemed to prove him right. It seemed to me that the darkness was less dense and that a kind of gray dusk was replacing the absolute blackness that had enveloped us thus far.

"Without even communicating the joyful thoughts to which that observation gave birth within us we increased our pace and felt reassured. Gusts of fresh air began to arrive, caressing our faces.

"It was Jean-Marie, again, who pointed out that certain sign of salvation. 'Lieutenant,' he said, 'Look straight ahead. Can't you see a glimmer of light, like a lamp throwing out its last flickering flame?'

"'I see it! I see it!' I cried, squeezing his hand forcefully. 'Nothing's desperate now! Light is life!'

"Still holding one another by the arm, we lengthened our stride toward the liberating gleam.

"Suddenly, I grabbed my companion's extended hand. 'Listen!' I said.

"'I'm listening,' he said. 'The sound of the sea is still dying down,'

"'Not that!' I murmured, too emotional to explain myself further.

"We had stopped, and sounds whose nature we couldn't mistake soon reached our ears.

"'Ahoy! Ahoy!' we shouted, with all our might, uniting our voices.

"Similar cries of 'Ahoy! Ahoy!' responded to us— and it wasn't an echo.

"Our comrades weren't dead! We were going to rejoin them!

"From then on, all our strength and all our courage was renewed; we marched forward, our eyes fixed on the light, which grew, in the midst of a dusk that was becoming less opaque with every instant. In less than a quarter of an hour, we were in daylight, and we observed that we were advancing through a broad and spacious grotto over fine sandy ground. An entrance, arched like the door of a Roman cathedral, was letting floods of light through, and visibly growing, until it took on monumental proportions.

"Then we saw the silhouettes of six men outlined in black against the brightness of the horizon, and we recognized them as our companions in disaster.

"Soon, we were reunited; we threw ourselves into one another's arms and embraced fraternally."

The orator took a swig of champagne and got his breath back before continuing: "You'll understand, Messieurs, what a flood of questions, interrupted sentences and truncated stories intersected at such a moment.

"'There you are! By what miracle did you escape!'

"'And you, my friends! Where did you spring from?'

"'And the Captain?...and Gros Claude?...and Pierre Le Dall?'

"We all asked questions, and no one waited for the replies. I finally succeeded in getting a little order into the hectic conversation. 'Come on, my friends, I beg you,' I said, 'let me direct the discussion. If we all talk at the same time, we'll never succeed in making ourselves heard.'

"They listened, and silence fell. Each one took his turn to speak. Thus we learned that our companions, carried against the rocks of the shore by the irresistible force of the waves, had been able to hang on to jutting projections, and that they owed their life to the sudden diminution of the tempest. A further wave, returning to collect them from the point where the first had deposited them, would infallibly have carried them out to sea and robbed them definitively of any hope of salvation.

"Jean-Marie and I told them in our turn what we knew about our epic. Both gripped by a submarine current, we had been drawn by the waters into the depths of the dark grotto, and the wave that had deposited us not far from one another on the sand of the cave had withdrawn, not deigning to return to seize its prey again.

"They had no news either of the captain or our other absent companions, but we had reason to hope that they had been no less fortunate than us and might have been able to reach land.

"'What about Pongo?' I asked, addressing Yvon. 'Doubtless he drowned?'

"'No, certainly not,' replied the Breton. 'Pongo hesitated at first, but I'd put him in a lifejacket, and when he found that he was floating he started imitating my movements. Thus, he managed to cling on to the rocks, and stayed there, like the seaweed the tide leaves behind as it ebbs.'

"'Where is he, then?' I asked.

"'Over there, behind that stony hillock, where he found a bed of dry heather uprooted by the tempest and is warming himself up in the sun's rays.'

"After satisfying the first, perfectly legitimate surges of our curiosity, we held council, and thought about the means we might employ to ensure that existence so miraculously snatched from the unchained elements.

"First of all, we made an inventory of the objects we'd been able to save, and observed, fearfully, that we had been literally stripped of everything. My compass and sextant had disappeared. My watch was still in my waistcoat, but the sea-water had got into it and it had stopped. My pockets were empty. As for my companions in misfortune, they had been no luckier than me. Three of them had conserved their lifejackets, and Pongo, they told me had retained his collar, his bracelets and his diadem, which were no use to us.

"Everything we still had in our pockets was gathered together on the sand in a little heap, and we were very chagrined to realize that we had none of what was necessary to maintain material life.

"For some time we remained plunged in profound despair, but as I've said, hope survives in the human heart in the most frightful situations.

"We made sure of our first meal with the shellfish that the storm had deposited in large numbers on the sand of the cave. One of us, the matelot Pierre-Antoine, went to look around and brought back a little fresh water in his leather cap.

"As soon as we felt a somewhat renewed by that anchorite's meal, we set out to explore, but didn't take long to ascertain that the land on which we'd been cast up was a desolate mass of rocks devoid of vegetation, with no fruit trees, vegetables or cereals. How were we ever going to combat hunger on that accursed island?

"It was necessary to think of the most urgent matter; we recognized that the cave where we had met up constituted, when we penetrated a little further into it, a salubrious dwelling. We transported into it heaps of seaweed that we collected on the rocks of the coast, with which we made passable beds.

"What more can I tell you? The details of our wretched existence are consigned to our journal. We had no weapons and no tools, and were threatened with soon having no garments. We did what we could to replace the most necessary objects. Our only knife served us at first to dislodge shellfish from the rocks to which they were clinging; then, when we explored the island, we found deposits of flint, which furnished us with axes, knives, hammers and other tools that we invented to satisfy our needs.

"Our first trials did us little honor, but we didn't take long to become increasingly skillful in the art of shaping hard stone splinters, and, little by little, our armaments and our equipment improved.

"We made circuits of the island several times, crossing it in all directions, but in vain; we found no trace of the Commandant or our vanished companions. We soon acquired the certainty that, less fortunate than us, they had perished during the tempest.

"It was then that the survivors gave me command, and I continued to keep the journal miraculously saved from the wreck by matelot Mathieu, who, on Captain Joly's order, had tied it securely to his breast, sheltering it as best he could from the seawater by means of his sheepskin jacket and his lifebelt."

Lieutenant Lefort fell silent, and noticed that all the scientists making up his audience were looking at one another minutely, with anxious and consternated expressions.

Arthème Charmillon was the first to break the silence and to speak in the midst of general attention.

"So, he inquired, "You were forced to pass, like primitive humans, through the miserable age when people covered themselves in animal skins?"

"Yes, Monsieur," Lefort replied, "and no one could imagine what efforts of imagination and labor the creation of those primitive and barbaric instruments cost us."

"Can you tell me," the French geologist went on, "where this grotto is of which you made use as a primary dwelling, and how long you lived there?"

"The cavern that was our refuge wasn't far from here. Although one can't distinguish the entrance from here, which opens into a little bay, I can point out the high rocks that are massed above it. It wasn't until ten years after our shipwreck, when we felt that we were sufficiently well equipped to create more comfortable habitations, that we abandoned this coast of the island and went to establish ourselves on the northern coast, better sheltered from the cold southerly winds that often blow in the winter."

As he pronounced these words, Lieutenant Lefort got up and, followed by Monsieur Charmillon, went out of the dining room. When he was on the strand, he directed his indicative finger westwards.

"It's underneath those high rocks," he said, "that our former dwelling opens."

"Damnation!" cried the French scientist. "That's what I feared. It's the Grotto of the Sphinx! All of our scientific scaffolding collapsed at a stroke!"

His features pale and distressed, he went back into the dining room. "Messieurs," he said, "the terrible anticipations that I read in our eyes have been realized. The Grotto of the Sphinx served as a refuge for those unfortunates, and what we took for instruments of the Stone Age were produced by their industry, stimulated by necessity!" After a few moments of silence, troubled only by the sound of the distressed respiration of the assembled scientists, he added: "The evil is irremediable, alas! At the present moment, the *Glorieux* is heading for Australia, carrying the fatal report that will testify to our error before all the scientific societies of Europe, and render us the most ridiculous of men in the eyes of all civilized nations."

"Stop! Stop!" cried the English naturalist William Johnston. "I think that you're going a little too rapidly Master, and I'd like to continue to the interrogation."

"Please do, my friend," said Monsieur Charmillon, simply.

"Well, come with me," said Mr. Johnston to the castaways.

He went out of the large wooden building that contained the dining hall and meeting room and headed for a more modest edifice. The members of the expedition understood the objective of his step, and, after allowing the castaways to precede them, they set out in their wake, and the numerous company went into the building designed to house the scientific collections.

Johnston went to fetch various flint weapons and tools made of animal bone or fish bones from a shelf. The castaways recognized them without hesitation as being of their manufacture.

Suddenly, Monsieur Charmillon had an idea. He went to take from a carefully-closed display-case the little plaque of horn beveled at either end and perforated with two little round holes. He presented the object abruptly to the eyes of the lieutenant.

"What is this?" he asked.

"It's the plate from the hilt of my knife, saved from the wreck," replied Monsieur Lefort, immediately.

"Alas!" moaned Monsieur Charmillon. "Jean-Pierre was right!"

Without giving up completely, however, he put before the castaways' eyes the instrument made from an antler found by matelot Le Dall, the bizarre form of which had so intrigued the explorers. You will remember that Monsieur Charmillon had emitted the opinion that the grooves traced on the implement demonstrated victoriously that it had been a staff of command. John-ston had even profited from the occasion to obtain and approving vote for his scholarly French friend—almost a vote of confidence.

"Could you enlighten me," the geologist asked, "as to the origin and employment of this instrument?"

"Of course," said Monsieur Lefort, without the slightest hesitation. "As its form indicates clearly enough, it's an old shoe-horn that the captain used, when he was alive, for putting his boots on. It was saved, along with a few other toilet objects of no importance, by the matelot Jean-Marie, into whose pockets the cap-tain had slipped them."

"And what purpose do these stratified lines serve on a shoe-horn?" asked Monsieur Charmillon, not without a hint of ill-humor.

"That's the result of an idea I had," said the matelot Jean-Marie, "but which I eventually abandoned. When we arrived on the island we had no calendar, and I thought that if we stayed here for a long time, we might lose count of the dates, the months and years that went by. In consequence, I made a mark every day for a month, and then, at the end of the month, I made a notch on the other side of the horn, resuming the series of thir-ty days every month, and making a new notch, thus fab-ricating a perpetual calendar that served me until the day when both sides were full, when I replaced the tool with another, simpler one made of wood, which I've kept and which I'll show you. It's just a mark similar to the only provincial bakers use to mark the number of kilos of bread furnished to their customers."

Monsieur Charmillon listened to this explanation, which demolished his brilliant hypothesis, with less im-patience and ill grace than one might have expected.

After a moment's reflection, he murmured in a low voice: "At any rate, I wasn't mistaken in deducing that the grooves engraved on the horn were designed for numeration. The days are, in sum, the soldiers of a company that's known as a month, and twelve similar companies make a regiment, which is a year."

Chapter XVIII

In spite of that reasoning, with which he sought to console himself, Arthème Charmillon experienced a profound chagrin. He saw the entire scaffolding of his scientific research collapsing before his eyes. He was too generous and too profoundly humane to find any alleviation of his distress in the egotistical thought that his friends shared it.

"Messieurs," he said, "you can see how fragile human science is, since we, who are its torches, have allowed ourselves to be grossly deceived by appearances."

"My God, Monsieur Academician," said Mr. Wilson of the Royal Geographical Society of London, "It seems to me that you're being a little hasty in establishing our defeat. I'll be glad, since he evidence is there, to admit along with you that these weapons, these tools and this debris of bones and shells, that all the evidence of prehistoric humans in the Cavern of the Sphinx, were left there by these unfortunate shipwreck victims. Anyone else would have been deceived, as we were, and no one has the right to throw stones at us.

"In any case, weren't those objects produced in circumstances analogous to those which must have existed in the epoch when primitive humans lived? Cast up naked on to this inhospitable coast, these mariners were obliged to pass once again through the ages of the infancy of humankind. There's nothing surprising in the fact that men of good faith, ignorant of their existence, were able to believe that they were in the presence of instruments dating from the remotest eras."

Becoming increasingly animated, he went on: "How do you know, anyway, that we've been completely deceived? The Grotto of the Sphinx, which gave shelter to these castaways, might also have served as a shelter for the first humans thousands of years ago."

As he spoke he headed toward a display-case placed in the very center of the room serving as a museum. "Would you please come here, Lieutenant Lefort?" he said.

The leader of the castaways took a few steps forward and found himself confronted by the glass-fronted box in which the prehistoric man was lying. "Do you recognize this cadaver?" demanded the English geographer, in a thunderous voice.

"Pongo! Poor Pongo!" cried the castaway. "Is that all that remains of you?"

"What are you saying?" cried William Johnston. "That skeleton belonged to...."

"To our unfortunate Pongo, the captain's monkey, which the cold of the first winter removed from our affection."

"That," said the English naturalist, turning to his colleagues, "seems to me to surpass the, limits of a joke. What monkey, including the orangutan of Sumatra, could attain the dimensions of this skeleton? I'm beginning to believe that these Messieurs have invented a farce, which, for my part, I declare to be in rather poor taste."

"Alas, Messieurs, nothing is truer than what I've just had the honor of telling you. That really is what remains of Pongo, the gorilla that we brought with us from Africa. Look! He still has his collar and his bracelets of shells, and I even perceive the remains of his diadem around his head. That red dust visible in front of him was produced by his muzzle, for we buried him with everything that belonged to him."

"A gorilla! A gorilla!" murmured the naturalist. "Why didn't that idea occur to us?"

In the meantime, Lieutenant Lefort paraded his gaze around, recognizing every object displayed, indicating its usage and naming the person who had fabricated or possessed it.

His eyes fell upon two objects placed preciously to a crimson velvet cushion. "Oho!" he said, smiling. "You've even found those two teeth!"

"Yes," said Monsieur Charmillon, not taking his eyes off the castaway. "To what animal did those teeth belong?"

"Well," replied Lefort, without hesitation, "they're two of Pongo's canines. As soon as he was dead we realized that we could utilize those four formidable fangs, and we made hooks of a sort out of them, which were valuable to us for ridding the inner surface of sealskins of the fibers and threads of grease that were stuck there. Those two tools, which have a veritable place of honor here, were mislaid by Jean-Marie, and we regretted their loss greatly. Fortunately, we still had the other two, of which we still make use, and which we'll be glad to show you."

From then on, no further doubt remained possible. The scientists had fallen into a series of fatal errors; that was absolutely certain.

Monsieur Charmillon turned to Wilson. "Well, my friend," he said, in a tone of voice shot through with irony, "can you still find any means of consolation, any attenuating circumstance? Are you quite convinced that we're condemned from now on to eternal ridicule?"

"Perhaps you're exaggerating the gravity of the situation. We were mistaken, that fact is unfortunately incontestable, but after all, we made the mistake with the best faith in the world, and people will take account of our disinterested sincerity." He headed toward the bookshelves placed at the back of the room and took down a superb quarto volume, richly bound. "Besides which, our error isn't unprecedented, and here's an analogous case with which European science has been familiar for a long time. This is what Henri Du Cleuzon relates in his beautiful book *L'Art national*:

"'At the beginning of the last century, in the quarries of Ehnignen, a few leagues from Lake Constance, a layer of schist was discovered containing a bizarre imprint equipped with arms, at the extremity of which little hands were outlined. The head was enormous, the dorsal spine very characteristic. A knowledgeable local physician wrote a paper about the individual conserved in that schist, proclaiming in a learned manner: "It is irrefutable! This is a portion, slightly more than half, of a human skeleton; the very substance of the bone, and what is more, of the flesh, is incorporated into the rock; in a word, it is one of the rarest relics we possess of the accursed race that was buried under the waters. We possess the man of the deluge: *Homo diluvii testis*."

"'That physician was named Scheuchzer. When the matter was presented to Cuvier, the savant professor of the Museum completed the interrupted design with his expert pencil, putting in the other two feet of the pretended biped, prolonging the dorsal spine into a long tail terminating in a point and contented himself with writing underneath it: *Giant Salamander*.

'The disappointment was considerable. The stone was examined again. The celebrated naturalist as summoned to the task. He was even permitted to extract the debris with his hands in the presence of several distinguished scientists. The operation laid bare before all eyes the entire skeleton that he had indicated with marvelous precision. The man of the deluge became a simple batrachian reptile of the family of *Urodeles*."[34]

That reading was very appropriate to create a diversion from the chagrins to which the discovery of their irreparable error had given birth in all the members of the international scientific expedition.

Until this point, the two German scientists had maintained the most profound silence. One of them, Walter Müller, said: "It seems to me, Messieurs, that the discovery we've just made is sufficiently important to necessitate a general meeting, in which each of us can be called upon to express his opinion on the line of conduct that it's appropriate for us to follow. My compatriot Franz Henrich and I propose that the meeting in question should be held without delay."

Monsieur Charmillon consulted his colleague with his gaze. "Does anyone have any objection to Monsieur Müller's proposal?" he asked.

No one said a word.

"Monsieur Müller's proposal is accepted unanimously," proclaimed the French Academician. "All the

---

[34] In fact, it was not until long after Johan Jakob Scheuchzer's death in 1733 that Georges Cuvier demonstrated, in 1811, that the so-called "diluvian man" identified a century before by the Swiss naturalist (a devout believer in Biblical chronology, who believed that fossils were "sports of nature") was actually a giant salamander—whose species was, somewhat ironically, named after Scheuchzer. Modern readers of speculative fiction will recognize the anecdote as the seed of Karel Čapek's classic satire *War with the Newts* (1936).

members of the expedition are summoned to the meeting-hall, and requested to assemble there in ten minutes."

While the castaways were escorted back to the dining room, where new refreshments were waiting for them, Monsieur Charmillon went straight to his lovely chalet, where he found Émile Colin deep in conversation with Angèle. The old scientist was so struck by the joy that was resplendent in their faces that he did not feel that he had the courage to trouble so much gaiety by revealing to the young people the frightful news that had just reduced all is hopes to nothing. He contented himself with informing his secretary that an important extraordinary meeting was about to take place, and asking him to come along immediately in order to exercise his functions.

No meeting of serious men had ever presented such a grave and somber appearance. Each of the members went to his seat without saying a word. When Monsieur Charmillon rang his parliamentary hand-bell and declared the session open, a mortal silence reigned in the vast hall.

Walter Müller of Berlin requested the floor, which was granted to him.

"Messieurs," he said, "the fatal event that has just struck us is not only a personal disaster for each of us, but assumes the proportions of a public calamity. If people in Europe learn that the most erudite men in the entire would have allowed themselves to be taken in, grossly—allow me that expression because of is exactitude—misled by appearances, that they have unanimously concluded in favor of false ideas, that they have represented as incontestable discoveries that do not contain an atom of truth, not only will we be dragged through the mud by the great and petty press, but all scientific axioms will become the object of the crowd's mistrust.

"The recantation of the unfortunate report that we were, alas, in too much of a hurry to send to Europe will dead a mortal blow to science in general. When the ignorant public find out that we have mistaken the skeleton of a gorilla for a human being, what do you expect them to think of the marvelous anthropological theories of Broca, the fact-filled studies of Quartefages, the admirable discoveries of Boucher de Perthes, the fossil man fund in the Cavern of Menton by Rivière, and everything hat constitutes in our day the scientific absolute?

"Let us put aside, if you wish, our personal self-respect; let us consent, following the example of a great French revolutionary, to allow our memory to perish, but let us save the sacred deposit, placed in our hands, of science itself!"

A murmur of approval from all parts of the room greeted these words. Cries of "Go on! Go on!" were heard from several directions.

The orator continued: "Certainly, Messieurs, no one is more opposed than I am to violent procedures, and no one has protested more loudly than I have against radical measures. There are, however, circumstances in which duty imposes then, no matter how terrible they seems, and in which it is necessary to say, along with the great Chancellor of my country: 'Might makes right!'"

A slight murmur interrupted the naturalist, but silence was soon reestablished and he continued.

"I have a horror myself, Messieurs, of the measure that I am about to propose to you, and the words necessary to express it refuse to emerge from my throat. Let one of you propose another means of salvation and I shall bow down before him as before a savior. But alas, the fatal report is on its way to Europe; any possibility of getting it back is gone. Now, it is necessary, it is important, it is vital that the conclusions of that report are not called into doubt; I have, in consequence, the honor of reminding you that the five castaways who have overturned the entire edifice of our studies are old and infirm, that the life they lead here is an intolerable burden, that they are poorly armed—or, to put it better, have no weapons at all—that no one in the world will ever think about looking for them and that for them, an easy death would be the supreme benefit...."

A long cry of horror interrupted the orator; insults were hurled at him from all sides of the room.

"That's horrible!"

"That's monstrous!"

"Blackguard!"

"Murderer!"

The president shook his hand-bell violently. "Monsieur Walter Müller," he said, in a firm voice, "I call you to order and withdraw the floor from you."

Without protesting against the general outcry, the Prussian naturalist stepped down from the podium.

"Monsieur William Johnston, you have the floor," said the president.

"I shall not refer to the motion whose formulation you have not wanted to permit in its entirety," said the noble English scientist. "Personally, I believe that it is important that those imprudent words are effaced from the memory of everyone here and that the secret be conserved eternally. Our colleague, Messieurs, has allowed himself to be carried away by his love of science; let us not forget that, and let the memory of it be, in our consciences, the attenuating circumstance that allows us to pass a sponge over a proposition that I do not hesitate to qualify as criminal."

Unanimous applause burst forth in the auditorium.

Johnston continued: "While rejecting with horror the solution proposed by our colleague, I do not hide the gravity of the question and the importance of the European public not being informed of the errors, pardonable as they might be, that we have committed As my predecessor has said, it is not only our persons, but science itself, sacred science, that will be called into question. I can glimpse one means of salvation, which, I hope, will obtain our approval.

"These five castaways, abandoned on this island for thirty years, no longer have any hope of finding relatives or friends in France. Their fortunes, if any of them possessed one before their departure, have doubtless passed into the hands of strangers, and have doubtless, by virtue of modern economics, been sufficiently dispersed for it to be impossible to discover any trace of them. Nothing, therefore, recalls them to their fatherland, while everything ought to make them love this island where they have suffered and struggled.

"I propose, in consequence, that instead of repatriating them, we leave them here with everything that might ameliorate their lot: abundant food, weapons and ammunition, comfortable clothing, the elegant constructions that shelter us—everything that, at the moment of our departure, is not absolutely necessary to ensure our voyage as far as Melbourne,"

A few approving murmurs were heard, and the orator continued.

"What I propose, in sum, has nothing inhuman about it, nothing that injures common rights or justice. These men have become involuntarily, an obstacle to our future, and instead of striking them, instead of abandoning them, as might be within our right to do, strictly speaking, let us cover them with benefits, let us render them happy and rich. I have spoken."

When Johnston descended from the podium, several hands were offered to him, and merely by studying the physiognomy of the assembly it was certain advance that the English naturalist's motion, if put to the vote, would be adopted with an enormous majority.

Monsieur Charmillon stood up. "Monsieur de Kolikoff," he said, "would you be god enough to take my place in the presidential chair? I believe that the question is sufficiently serious for me to contribute to the debate."

The noble Russian nodded his head as a sign of assent, and immediately took the place of honor offered to him.

Monsieur Charmillon went to the podium.

"My dear colleagues, my dear friends," he said, in his mildest voice, "I have no intention of diminishing in your eyes the gravity of the situation in which we have been placed by the discovery of these unfortunate castaways, all the more so as I am, by three different titles, the individual whose reputation is most gravely threatened—firstly as the official leader of he expedition; secondly by virtue of being, in that capacity, the first signatory of the fatal report; and thirdly, because my capacity as a geologist, a member of the Académie des Sciences de France, and my anterior works cause the responsibility for errors made in matters of which I have made a special study to weigh most especially upon me.

"Alas, Messieurs, whatever might happen, and however disastrous the mockery with which the entire world will cover us might be for our glory and reputations, I think, and I firmly believe, that there is something that must come before our personalities, and before science itself, and that is humanity.

"I will admit, if you wish, for a moment, that the means of salvation proposed by my excellent friend Monsieur Johnston would be successful, and would assure us of eternal secrecy, but we could not accept it, because it would be the most abominable of crimes to leave these unfortunates who have been mourning their absent fatherland for thirty years, even in comfort, even in wealth."

The absolute silence that reigned in the hall demonstrated superabundantly the importance that the audience attributed to the speaker's words.

Without appearing to pay any heed to those signs of hesitation, the latter continued: "I have said to you, my dear colleagues, that I would only admit for a moment the efficacy of the expedient proposed by Monsieur Johnston. You will see how right I am. Even if we suppose that none of the matelots, workmen or employees who surround us has caught wind of the error that we have committed, we cannot dissimulate from them the presence on the island of the castaways. On arriving in Europe they would hasten to talk about those unfortunates, to depict their distress and their misfortune. Do you think that we would not be held to account for our inhumanity, that people would not seek to know what motive had prevented us from returning them to their fatherland?

"It might also be the case that tomorrow, in six months, or next year, a ship calling at Seal Island will return these poor mariners, imprisoned by the sea, to their homeland. Do you think that they would then be inhibited about making known the true motives for our barbaric abandonment? Europe, and the entire would, would add to the ridicule that our error will fatally bring in its wake, the odium that our inhumanity would merit."

A few expressions of approval formulated in the hall informed the orator that his stern logic had found a path to hearts.

"I have kept my most serious argument for last," he continued. "It is not outside of us but within us, in our consciences, that I encounter it. Can we, the scientists, the professors, who obtain our glory from instructing and moralizing the masses, consent to keep secret a deceit, a lie, a delusion? No, no, a thousand times no! My dear colleagues, if you abandon the castaways, oblige me to share their fate, for on arriving in Europe, even touching the first civilized land, my first word, my first cry, will be an indiscretion. I shall hasten to tell all, even if I must die thereafter of shame and chagrin."

The effect of that speech was decisive. The entire audience ran to the podium; the orator was embraced and thanked, his hands were shaken. Johnston, habitually so cold, took him in his arms and hugged him.

"No vote! No vote!" was proclaimed on all sides. "We're all in agreement, and it would be an insult for any of us to believe in the possibility of a lack of unanimity.

Thus it was, after a brief session in which the most contrary opinions had been voiced, everyone withdrew in accord—which is, for sure, a result very rarely obtained in parliamentary assembles.

From that day on the blackest melancholy invaded all the members of the scientific expedition. The more they thought about the disastrous effect that the revelation of the error they had made would produce in Europe, the more they sensed how heavily the ridicule would weigh upon them that attaches so easily to intellectuals. More than anyone else, Monsieur Charmillon was inconsolable. His nights were sleepless; as for his days, he spent them wandering along the strand, somber and mute.

In addition to the irremediable personal check that threatened him, another bitter thought laid incessant siege to his mind. Émile Colin, his secretary, his protégé and his pupil, whom he had believed to be attached to his person by bonds of amity and gratitude, did not appear to be moved by the catastrophe. As before, he spent a part of his days hunting, and when he returned he hastened to visit Angèle and to have long conversations with her that the Academicians carefully avoided trying to overhear.

"Sow benevolence," the new misanthrope muttered between his teeth, "and you harvest ingratitude. That young man, whom I loved almost as if he were my own son, cannot entirely hide the secret joy that the fall of his master and all my honorable colleagues procures him. A disaster that overtakes the old is a certainty of advancement for the newcomer. Doubtless Émile Colin is already glimpsing the possibility, on our return, of replacing me in my teaching at the Sorbonne."

Bitter thoughts acted with so much force upon Monsieur Charmillon that his health was affected by them, and it was visibly deteriorating.

One morning, Monsieur Colin, with his game-bag on his back and his rifle over his shoulder, was getting ready to depart for his favorite occupation, when Angèle, having risen earlier than usual, emerged from her room and beckoned him to approach.

"My dear Émile, the moment has come to attempt the great enterprise. Perhaps we could have waited a little longer, for the sharper my uncle's chagrin is, the more chance I think we would have of success, but I don't have the courage to see him suffer any longer. Prepare yourself then, my friend, to undertake the great battle that must ensure our lifelong happiness."

"Mademoiselle," replied the secretary, "I am, as you know, entirely at your disposal. You know that, in spite of my personal ideas. I have obeyed you to the letter. I will not hide from you, however, that it is not without a sharp secret emotion that I shall go to find Monsieur Charmillon. Will he ever forgive us for this little comedy? You tell me that he will; I believe you, but I tremble."

When he finished speaking, Émile Colin went back into his own room. He soon emerged clad in a black frock-coat, his hands irreproachably gloved, in the perfect image of a suitor or an ambassadorial attaché. Under his arm he was carrying a black morocco case, a kind of large portfolio, carefully closed, which completed the appearance of an official personage.

He headed toward the strand where he was sure to encounter the old Academician. Indeed, he soon found himself in his presence. He bowed profoundly and aid: "Monsieur Charmillon, would you do me the honor of according me a few minutes of your time?"

In any other circumstances, the attire of his secretary, the pomposity of his language and the gravity of his manner would have seemed odd to Angèle's uncle, but his personal preoccupations prevented him from noticing anything outside of his dolor.

"Speak," he said. "I'm listening."

"I will venture to remark to you," said the young man, his voice trembling with emotion, "that the location is perhaps ill-chosen for a conversation that I judge to be of capital importance, and I beg you to listen to me in your study, if you have no objection to that."

"What the devil can you have to say to me?" Monsieur Charmillon demanded, all the ceremony beginning to arouse his suspicions.

"I have the intention of talking to you about the subject of the report addressed to the Académie des Sciences in Paris."

"I don't know what sentiment is driving you to torture me by reminding me about that fatal report, which I'd buy back at the price of my blood, but nevertheless, I'll drink the cup of bitterness to the dregs and listen to you in my study."

The old man and his secretary went back into the pretty chalet that served them as a dwelling. Monsieur Charmillon sat down in his vast armchair, like a man determined to immolate himself to the end. As for Monsieur Colin, he remained standing respectfully before his master, who gestured to him to sit down.

He obeyed.

Monsieur Charmillon then said: "I'm listening."

The young man finally started speaking.

"However singular the question that I have the honor of putting to you might seem, I beg you, my dear Master, to consent to answer it."

"Go on!"

"I know, Monsieur," the young man continued, "how the sudden discovery of the castaways at the very moment when the departure of the *Glorieux* for Melbourne rendered the error into which you and your colleagues had fallen irremediably, and fallen in such a logical manner, has brought chagrin into your soul. It is not to try to console you that I have requested this conversation, but it would only be just to demonstrate to you that the evil is not as serious as you believe. Your research, your studies and your observations have been as serious as they could have been. The error committed cannot diminish the just esteem that all the true friends of science have for you. Is it your fault that on this desert island, men cast up by the tempest, without tools, without vestments and without the means of existence have been obliged to recapitulate the period of the infancy of humankind? I shall say more: the error to which you have fallen victim is one of those that strongly confirm scientific discoveries."

Monsieur Charmillon made a hand gesture to indicate that he wanted to put a word in.

"I thank you for that, Émile," he said. "It demonstrates to me that I was wrong to doubt the goodness of your heart, but I'd be grateful to you for not persisting in this dolorous theme. I've told myself everything that you've just said; I've entered into my conscience and I've asked myself severely whether my work was conducted with sufficient application, My intimate thought replied yes, and I'm certain that anyone else would have been afflicted by the same fatal blindness. Alas, the malign public will not pay much attention to the attenuating circumstances that we might evoke. I shall die under the weight of an eternal ridicule. The story of the fossil gorilla will take its place in the textbooks alongside that of the salamander that witnessed the deluge."

"Well, my dear master, what would you do in favor of the man fortunate enough to be able to spare you that embarrassment—in favor of the man who could stop that fatal paper *en route*?"

"What use are such hypotheses?" said the scientist bitterly. "Where there is material impossibility, the right to reason stops. Do you have the wings of Icarus in order to fly after the *Glorieux*, and if you had, would they be sufficient to accomplish the task?"

Émile Colin stood up. "My Master and benefactor," he said, in a tender voice, "you know that it would never enter my head for a moment to lack respect for you, but I beg you to answer my question. What would you do for the man who could return the accursed document to you?"

"I would give him my fortune, my life—anything, anything at all, without bargaining."

"Would you give him Mademoiselle Angèle's hand in marriage?"

"I would even do that, I swear," said the Academician, "on the condition, of course, that Angèle consented."

"Well then, my dear Uncle, you're saved, and I'm the most fortunate of men."

On saying those words, Émile Colin took a long envelope out of his briefcase, broke its seals, and handed the scientist a piece of paper, which he recognized at the first glance as the terrible and fatal report.

He put his hands to his forehead, which he pressed in order to assure himself that he was not dreaming and had not suddenly gone mad.

"Please, Émile, explain this miracle to me! Tell me that I'm not the dupe of a fatal illusion!"

Sitting down again, Émile Colin commenced the narration of the facts that were to cast light on the confused mystery.

"Firstly, know that Mademoiselle Angèle wishes to take sole responsibility for what has happened. Personally, I have only obeyed, blindly, the orders of the woman I love more than anything in the world."

He then told the aged scientist, returned to serenity by the sight of the report, that in the course of his long hunting excursions on the island, he had encountered the leader of the unfortunate castaways, that he had learned from his mouth the story of their terrible existence during their thirty years of exile, and that he had written that epic, with the assistance of the castaways' own journal.

"I thought it my duty," he continued, "to tell Mademoiselle Angèle, your niece, that moving story, as well as the fatal consequences that it would have for your discoveries. I questioned her as to the oratory precautions I ought to take in order to make that disagreeable revelation to you. She initially advised me to go to you immediately and tell you the whole truth, straight out. 'My uncle will understand, I hope, the importance of the service you have rendered him, and perhaps he will condescend, out of gratitude, to grant you his consent to the marriage about which neither you nor I have ever dared speak to him.'

"I was about to do that when she abruptly changed hr mind. 'No, Monsieur Émile,' she said to me, 'there's a better way. The antipathy that my uncle harbors against marriage is so profoundly anchored in his mind that gratitude might not suffice to cure it. I think that we'll more certainly extract is approval if we make it the essential condition of a bargain that will put his entire scientific past at stake,'

"It was then that she developed the whole of this Machiavellian plot, thanks to which I've been able to obtain your word and can call you my uncle."

Émile then told the guardian of his future wife how, by following the latter's instructions, he had copied the story of the shipwreck on paper identical to that of the report, and how, at the moment of the *Glorieux*'s departure, he had substituted that document for the one the scientist had so deeply regretted sending.

Monsieur Charmillon reflected momentarily, but it was easy to see, by his expansive features, that joy had reentered his heart.

"That," he said, "is a plan full of feminine cunning, and I congratulate you, my dear Émile, for the courage you're showing in consenting to take such a diplomat for your wife."

With those words he dismissed his future son-in-law with a gesture, and hastened to summon his colleagues to a new meeting in the conference hall.

We shall not insist on the joy of the revelation that the French scientist made in his turn to all those erudite souls. The most vivid gaiety succeeded, without transition, the somber melancholy that had taken possession of the little colony. Everyone felt reborn on learning that they were all saved, and that the fatal report was not on its way to Europe.

Only the Germans, Walter Müller and Franz Henrich formed a dark patch in the midst of the general lightness. The more their colleagues yielded to joy, the more somber they became. The savant and amiable Russian geologist Pierre de Kolikoff attempted in vain, several times, to extract the secret of their black humor from them. The two Berliners opposed a stubborn silence to the most amicable demonstrations.

A lugubrious event even seemed liable to trouble the general happiness. Only hazard, aided by the valet Jean-Pierre, prevented an irremediable denouement.

One day, Jean-Pierre was strolling on his own in a little valley that opened on to the strand from the interior of the island, walking pensively, perhaps thinking about some new transcendental theory to profess before those members of his usual audience whom the *Glorieux* had not taken away, when it seemed to him that he saw something strange swaying beneath an arborescent fern that had grown there, sheltered from the cold southerly winds. He drew closer, and was utterly astonished when he realized that it was a human being hanging by the neck, who was agitating in the anguish of the most terrible agony.

Without paying any heed to the identity or nationality of the patient, Jean-Pierre launched himself toward the tree and cut the rope with a single sweep of the blade of his knife.

In the hanged man, he had recognized Walter Müller.

After laying him down on the grass and loosening the slipknot that was strangling the unfortunate fellow, the valet ran to tell his master, who arrived at the scene of the disaster accompanied by Dr. Despierre.

The latter observed that, fortunately, the asphyxia had not been complete, and lavished the cares of his art on the hanged man.

Müller, having returned from the journey that had so nearly been definitive, ended up confessing the cause of the despair that had driven him to such a determination. It was Pierre de Kolikoff, more fortunate this time than on previous occasions, who received the confidences of the Prussian naturalist.

He learned that, contrary to the engagement of honor made by all the members of the expedition not to make any individual report external to the official report, even a simple note, concerning the discoveries made in the Grotto of the Sphinx, the two Germans had addressed a separate document to the Scientific Acadeemy of their own nation specifying the studies undertaken and the part that they had personally played in them.

That broken word clearly explained the chagrin that had taken possession of the two scientists, and why the joy of their colleagues seemed to render it more intense. In fact, they alone were compromised henceforth, and they would be mocked all the more because they would pass for naïve dupes tricked by their colleagues.

A sin confessed is half-pardoned, the proverb says. No one had the courage to criticize the unfortunate Prussians for their treason, and everyone strove to console them as best they could. Let us say that, in the early days, no one succeeded in that philanthropic enterprise.

One day, however, Müller, who, since his suicide attempt, never showed himself at the communal table, came to sit down for the morning meal. Everyone was struck by the profound change that had overtaken his physiognomy.

Batschkoff having made the observation aloud, the Prussian naturalist said, almost cheerfully: "In truth, Messieurs, I made a series of reflections last night that almost consoled me. The harm is done, that's indisputable, but at the end of the day, it's necessary I get out of it as best one can. My colleague Franz Henrich and I have resolved not to abandon ourselves to despair. As soon as we arrive in Germany, we shall publish volume after volume to demonstrate that the discovery of the antediluvian human and all the other finds made in the Grotto of the Sphinx are indisputable verities. We shall affirm that the ridiculous stories printed in neighboring countries concerning the pretended shipwreck are a tissue of lies, invented with the sole aim of discrediting us. There will be people in my homeland, and even in yours, Mes-

sieurs, who will believe us. Hence, there will be interminable polemics, which will shine a spotlight on our
names."

The guests could not help smiling at the ingenious
indecency of their colleague, and subsequently avoided
any allusion that might have reminded them of the sorry
adventure.

Epilogue

The days went by cheerfully, and the moment finally arrived to carry out the observation of the famous transit of Mercury across the face of the Sun. Unfortunately, the sky was so completely covered with cloud that day that it was necessary to renounce any attempt to view the day star.

The *Glorieux* returned from Melbourne two days later, and the members of the expedition, having nothing more to do on Seal Island, hastened to embark and resume the route to Europe.

The five castaways were received aboard the ship, and throughout the journey, which was exceedingly fortunate, they were admitted to the scientists' table. On arrival in Europe, they were introduced to all the scientific societies, and made a tour of the Old World, but without making an appearance in Germany, where Müller and Henrich had commenced their intellectual campaign.

While those intrepid battlers were heaping up folio volumes in support of their thesis, Monsieur Charmillon, keeping his word to his savior, granted him the hand of his niece, Mademoiselle Angèle. The wedding was celebrated with great pomp and all of Parisian scientific Society was invited. The young husband's witnesses were William Johnston and Wilson, who made the journey from London to Paris expressly. The two amiable Russian scientists Pierre de Kolikoff and Batschkoff did not want to be found wanting in amiability, and waited until after the ceremony before resumed the route to their homeland; they served as witnesses for the bride.

Finally, Monsieur Charmillon was proved wanting in his diagnosis regarding the marriage of his niece and the dangers that her subtle mind posed to her husband. The two spouses formed the most united household in Paris, soon animated by two children. The first, who was a boy, promises, the old scientist assures us, to be one of the glories of French science. As for the little girl, she is already as pretty and gracious as her mother.

SF & FANTASY

Adolphe Alhaiza. *Cybele*
Alphonse Allais. *The Adventures of Captain Cap*
Henri Allorge. *The Great Cataclysm*
Guy d'Armen. *Doc Ardan: The City of Gold and Lepers*
G.-J. Arnaud. *The Ice Company*
Charles Asselineau. *The Double Life*
Henri Austruy. *The Eupantophone; The Olotelepan; The Petitpaon Era*
Barillet-Lagargousse. *The Final War*
Cyprien Bérard. *The Vampire Lord Ruthwen*
S. Henry Berthoud. *Martyrs of Science*
Aloysius Bertrand. *Gaspard de la Nuit*
Richard Bessière. *The Gardens of the Apocalypse; The Masters of Silence*
Albert Bleunard. *Ever SMalher*
Félix Bodin. *The Novel of the Future*
Louis Boussenard. *Monsieur Synthesis*
Alphonse Brown. *City of Glass; The Conquest of the Air*
Émile Calvet. *In a Thousand Years*
André Caroff. *The Terror of Madame Atomos; Miss Atomos; The Return of Madame Atomos; The Mistake of Madame Atomos; The Monsters of Madame Atomos; The Revenge of Madame Atomos; The Resurrection of Madame Atomos; The Mark of Madame Atomos; The Spheres of Madame Atomos; The Wrath of Madame Atomos* (w/M. & Sylvie Stéphan)
Félicien Champsaur. *The Human Arrow; Ouha, King of the Apes; Pharaoh's Wife; Homo-Deus; Nora, The Ape-Woman*
Didier de Chousy. *Ignis*
Jules Clarétie. *Obsession*
Michel Corday. *The Eternal Flame*
André Couvreur. *The Necessary Evil*; *Caresco, Superman; The Exploits of Professor Tornada* (3 vols.)
Captain Danrit. *Undersea Odyssey*
C. I. Defontenay. *Star (Psi Cassiopeia)*
Charles Derennes. *The People of the Pole*
Georges Dodds (anthologist). *The Missing Link*
Charles Dodeman. *The Silent Bomb*
Harry Dickson. *The Heir of Dracula; Harry Dickson vs. The Spider*

Georges Le Faure & Henri de Graffigny. *The Extraordinary Adventures of a Russian Scientist Across the Solar System* (2 vols.)
Gustave Le Rouge. *The Mysterious Doctor Cornelius* (3 vols.); *The Vampires of Mars; The Dominion of the World* (w/Gustave Guitton) (4 vols.)
Jules Lermina. *Mysteryville; Panic in Paris; To-Ho and the Gold Destroyers; The Secret of Zippeliu; The Battle of Strasbourg*
André Lichtenberger. *The Centaurs; The Children of the Crab*
Listonai. *The Philosophical Voyager*
Jean-Marc & Randy Lofficier. *Edgar Allan Poe on Mars; The Katrina Protocol; Pacifica; Robonocchio; Return of the Nyctalope;* (anthologists) *Tales of the Shadowmen 1-11; The Vampire Almanac*
Xavier Mauméjean. *The League of Heroes*
Joseph Méry. *The Tower of Destiny*
Hippolyte Mettais. *The Year 5865; Paris Before the Deluge*
Louise Michel. *The Human Microbes; The New World*
Tony Moilin. *Paris in the Year 2000*
José Moselli. *Illa's End*
John-Antoine Nau. *Enemy Force*
Marie Nizet. *Captain Vampire*
C. Nodier, A. Beraud & Toussaint-Merle. *Frankenstein*
Henri de Parville. *An Inhabitant of the Planet Mars*
Gaston de Pawlowski. *Journey to the Land of the 4th Dimension*
Georges Pellerin. *The World in 2000 Years*
Ernest Pérochon. *The Frenetic People*
Pierre Pelot. *The Child Who Walked on the Sky*
J. Polidori, C. Nodier, E. Scribe. *Lord Ruthven the Vampire*
P.-A. Ponson du Terrail. *The Vampire and the Devil's Son; The Immortal Woman*
Georges Price. *The Missing Men of the Sirius*
Edgar Quinet. *Ahasuerus; The Enchanter Merlin*
Henri de Régnier. *A Surfeit of Mirrors*
Maurice Renard. *The Blue Peril; Doctor Lerne; The Doctored Man; A Man Among the Microbes; The Master of Light*
Jean Richepin. *The Wing; The Crazy Corner*
Albert Robida. *The Adventures of Saturnin Farandoul; The Clock of the Centuries; Chalet in the Sky; The Electric Life*
J.-H. Rosny Aîné. *Helgvor of the Blue River; The Givreuse Enigma; The Mysterious Force; The Navigators of Space; Vamireh; The World of the Variants; The Young Vampire*
Marcel Rouff. *Journey to the Inverted World*

Léonie Rouzade. *The World Turned Upside Down*
Han Ryner. *The Superhumans; The Human Ant*
Pierre de Selenes: *An Unknown World*
Angelo de Sorr. *The Vampires of London*
Brian Stableford. *The New Faust at the Tragicomique;The Empire of the Necromancers (The Shadow of Frankenstein; Frankenstein and the Vampire Countess; Frankenstein in London); Sherlock Holmes & The Vampires of Eternity; The Stones of Camelot; The Wayward Muse.* (anthologist) *News from the Moon; The Germans on Venus; The Supreme Progress; The World Above the World; Nemoville; Investigations of the Future; The Conqueror of Death; The Revolt of the Machines; The Man With the Blue Face*
Jacques Spitz. *The Eye of Purgatory*
Kurt Steiner. *Ortog*
Eugène Thébault. *Radio-Terror*
C.-F. Tiphaigne de La Roche. *Amilec*
Simon Tyssot de Patot. *The Strange Voyages of Jacques Massé and Pierre de Mésange*
Louis Ulbach. *Prince Bonifacio*
Théo Varlet. *The Golden Rock. The Xenobiotic Invasion; The Castaways of Eros; Timeslip Troopers* (w/André Blandin); *The Martian Epic* (w/Octave Joncquel)
Pierre Véron. *The Merchants of Health*
Paul Vibert. *The Mysterious Fluid*
Villiers de l'Isle-Adam. *The Scaffold; The Vampire Soul*
Philippe Ward. *Artahe ; The Song of Montségur* (w/Sylvie Miller) *Manhattan Ghost* (w/Mickael Laguerre)

MYSTERIES & THRILLERS

M. Allain & P. Souvestre. *The Daughter of Fantômas*
A. Anicet-Bourgeois, Lucien Dabril. *Rocambole*
A. Bernède. *Belphegor; Judex* (w/Louis Feuillade); *The Return of Judex* (w/Louis Feuillade); *The Shadow of Judex*
A. Bisson & G. Livet. *Nick Carter vs. Fantômas*
V. Darlay & H. de Gorsse. *Arsène Lupin vs. Sherlock Holmes: The Stage Play*
Séamas Duffy. *Sherlock Holmes in Paris*
Paul Féval. *Gentlemen of the Night; John Devil; The Black Coats ('Salem Street; The Invisible Weapon; The Parisian Jungle; The*

Companions of the Treasure; Heart of Steel; The Cadet Gang; The Sword-Swallower)

Émile Gaboriau. *Monsieur Lecoq*

Goron & Émile Gautier. *Spawn of the Penitentiary*

Paul d'Ivoi. *Around the World on Five Sous* (w/Henri Chabrillat)

Rick Lai. *Shadows of the Opera: Retribution in Blood; Sisters of the Shadows: The Curse of Cagliostro*

Steve Leadley. *Sherlock Holmes: The Circle of Blood*

Maurice Leblanc. *Arsène Lupin vs. Countess Cagliostro; Arsène Lupin vs. Sherlock Holmes (The Blonde Phantom; The Hollow Needle); The Many Faces of Arsène Lupin; The Island of the Thirty Coffins*

Gaston Leroux. *Chéri-Bibi; The Phantom of the Opera; Rouletabille & the Mystery of the Yellow Room; Rouletabille at Krupp's*

Richard Marsh. *The Complete Adventures of Judith Lee*

William Patrick Maynard. *The Terror of Fu Manchu; The Destiny of Fu Manchu*

Frank J. Morlock. *Sherlock Holmes: The Grand Horizontals; Sherlock Holmes vs Jack the Ripper*

Jean Petithuguenin. *The Adventures of Ethel King*

Antonin Reschal. *The Adventures of Miss Boston*

P. de Wattyne & Y. Walter. *Sherlock Holmes vs. Fantômas*

David White. *Fantômas in America*

Pierre Yrondy. *The Adventures of Thérèse Arnaud*

Victor Margueritte. *The Bacheloress; The Companion; The Couple*

SCREENPLAYS

Mike Baron. *The Iron Triangle*

Emma Bull & Will Shetterly. *Nightspeeder; War for the Oaks*

Gerry Conway & Roy Thomas. *Doc Dynamo*

Steve Englehart. *Majorca*

James Hudnall. *The Devastator*

Jean-Marc & Randy Lofficier. *Royal Flush*

J.-M. & R. Lofficier & Marc Agapit. *Despair*

J.-M. & R. Lofficier & Joël Houssin. *City*

Andrew Paquette. *Peripheral Vision*

Robert L. Robinson, Jr. *Judex*

R. Thomas, J. Hendler & L. Sprague de Camp. *Rivers of Time*

www.ingramcontent.com/pod-product-compliance
Lightning Source LLC
Chambersburg PA
CBHW030359020726
47493CB00003B/885